PRAISE FOR
JAN SHAPIN

RED YEAR

"SET IN RUSSIA AND CHINA during the 1920s, this beautifully written novel tells the story of a true American dreamer—a woman who charged into danger in search of passion, justice and some money to pay her bills. A fascinating story."
—Susan Breen, author, Maggie Dove mysteries

A SNUG LIFE SOMEWHERE

"SHAPIN'S FIRST NOVEL IS DENSE AND EVENTFUL...."
— *Historical Novel Society Review Online*

"A SWEEPING PICTURE OF A WOMAN"S LIFE, one that is at times heartbreaking and funny, ordinary and amazing.... How many of us know even the first thing about early 20th century labor unions and the rise of Communism? How many of us have heard of the Everett Massacre and the Seattle General Strike? Through this book we see them both, with Penny as our eyewitness..."
—*Estella's Revenge, A 'Zine About Books!*

"LIVELY AND DESCRIPTIVE... A Snug Life Somewhere* offers insight into an era when labor and capital were locked in an often-bloody struggle..."
— *Tacoma Weekly*

"PENNY JOE'S ADVENTURES held my attention and wouldn't let me go."
—*The Road to Here Blog*

"INTRIGUING AND GRIPPING... I couldn't stop thinking about this book."
—*Unabridged Chick Blog*

A DESIRE PATH

"POLITICS IS POWER AND POWER ALWAYS ATTRACTS. A Desire Path is a novel of romance and politics set amongst the aftermath of World War II, with the frost of the Cold War coalescing. An affair between a union leader and a lawyer's wife leads to cruel intentions, as well as a woman driven to defect to the Soviet Union. A riveting novel with much romance and intrigue, *A Desire Path* is…not to be missed."
— *Midwest Book Review*

" I REALIZED I WAS IN OVER MY HEAD, but in a pretty wonderful way… I love when books push me to learn and grow."
— *Tiffany's Bookshelf Blog*

"A GENUINE STORY WITH HEART and possibly a message about the human spirit."
—*Lavish Bookshelf Blog*

RED YEAR

by Jan Shapin

Cambridge Books

an imprint of
WriteWords, Inc.
CAMBRIDGE, MD 21613

𝕮𝖆𝖒𝖇𝖗𝖎𝖉𝖌𝖊 𝕭𝖔𝖔𝖐𝖘 is a subsidiary of:

Write Words, Inc.

2934 Old Route 50
Cambridge, MD 21613

ISBN 978-1-61386-402-9

Fax: 410-221-7510

Bowker Standard Address Number: 254-0304

Part I
Never Go Home

CHAPTER 1

She'd first become aware of Mikhail Borodin on a sweaty day in November, 1926, not long after she and Bill had arrived in Canton, on the south coast of China. Borodin and his Russian advisers were engaged in what looked like a jousting match against some Chinese cadets at the Whampoa Academy. Bill and Eugene Chen were foraging for refreshments as Rayna shielded her eyes against the glare and examined the stocky Russian on his huge gray gelding. He was dressed in a white smock and billowing white trousers, his dark chestnut hair lifting in waves as his horse pivoted and raced down the field, then reversed. With each turn her stomach reversed as well, rising and flattening with longing or desire or something else she could not name. Perhaps she was coming down with the flu. Checking to see that Bill was still occupied, she decided to escape to the shady overhang of the stable roof.

The game was like polo, she concluded, some Chinese version where they used paddles to steady the ball, position it and then take great whacks. Quite like the game she and her brother Reddy used to play with sticks and clods of earth in the corn fields at her father's farm, where if you got hit you were dead. Tufted hunks with worms hanging out were Reddy's favorite weapon, or better yet, cow pies. He'd fling them with great glee, bellowing his fierce Indian yell, *Comancheeee!*

That was more or less what the Chinese were yelling now as the teams dismounted and fell into opposite lines to make their ritual bows. A break to change horses, and the Russian in the sweaty tunic and muddy breeches was walking toward her. She knew who he was, of course, he was in charge of everything having to do with the revolutionary Chinese government, but she had yet to meet him. She took in a deep draft of air, straightened her back against the whitewashed boards. Behind his heavy moustache, a flushed face. His lower lip, what she could see of it, broadened into a toothy smile. She regretted her not-so-recently washed dress, the dull green thing that hung loose but at least showed off her red hair. In her confusion she blurted out the first thing that came to mind. "I hear you come from Chicago." Should she smile? No, look him straight in the eye. "I do too."

He absorbed that. "You must be Mrs...." She watched him grope for Bill's last name.

Then, as if on command, his wife appeared. Mme. Borodin was a formidable figure, unhappiness radiating from her in a way that was almost visible. Fanya was her given name, but the foreign journalists called her Fanny, a reference to her enormous backside. Madame, in the French manner, was the title she preferred. Rayna stuck out her hand. "Mme. Borodin." Rumor had it her husband's staff found her imperious. Getting no response, Rayna drew back the offer. Mme. Borodin was speaking to her husband in swooshy Russian.

His response was short and guttural. Then he turned to Rayna. "My wife thinks I'm going to break my neck." She thought there was more to it than that, but then, in the second chukka or whatever it was, he nearly did break his neck, falling hard from his horse and injuring his left shoulder and arm. The game stopped. She watched him limp away to the stable while they called a doctor and everyone repaired to the half-finished auditorium where speeches were in order.

She sat with Bill through the first two, then pleaded a headache and wandered back to the exhibition field, following the direction Borodin had taken to the stables. She found him in the tack room, resting on an old leather couch, his face turned to the wall. She feared he was asleep, and wondered why no one was guarding him, then thought maybe he had insisted on being left alone. She wondered where his wife was, whether Mme. Borodin would burst in and accuse Rayna of coveting her husband. Just as she had decided to slip away, Borodin turned and cleared his throat.

"Nice of you to look in on me."

She became flustered. "The speeches gave me a headache. Not the speakers, the room."

"With me it's the speakers. And now this." He pointed with his chin at the strapped-up shoulder.

He was looking at her with great stillness. She tried to return that stillness while her mind raced.

He waited.

Finally, to say something, she came out with, "Is there anything I can do?"

He closed his eyes. "Tell me how you washed up on these shores."

So, like Scheherazade, she stood twisting her fingers and burbled on. "Bill and I left the States in the fall of 1925, spending two months in Hawaii. I liked Hawaii but I was anxious to move on. China was my aim. I had been there before, for just a few months in 1923. Then I was traveling alone, gathering material for an anthropology thesis on Chinese religious thought, but I had to come back." She didn't tell him about the loneliness, her abortive attempt at freedom, how in the villages they ignored her, spit at her and called her 'Red Hair', a slur, she came to learn.

"When Bill said he was interested in what was going on in revolutionary China — at that time I had not much interest in such things, but I wanted to go back, to make a second try, and he was an experienced newspaper man, and so we thought…"

Here her narrative ran out. Borodin had his eyes closed and she couldn't tell if he was listening or not. "Japan was our first stop. We stayed only a few months, just enough time to make some money to get here." Then she told him about the dance floor in Peking where she'd first heard of Eugene Chen. She watched his chest rise and fall. "I'm not going back there, Chicago, I mean. What about you?" Then she became concerned that Bill would be looking for her, that Mme. Borodin or the doctor would appear and demand to know what she was doing. So she crept up and leaned over and whispered that she was honored to be of help, that she believed in his cause. Then Rayna backed out the door and made her way to the auditorium for the applause at the end of the second-to-last speech.

CHAPTER 2

In the summer of 1925, after she and Bill had decided to abandon their Stateside lives and go to Japan, she had written to her ex-husband Raph, asking for help in making contacts. He had not replied, busy mounting a new play, or perhaps offended by the request that he help his replacement. But midway through that first cold year, in damp quarters, that disappointing year in which Bill's job had not panned out, his book remained unfinished and his lungs got worse, a letter from Raph arrived, forwarded and forwarded again.

Then, as now, she responded with half-truths. Japan was fine, she wrote, but she and Bill had decided to go to China, to join an 'honest-to-God' revolution. Something real, she meant to imply, not a Broadway play. And so, arriving in Peking on the last of their funds, she'd set out to find work, getting nowhere until she met an American on a rooftop dance floor set up so the hotel patrons could watch the night fighting on the southwest plain. The bombs were like fireworks, the dance music ragged, but she learned in mid-foxtrot of an English language newspaper financed by the Soviets. The next morning she set out to find the editor, a Mr. Chen, while Bill shivered in their room. The Palace was a grand hotel, but a bomb had damaged its furnace lines.

When she found Chen she showed him samples of Bill's work, told him of the prizes he had won at the *San Francisco Examiner*, explained that Bill was brilliant, almost finished with a book that would lay bare the intricacies of Germany's rearmament in the Ruhr. Chen said he needed someone to set type. She'd volunteered on the spot, although she knew nothing about typesetting. Chen looked over his full-moon glasses, told her if she would agree to set type, he would consent to talk to her prize-winning husband. That's how the misinformation began, that she was married to Bill, but she let it stand.

The Peking paper where Chen first assigned them was really a clipping service, translations of press reports on the Kuomintang government's doings down in South China that Chen sold on a subscription basis to embassies and news organizations. Bill was put in charge of cleaning up the execrable prose while she did rounds delivering the copies. For her assignment, Chen thought some tutoring on the current political situation was in order: "Keep your mouth shut about what General Chiang is doing in Shanghai. Only answer direct questions. Say: 'No I haven't heard of any split between the Canton government and the army. No, I don't know which armaments the Soviets are shipping or where they are going.' Above all, don't get into any discussion about the Chinese Communist Party. You don't know anything, got that straight?"

She didn't, although she would have liked to know the answers to all those questions, because she sensed that what was unspoken was what was really going on. "How about the Soviet Embassy? Can I ask questions there?"

"Yes," he said, "go right ahead." He gave her a name, a guy named Josef on the political desk, and mentioned that there was a Chinese scholar hiding out there who might be able to give her some help understanding the history.

She never got in to see the Chinese scholar but she did pump Josef, a wild-haired young man whose English was more than adequate, about what was going on in Canton. Over mugs of black tea he told her about Lenin's response to Dr. Sun's plea for help in 1922. "Sun had reached the bottom of the barrel in terms of getting money to finance his troops, which were mostly hired from local warlords and not reliable unless they got paid. Up till then Sun had gleaned most of his cash from overseas Chinese merchants who stood to improve their business with a less chaotic government in place. But by 1922 Sun had come up short. His decade-long effort to unify China had been reduced to the southern coast around Canton.

"Lenin sent Joffe to strike a deal, and we wound up putting in money and advisors and agreed to build a military academy that also trained propaganda officers. That, at least, is now bearing fruit."

She told him how she longed to go to Canton and see for herself. Then asked about the other part of the Soviet deal, the part Chen had warned her not to talk about. "I gather you are trying to build a Chinese Communist Party?"

"You bet. They're now part of the government. We've negotiated a half-dozen ministerial posts and have tucked away loads of tactical support underneath. Needless to say, the Chinese merchants and Western powers don't like it one bit."

She asked about the stories coming out of Shanghai, that Moscow-trained General Chiang, a favorite of Dr. Sun's, was now denouncing the Soviet presence in Canton.

Josef didn't answer directly. Said it was a game of keep away, and left it at that.

As winter set in, Bill's lungs got worse. Then the warlord who ran Peking changed sides and ransacked their printing press. Rayna and Bill implored Chen to bring them to Canton, where the real action was, and the climate better, or so they thought. The pay was meager, one salary for them both, and Canton was hot, dreadfully hot, but Bill's lungs improved and the madhouse tempo of strikes, demonstrations and trade embargoes was energizing.

But they were woefully short of funds. She considered writing to her father, asking for money from her mother's trust. The day before she and Bill left California, her father had written to ask if she wanted money transferred, but she'd said no, that when they got back would be soon enough. She hadn't told Bill about the trust and to bring it up in Canton would mean explaining why she had never mentioned it in the first place. Besides, she felt uncomfortable bringing an inheritance to a revolution.

In Canton, as she feared, she was assigned to set type. What little she knew about leads and ligatures and kerns she'd picked up from watching Chen's newsletter production in Peking. Canton had the same kind of machine, an ancient monster that required inking and oiling and laborious loading of type into composing sticks and formes, then sizing the chase with a cranky adjustable knee. Fortunately Nils, who ran the press, took pity and helped her out for the first weeks. She never got any good at it, but discovered a much needed talent for finding words without the letter e which turned out to be vital because their various trays of moveable type were all woefully short of that vowel.

Soon enough she was promoted to managing the office. Nils kept the ancient press lumbering along, as well as the three-wheeled jitney they used to haul copies around town and to the port for posting. On its masthead, *The People's Tribune* proclaimed Eugene Chen as its editor and Bill the features reporter and she and Nils as the production staff, but in practice it all got hopelessly mixed. Chen spent his days hanging around Russian headquarters angling for meetings with Borodin, who had the title of Advisor to the Kuomintang Government, but that too was misleading. Ostensibly in China to set up a military academy, Borodin ran things for the KMT, and spent most of his time locked in an office over the Imperial Stables, figuring out how to keep General Chiang's right-wing KMT army that was centered in Shanghai from breaking off from the official government in Canton.

It was the job of *The People's Tribune* to rebut any suggestion of trouble between the KMT left and right wings. This Chen and Bill regularly did, downplaying any disagreement between the two factions, but Nils, as he was tinkering with the inky press, would grumble. He was an old newspaper hand, troubled by inaccuracy in a story.

A week after the ill-fated match that resulted in a broken arm, Borodin invited her to sit in the dignitary box on the flag decorated platform at the Whampoa graduation ceremonies, while Bill and Chen sat far back in the blazing sun. While the band warmed up, Borodin made a point to introduce her to Mme. Sun, the widow of the revered leader. Serene, beautiful, Mme. Sun didn't look like a widow, couldn't have been much older than Rayna, who was still in her early thirties. Mme. Sun welcomed her in precise English.

"Your command of English is very good," Rayna responded, shaking the small hand that was offered.

"I was educated in the United States," she said. "My father was quite progressive, sending all his children, including his three daughters, to study there."

Rayna was reluctant to release the hand, lost in the porcelain cool of it. The dress Mme. Sun wore was black silk, cut in the close-fitting manner favored in the smart shops of Shanghai. Her face was a perfect oval, brows smoothly arched, lids motionless above eyes so still that Rayna felt she was talking to a mannequin. Then Borodin laughed.

"Mrs. Prohme is quite the progressive herself. She says she's here to serve our cause."

Rayna flushed. Had he heard what she'd whispered in the stables?

Mme. Sun's response was gracious but perfunctory. Rayna felt she was in danger of losing the woman's attention. "I want to serve the women of China," she found herself saying.

The Chinese widow's cheeks rose. "We shall have to find an opportunity for that." Then she turned away to handle some request by a cadet who appeared at her elbow.

While they waited, Borodin filled Rayna in on Mme. Sun's

family. The father, Charlie Soong, was a wealthy bible merchant, a Methodist minister by training and an early supporter of Dr. Sun. The oldest daughter, A-ling, had married into the fabulously wealthy Kung family, while a brother, known as T.V., was a banker who doubled as Finance Minister for the KMT.

Borodin was just about to explain how the beautiful middle daughter had come to marry the elderly Dr. Sun when Mme. Sun completed her task and turned back to the two of them. "Commander Borodin has been most vital to my husband's cause." She said this smiling at Borodin in a way that Rayna found interesting. She likes him, Rayna decided, likes his straightforward manner, how his decade in Chicago made him seem more American than Russian.

Borodin was making a joke about Rayna's lack of deference. "She came in on me when I got this." He lifted his bandaged arm. "Her whole manner bordered on impertinence. Announcing she came from Chicago. As if that entitled her to ask anything."

Mme. Sun nodded. "Those are qualities I most admire in Americans. They are optimistic and straightforward. We Chinese, you know, are not." She began to reminisce about her college days in Macon, Georgia.

Borodin then started to tease her about that special brand of Georgia impertinence, Southern slyness masked by perfect manners.

She laughed, said slyness was also very Chinese. "My clothes at school were a disaster. I had no idea how to dress in the American fashion. But my sorority sisters were always telling me how beautiful I looked. When I got back to China with my new American outfits, my Shanghai aunties said the same thing."

Borodin extended the comparison. "But neither Shanghai nor Georgia impertinence comes anywhere near to Chicago impertinence." To prove it, he took up Mme. Sun's hand and kissed it, which made her return a look both stern and amused. Adjusting his sling and quite pleased with himself, Borodin craned his neck to check progress on the podium. "Don't let on," he whispered, "don't say anything about our special three-handed mutual bond." Then he winked, gathering Rayna's arm to escort her to her seat while the waiting cadet took Mme. Sun's.

After the speeches, when the dignitaries were making their farewells, Mme. Sun pressed Rayna's arm and murmured something to Borodin. They were talking about her, Rayna knew, and had the sure sense it was all to the positive.

Back in the newspaper office, Bill and Chen demanded a full account. Nothing of importance, she told them, just chitchat. Then, of course, they wanted to know about that. Instead, she told them that Borodin had been rehearsing his upcoming speech, explaining how his time in China had taught him the long view. Bill wrote that up as the headline, cropping Rayna out of the photo. "Mme. Sun Counsels Borodin on The Long View," the headline read. The next day Rayna ran into Borodin, literally ran into him as she was hauling newspapers out of the jitney. He was coming from his doctor's office and groaned as the wired newspaper bundle glanced off his new white cast. When she stammered a shamefaced apology, he asked in a sour tone if she were the one to thank for the headline which put the Chinese cart before the Russian horse. She blushed and, mumbling a second apology, hurried away.

Months later, as she was making her last trip down the Yangtze, she wondered about that moment on the street in Canton, he with his aching arm and she with her crimson face. If both of them had known then how things would turn out. If her loyalties, even then, had shifted. Would things have been different if Bill hadn't written that snide headline? If she hadn't looked the Russian commander in the eye that first day at Whampoa and asked about Chicago?

She had been attracted to Bill because of his belief, his

utterly convinced Marxist view of history. Not that she shared it then. Then she had imagined belief as something beyond her, a second sight she could never possess. She had since learned differently. When she bumped into Borodin with her wired newspaper bundle and sent shooting pains down his arm, once again she had been stirred by the sense of a man's deep belief. And once again she mistook that belief for confidence, not yet knowing that the two were not the same.

Somewhere along the road from Tokyo to Peking to Canton, Bill had lost confidence, though not yet his belief. In Canton's lovely late autumn, with the sycamore leaves wetted to a papery brown, that confidence had revived a bit, his elegant brand of Marxism burnished by his job on the KMT newspaper. Reflected glory, she thought. Chen and Bill were given to indulging themselves in the illusion that they were part of the army of the victors, elevating this shared belief to dogmatic certitude as they churned out stories for *The People's Tribune*. Only Nils, cajoling the balky press, grumbled the truth, that what they were writing was no news at all, that the Canton government was getting weaker, that the long awaited Northern Campaign was an act of desperation. But she kept silent, knowing how fragile Bill's confidence was, knowing the doubt all newspapermen have as to their ultimate importance.

They argued about that, whether it was the job of a newspaper to expound beliefs or report facts. "Newspapers don't make history," she told him, "history is made in the streets, in Commander Borodin's office with his maps and plans, in the armies the Whampoa Academy is churning out."

He had looked at her with barely disguised impatience.

"General Chiang's army has its own newspaper," she pointed out, "its own cache of bullets and propaganda units and maps and plans."

"You think it's our job to give weight to his side's version of history?"

"No, no. Our job—" Rayna tried to puzzle out what she did mean. It had something to do with who was helping whom. "Our job is to deepen Russia's belief in China's destiny."

That shaky reasoning confirmed Bill's analysis of her limited capacity for political thought. He corrected her logic. "It's not a matter of Russia's belief. Marxism is scientific, it's the way history unfolds. We are not competing with General Chiang to see who rules China, not trying to get the Soviet higher-ups to bet on us over him. We are engaged in the complex expression of an inevitable historical process." His tone of voice, as always in these arguments, made her head ache.

Nevertheless, for his sake, or maybe her own, she tried again. "If it's ordained — heads we win, tails they lose — then why are we the ones packing to move north?" The goal of the Northern Campaign was to defeat or make alliance with key warlords in order to bolster the government's position with respect to General Chiang.

He had not liked that question one bit. He spoke again, this time with any pretense of patience gone.

"Your job is to handle production." He waved at the stacks of newsprint, the hopeless office clutter.

And because she disliked his bullying tone, she retreated, in her usual way, into vague disavowals.

Satisfied, he put on his hat and went off to meet Chen at the now empty Commodore's Club where the foreign merchants sat behind military checkpoints, a watering hole the two men retired to each afternoon to hatch the next day's lead story.

As it happened, Bill and Chen were planning a trip to the countryside, and she asked to go. Demanded to go, announced she couldn't stand being cooped up another day in Canton. They exchanged glances, but finally consented.

Chen had commandeered an army car, with leather seats and a Russian driver, for the three hour drive south. Their destination was a beautiful hamlet, medieval in its feel, with cobbled streets and tile-roofed houses stacked along the contours of the bay. As the car zigzagged up hairpin turns, red roofs dropping off in staggered rows below them, a drizzle turned into a deluge that cleared as suddenly as it arrived. Steam rose all around them turning the clay roofs and gray cobbles gauzy and sunlit. It was then she announced her plan to find a dead baby depository. The men were not pleased. They had a meeting with the mayor, they pointed out, seeming to believe a three hour lunch with an appointed village leader would be an accurate gauge of morale.

The car took a last hairpin turn into an opening, a flat area with a stone well. A sign marked where the road ended. The driver pulled to a halt and looked at Chen. Bill leaned forward and directed him to turn back. Rayna, raising a hand, insisted she wanted to stay, to find out if there were such things as dead baby depositories, some dark rumor she had picked up on the street. Without asking permission, she got out and walked over to the well. Bill opened his door and followed, caught her by the arm and hissed that she was being irrational. "Even if there were such things," he said in his pasted-on calm voice, "they don't exist now."

"Old wives' tales," Chen agreed, having taken up a precarious perch on the car's back bumper. He motioned to the driver to bring him a handkerchief soaked in water which he used to cool his face. Then he stood and rubbed his neck with the cloth. "That's why I left Trinidad, everything there voodoo, omens." Chen's family had lived on the island for generations.

The men took turns assuring Rayna that her quest was an illusion, a scare story for foreigners, the idea that Chinese villages had special places to put dead babies, sick ones, stillborns. If there had been such a practice, they pointed out, Dr. Sun's revolution had put an end to it. This was modern China. No queues. No bound feet. Rayna turned her face away, silently adding to the list: no girl-babies, dead ones, unwanted ones too costly to raise.

"Have lunch with your mayor," she told them, "then pick me up here." An old woman was filling a jug. Rayna went over and asked in loud English where the baby depository was. No response. She made a halfhearted effort to commandeer Chen into translating but found his command of the dialect insufficient. So she resorted to pantomime, crooning and rocking an imaginary infant, then putting on a mask of grief. A smile from the toothless woman. This followed by a frown as Rayna pantomimed her follow-up question: where to dispose of the dead baby? Reluctantly, the woman motioned up the hill. "Ten minutes," Rayna pleaded with the men. "It will only take us that long to check."

The men pointed out they were wearing good shoes, that the old woman was confused, that they were late for their lunch. Rayna held her ground, saying she would go alone if need be. Bill, perhaps because he feared the impression this quarrel was making on the Russian driver, who sat smoking his long cardboard Russian cigarette and examining the skyline, finally agreed. Chen shrugged and fell in behind.

The path was running with mud. They marched single file, Chen cursing his shoes, Bill whistling his customary seven-note warning. After five minutes, they came out at the top and discovered a paved path that cut behind the hill. Across the clearing was a cement bunker streaked with rust from reinforcing bars that formed a cage opening. A locked metal door on the side confirmed that the building couldn't have been more than a dozen years old. Rayna hid her disappointment but insisted she wanted to look. "Garbage," Chen said, "you've taken us to the garbage dump."

Not paying them attention, she picked her way across the clearing. "Nothing inside," Chen called out. "The Chinese don't make garbage."

The two men waited at the far edge of the bluff, the tension in their bodies belying their apparent disinterest. Two men in dress suits and muddy shoes silhouetted against the hazy sky. Behind them, the waters of the bay, a packet boat churning out a white wake.

Even if it were not true, she reasoned, it could be, and that's why the men are afraid. She examined the rusty bars that swung open over a foot-square opening. A stepping stone was placed off to the side so someone with a package did not have to look while making a deposit. But she wanted to look, because she suddenly realized there was no smell. It was not like the incinerator back in Elmhurst, Illinois, the one behind the public works garage near her father's farm. No black crows reeling in angry arcs. Here the birds were small, gray and silent. They looked like sandpipers, tiny scavengers with long curved beaks. Inside she could hear the flutter of wings, something shift and settle.

Rather than standing on the stepping stone and leaning sideways, she decided to stay where she was and jump. To see what was inside, rotting vegetables or old clothing, although she knew the Chinese used everything that decomposed in their fields. She took a deep breath and dropped down to spring herself up. A flash of black walls, birds picking over gray ash.

"Come on," Bill called out. "You've had your look."

She jumped again. A bleached area in the far corner.

"Rayna." Bill's warning voice.

"In a minute." She jumped and saw something two inches long, a bone, she thought, a small leg bone. Again she jumped.

"Rayna."

"In a minute." Her voice was whiney, insistent. This time she saw fabric, a bit of red cloth near the white thing she thought was a bone. In the next jump, against the gray ash, blue dots. She was starting to jump yet again when the circle of blue dots registered and her stomach turned. Beads, a tiny ring of beads. She dropped down on her haunches, head between her knees, as she tried to stop the sick feeling from spreading.

"You see." Her husband's voice, just over her shoulder, sounded pleased. "You've got yourself winded. And what did you find? Nothing."

"I saw bones," she said after a bit, testing with her tongue the dead certainty of it. "Small bones."

"Rodents." Chen, now behind Bill, explained in a cheerful voice. "Chinese eat everything, but not rats. Oh, water rats, yes, but not ship rats. Even ignorant villagers know ship rats will kill you."

Rayna got up and smoothed down her rucked-up dress and didn't tell them that the bones were too big for rats, or about the red fabric that looked like a baby's sleeve, or the circle of blue beads. She stood and looked at the hazy hot sky and let her head clear, let the confidence in what she had seen solidify against their smug view of what they hadn't witnessed. Something had shifted in her along with that shifting and settling inside the cement enclosure. A certainty that was new to her, a confidence born of direct knowledge. Knowledge that must be protected from shallow minds, the men who stood over her. It was knowledge that armed her. She was not going to give it up.

The next day in Canton, the men told her she couldn't accompany them north. The overland trip would be too treacherous, she wasn't strong enough. Not reliable enough, she wanted to say, but didn't. She should stay and look after the printing press, they told her, wait until she was sent for. Then she should box up the press, the trays of type, escort it all by packet boat to Shanghai and then by steamer up river. Two months, they told her, a month for them to get there and a month to send a message back.

"Why can't I pack everything now, go to Shanghai and save a month?"

They ignored the question and kept up their chatter about conditions en route.

"Bandits," she said. "I hear there are bandits in the mountains."

"And bad food, lice," Chen agreed, chuckling at the fun of it all.

"Mme. Sun is going. If she's strong enough, so am I."

"She's with the government," Bill pointed out.

"The going can't be that hard. The railroad takes you three quarters of the way."

"If they haven't blown up the tracks," Chen pointed out.

"I want to go," she said, stubborn, like a child.

"No," Bill said, menacing, like her father used to be.

She wanted to throw a tantrum then and there, just like she used to with her father, but she didn't. She held her breath and slowly let it out and thought about the piece of bone and the bit of red dress and the blue glass beads until it quieted her. Then she made a resolution to fight this her way, on her terms, for her own reasons.

The question of what she was fighting against, what she was fighting for, she hadn't yet figured out. But it had something to do with making a mark in this country, of having the Chinese people look up to her in spite of her red hair.

CHAPTER 3

With the men gone she found herself cold for the first time since she'd arrived in Canton. Maybe it was the apartment, two huge rooms echoing around marooned bits of furniture, damp patches running down the walls, rats nesting in the ceiling. *The People's Tribune* was housed in a cement building, the printing shop on the ground floor, offices above. Their living quarters were in the back with not much in the way of light, or air, so gloom and the musty smell often made Rayna's head ache.

Borodin lived and worked above the stables on the other side of the parade ground. The night before the men left, she'd slipped outside to check the newspaper bundles, looking across the scrubby grass at the lighted window of his apartment. She would not see him again for weeks, maybe months, and that made the prospect of being left in Canton even more bleak.

"Is Mme. Borodin going?" she asked Bill the next morning.

Bill frowned in a way that made his face seem spinsterish. "To Hankow?"

"Yes."

He considered the possible meaning of this question. "Not overland. She'll be taking the packet boat to Shanghai with Norman."

The younger son, Borodin's favorite. "Has she left?" Rayna didn't like the idea of being in Canton with Fanya Borodin. Bill shrugged; other men's wives were not his affair.

The whole contingent pulled out later that day. Chen's two daughters had joined the group, as had Mme. Sun's brother along with various servants, plus a half-dozen KMT ministers and their servants. That wasn't counting the forty Russian advisors with guns. All of a sudden, the city was quiet. Rayna had nothing to do, no one to tell her to get hopping. Alone, with no newspaper to put out, she took to wandering the streets, peering in the packed stalls that passed for shops, restraining herself from buying pairs of live chickens to set them free. She started writing letters, to Raph, her sister Grace, her best friend Helen.

With the KMT government gone, the city was reverting to ancient ways. Gangs reappeared, the strikers stopped striking, ships came back into port to stock the European trading houses. Oh, the Whampoa Academy was still in operation, down river a dozen miles, but she had no cause to go there. No instructions came, there was no urgent business requiring her to drop everything. It was as if the revolution, like a circus, had pulled up stakes. Once she saw a shiny black car, a large woman in the back, and her heart plummeted. She crossed the street to get away, fearing it was Fanya Borodin, that she would be stopped, hauled up, interrogated. *What designs do you have on my husband?*

Only revolution, Rayna's mind cried out, no other designs. The car passed. She tried to reason with herself. Mme. Borodin was in Shanghai. Then she turned the questions back on herself. *Why have they left me? Why am I not needed? Am I losing my mind?* That last thought stopped her cold outside a shop that sold caged parrots, blackbirds, magpies. It's being idle, she told herself, that's why I can't concentrate, can't sleep, why the dark islands on the ceiling seem to be spreading. I must wait these few weeks until Bill sends for me.

Then her cat disappeared. She feared he had been abducted, that Pooch would wind up in some street vender's stew. That worry brought back memories of her childhood cat, of the time Planter got chewed up in the threshing machine.

At the carved Blackwood desk that took up the middle of the huge damp room, she examined a half-written letter to Raph. It was about Planter. "All mangled meat and soaked fur," she had written, propping each page as she finished it against a Gideon Bible that was part of the room's furnishings. "It happened in an instant. There was Planter, clogged in the tines, his head sticking out, his hind legs lost to sight where the motor quit at the prospect of digesting his hip." Why had she written that? Why was she even thinking about Planter, a kitten rescued from a well, the only one alive in a sack of seven? At first her father had refused, only consenting when it became clear her stepmother disliked the idea of another cat even more than he did.

Fresh memories of that day shot through her, her father high on his enameled throne, the green Waterloo gas tractor. "Rayna." His voice grand, his body a black silhouette in the late afternoon sun. "I'm sorry. I didn't see him in the cane brake." They didn't have cane brake in Illinois, her father called the silage piled up at the edges of the furrows that. Planter had been stalking mice when her father cut across the field, late for supper.

He wasn't a real farmer, she didn't have to explain that to Raph. They lived in a big house in Chicago, her father was Vice President of the Chicago Board of Trade. But it seemed important to explain to her ex-husband how terrifying her father had looked that day, high on his tractor seat, that someone else should know exactly what had happened to Planter. How her father had said, "I'm sorry," and then, "I didn't see him," the one sentence disavowing the other, his claiming, in effect, that it was Planter's fault for being there, her fault for having rescued him from the well. As if her father could afford to be generous, to say "I'm sorry," knowing full well that Rayna was the culpable one, that it was her fault, hers and Planter's, not the fault of the Vice President of the Chicago Board of Trade.

Finally Bill's message arrived, a cable routed via Shanghai. She should box up the press and ship it by packet boat and then by steamer up the Yangtze. She was reduced to escorting printing equipment. That was her job. Nevertheless, she was glad to quit Canton and booked a straight passage with no stop-off in Shanghai because she didn't want to run into Mme. Borodin. But at the last moment, in memory of Planter, in recompense for Pooch, she bought a bony stray off a street vendor, a dog he probably didn't even own, brought it home and fed it the last of her canned foodstuffs. She went back to the ticket office and paid extra for boarding the dog, which she called Dan, only discovering after the fact that it was a she. She dragged the newly christened Dan into the hold, where they had sectioned off a filthy kennel, and promised to visit for the allotted ten minutes each day.

The packet boat took just overnight, but the river trip was slow, twice the normal time because of fighting on land. Trigger-happy soldiers of one stripe or another were given to shooting at anything that moved. Last week, the German captain told her, two passengers had been badly wounded while sight-seeing at the rail. His remedy was to stop each night in the middle of the river and throw search lights over the hull, then lower a banner that said in Chinese, 'Neutral Vessel.' She hadn't the heart to tell him the soldiers were almost certainly illiterate. Nevertheless, the ploy worked and they had no casualties, nor were they boarded by pirates although some other vessels they passed seemed to have suffered ransacking.

There were two journalists aboard, a Frenchman and a Canadian, going upriver to see for themselves what had become of Dr. Sun's revolution now that General Chiang had overrun big chunks of the south. Her mood lightened as she spent long hours on deck, peering through the haze at the endless land, talking to her new companions with that slight edge of madness that had settled upon her in Canton.

It seemed both were members of the Communist Party. "So's my husband," she said with a kind of glee, "you'll have to meet him."

They agreed and then wanted to know what she thought of Moscow's line in China. She knew this question had something to do with whether she favored Trotsky or Stalin, but she was unsure of the right answer and besides, she didn't know the details of the difference.

So they gave her a lesson on that, how the war hero Trotsky favored permanent revolution, which translated into strong support for Communist revolutions wherever they might emerge. Stalin, they said, was more concerned with strengthening Russia's power in response to threats from its enemies.

She observed that the Chinese situation didn't fit neatly into one side or the other, that the KMT government was composed of three-quarters merchant interests and about one quarter Communists. If the Communists pushed too hard they'd lose the merchant support. Borodin's strategy, she supposed, was to keep things rolling and build up the influence of the CCP over time. Then she felt the sting of embarrassment that she'd voiced that thought.

They rolled their eyes. "Won't work," they said. "Not in the long run. What's needed is decisive action. Flat out revolt. Let the chips fall where they may."

She wondered aloud how that was going to go over at the Russian-led conference they were attending.

"Not a problem," the Canadian said, "we're here to cover the speeches, not make them."

On the river, shooting the breeze with them she felt safe, marooned en route to a reckoning with Bill over the addition of her new dog, Dan. In spite of that, Rayna could feel herself readying for a great challenge, certain that in Hankow she would no longer be a bystander. As she talked a blue streak to her new friends, there came the sound of a single shot, an execution probably, who knows what was happening on land. What was she trying to tell these eager listeners, how could she explain the world-shaking nature of the revolution that lay ahead?

When she got to Hankow, the few remaining cherry trees were blooming along the quay. She no longer thought about headaches, the weight she had lost, the reason she'd cropped her hair. All the young Chinese women were chopping off their thick black hair. Maybe her curly red mop should suffer the same fate. When Bill met her at the dock he asked for an explanation, as if it were his hair she had cut. She rubbed the damp scruff, remembering a time when she had stared at herself in her childhood mirror. "I cut it when I was nine," she explained. "To get back at my father after my cat died." He gave her a strange look but didn't question her logic.

The Canadian and Frenchman had disappeared. She explained about her new friends while Bill, with his hand spread on her sweaty back, escorted her the mile or so to their living quarters. The rutted streets were wide, the buildings squat and ugly, rather like the industrial sections of Chicago. Their new apartment was over a garage that repaired bicycles. Two rooms, small and musty, and a bathroom that was tolerable for a night or two only. She asked to see the newspaper office, much better quarters, the whole ground floor of a granite building in the British Concession. Borodin's office was on the second floor and his living quarters on the third. Nils had not made the trip, and Bill was now trying to put out the paper with two Chinese assistants, one who handled the press and the other translations. They were both young, eager to please and pretty much incompetent. Bill showed her a desk piled high with unfinished work. "Sorry," he said. "I've been saving stuff."

"Fine," she said, dumping her bag on the floor. "I'll start now, but I want you to know I'm going to find us a better place to live." That's when she told him about Dan, still caged in the ship's hold, and how she must go back and retrieve her that instant.

On the way back to the steamer, she surveyed Hankow, one of three sprawling cities at the juncture of two rivers that made up the inland port of Wuhan. She could feel this place poised to consume her, the energy of its daily workers' strikes, its strident billboards and endless rallies. KMT army patrols were everywhere in the newly occupied British Concession. The European merchants and their government protectors had departed but kept their stranglehold by parking gunboats in the middle of the river, officially to protect the shipping lanes, but actually to maintain their diplomatic and commercial presence while the revolution played itself out.

She trotted Dan back to the office and made her sit under the new desk with its overflowing mound of paper. Once she'd selected copy and headed it for the first edition, she took Dan and scoured the streets of the British Concession seeking a better place to live. At last she found the Lutheran Mission, four stories high, with an abandoned first floor cafeteria she could see through a flapping shutter. She guessed there were sleeping rooms above and, after rousting a caretaker from the back shed, discovered that the top floor was a two bedroom furnished apartment. She asked the price for the whole thing and agreed to rent it on the spot. The sum was outrageous but she had the notion that foreign journalists could be persuaded to rent the dozen single rooms.

The furniture had been made in Grand Rapids, tags on the undersides to prove it. Also included was an ample supply of knickknacks, dancing ballerinas, silver candelabra, a porcelain cup collection in a glass front cabinet. Plain Lutheran crosses adorned each bedroom. To this she added her Chinese wall hangings and brass gong. "We can't afford it," Bill announced when she brought him up for an inspection. Nevertheless, he sat square in the middle of the curved beige couch, his legs spread wide as he surveyed the place. "Awful," he said, with satisfaction.

"I know," she agreed. "The world's coming to an end, and we're going to wallow in Midwest kitsch." She didn't tell him that she had arranged for her sister Grace to loan her money against the trust deposits that were accumulating in the Mercantile Bank in Chicago.

Bill coughed, a racking sequence that set her to fresh worrying as he took out a handkerchief and, after wiping his mouth, inspected the contents. The way he flipped the edges together and stuffed it away meant the news was not good. "I'm falling behind on the paper," he muttered, further admission that the tuberculosis had returned. "Chen's no help now that he's got the Foreign Minister job."

She knew this meant she would do Bill's work as well as her own, but not to tell anyone, so as to spare his pride. "Maybe we should get help, call on Millie from Peking?" Chen's Peking news service had closed when the resident warlord raided the office a second time and arrested all the Chinese who worked there. Millie, the American left in charge, was unemployed.

"We don't have the money," Bill said, irritated she had brought this up.

"Maybe I can talk to Bee." She had started calling him that, just his initial; it seemed intimate without going all the way to first name.

"No."

"Why not?"

"I don't want you asking favors."

Rayna buttoned her lip and resolved to do just that. Her husband was ill. They needed help on the paper. Something had to be done. That afternoon she cabled Millie and forwarded some of Grace's money for her travel.

A week later, after she had gotten settled, had managed to rent out all the rooms on the lower floors, and had coaxed the caretaker into calling back the chef, she inspected the newly opened cafeteria, greeting the new arrivals. As she went through the breakfast line, she was struck by the feel of the place, its battered meal trays, the ice cream scoops of bland food, the little cash box to pay at the end. Just like college, the first day.

That morning she had lain awake looking at the gray curls on the neck of her sleeping husband. He needed a haircut, she would remind him of that. Bill didn't see the hair on the back of his neck. As with most things in life, you saw what was in front of you. She had reached out and touched Bill's shoulder, then touched a strand of his too-long hair, tugged at the gray tendril that should have been springy, but wasn't, that she should have loved, but didn't. He'd turned over, eyes closed, his lips set in a hard line. Time to get up, she'd told him. Then she rose, put on her bathrobe, padded down the hall, turned on the faucet that dripped just a little bit of rust, and set about brushing her teeth with a frayed toothbrush and salt.

She studied the meager food selection in the cafeteria line. Bit her lip. She had her father's full lower lip, his cheeky face. Or had. Bill told her on the Hankow wharf that her face had become gaunt. "Elfin," she replied, "my father said it was elfin." She no longer felt elfin. Now in the cafeteria with her still-empty tray, she surveyed the row of white plates. In the center of each was a cone of brown rice with a sparse decoration of cucumber slivers. With visiting dignitaries and hungry journalists lined up behind her, she again had the sensation of being back in college.

This week's special guests were delegates to the Chinese Communist Party plenum. Fraternal colleagues from half the world had made their way across oceans and up river to sit at this cradle of revolution. According to the mimeographed sheet she had typed out the night before, Earl Browder from the U.S. was here, Tom Mann from Great Britain, a German whose name she didn't recognize. Plus the two journalists she'd met on the river trip and a dozen more. A great show was in the offing. Speeches, parades, a sort of Fourth of July. Except the fireworks in the distance were real and there was not much food. Banners, leaflets, food for the spirit, but the blockade was having its effect. She looked at the cucumber slivers and wondered how long the fresh produce would last. Over by the window, Tom Mann looked up and waved. She lifted her chin in greeting, tilted her head in another direction. He followed her look, nodded. She had business to attend to. A primary task of *The People's Tribune* was to butter up journalists. Mann pouted a resigned face and returned to his meal.

As the cook slipped a plate on her tray, she turned to see two tables pushed together that were occupied by rumpled men who sat smoking after their meals. She squeezed into the one empty chair next to an open-faced fellow. Unlike the others, who were dressed like laborers, this one sported blue suspenders against a pale yellow shirt, a white suit jacket with eggshell lining draped over the back of her chair. As she removed the jacket and presented it to him with a slight bow, she noticed his socks were argyle. Not the usual kind that came to revolutions.

"Join me?" The man stood and spread his hand like a *maitre d'* in a fine restaurant. He relocated his jacket to another chair. "I'm Vincent Sheean, my friends call me Jimmy."

Rayna slid the plate off her tray.

"First day?" he asked, seeming to sense, as well, the college feel of this place.

"Nope." She tried to keep her face sunny. "Been here a week. I'm with *The People's Tribune*." She lifted her hands in imitation of his gesture. "My job is to butter up journalists."

"At your service." A deep bow with a special smile. "Where do we start? The buttering, I mean."

She found herself blinking, knowing she should say something snappy, but her mind was blank.

He gave her a prompt. "You will call me Jimmy?" He said this in a lazy, probing way she wasn't sure she liked.

She shook her head to break her drift, looked down at her plate, at the cucumber haystack arranged against the small mound of brown rice. A scene of rural England, she decided, then snapped out of that mild hallucination. "Does all this seem real?"

"You mean this room, the events that bring us here?" Jimmy's voice seemed to take into account the confusion she was feeling. She narrowed her eyes to try to bring him into focus. He was waiting for a reply.

Then he let her off the hook. "What's real, a pretty big subject for this time of day." He smiled, to show he understood the essence of her confusion. "Reality is, after all, the ultimate question."

She decided he was teasing and shut off her interest, picking up a long-tined fork, surprised that the good flatware hadn't been melted down. "The revolution's real," she told him, stabbing into the haystack and demolishing its neat arrangement.

While she ate, he questioned her about the government, who were the important players. She said Mme. Sun was the most important even though she held only a minor ministerial post. He asked about the older Soong sister, the one who had married the huge fortune, and the miracle banker brother who'd stabilized the finances of the Canton regime. He asked about General Chiang, whether she thought his army was strong enough to take Hankow, as most of the world press believed.

She was evasive, referring all such questions to Commander Borodin. Now Sheean became forthright. "I'd like an interview. I hear you have access to the great man."

She laughed and said she had no such thing, hadn't seen Borodin since he'd left Canton weeks ago.

He tried again. "I'll buy you dinner, a half a dozen bourgeois dinners, if you'll arrange it."

She pointed out there were no decent restaurants left except the two in the remaining concessions. The Japanese and Germans had not joined the gunboats on the river and so were allowed to continue their operations.

"I like Japanese food and I'll take a rain check on the other five, good for any world capital of your choosing."

"When things are secure, maybe then." She was thinking about Borodin, how she would like a reason to call on him.

"Absolutely. I'll mark it down in my book." The reddish tint to his hair, the way it tumbled over his forehead, reminded her of her brother Reddy and gave rise to a feeling of kinship that made her answer his next question even though she shouldn't have.

"What do you think the great Borodin expected to accomplish? To cure the lepers and free the peasants overnight?"

"Of course not," she responded with a laugh. "He was sent here by his government with a particular mission. To build the military academy, to train an officer corps and put some spine in the government Dr. Sun left behind."

"Has he accomplished those objectives?"

She screwed up her face to let him know she was talking out of school. "The first two."

Then he asked another question. "What do you think are his current objectives?"

This she was more careful about. "To make the best of things. To trust that the investments Russia has made will bear fruit in the long run."

"Communist fruits?"

"I imagine so. Sure of it, in fact."

He snapped his baby blue suspenders and grinned. "I knew you were the lady to talk to."

For the next two days, Jimmy followed her around, digging for news, pestering her to set up his meeting with Borodin. She said she'd inquire, letting him think she had that much pull. It was an excuse, she decided, to test whether she did.

Later that week, having fortified herself with a sheaf of papers, questions involving the upcoming plenum, she climbed the stairway via the separate outside entrance to Borodin's private quarters. The Russian guard threw down his cigarette and looked her over, visualizing what lay behind the papers she clutched. She watched an armada of flies circle while Sheean made his way up behind her. With the arrival of an American male, the guard said he'd check with the commander. Another two minutes while they watched the flies, then the door opened and they were motioned in. Borodin was standing with his back to them, looking out the window at the gunboats. The late afternoon sun cast him in shadow. Leaving Jimmy by the door, she circled around to get a view of his face. Borodin turned, startled by this intrusion.

"My father used to stand like that," she said.

He examined her with a grave expression, Sheean ignored at the door.

"He was a commodities broker," she explained, "with an office overlooking Grant Park." She grinned to lighten the mood. "Very capitalist."

He played along. "Yes, and now I, too, have a capitalist office, a perch from which to view my antagonists, at least one set of them." He extended the thought. "And your father is no doubt pleased to have you here, helping us with our revolution."

Sheean coughed. Borodin flicked him a glance, then turned back to Rayna.

"Yes, indeed," she answered, pulling a straight face. "He believes we Chicagoans need to stick together." She looked at Sheean to indicate she'd get to him in due course. There was a pause while Borodin seemed to think about Chicago. She hesitated, then remembered his saying that she was impertinent, that because she came from Chicago she felt she could ask him anything. "Do you ever think of going back?"

He barked a short, painful laugh, motioning to the row of gunboats. "Yes, often these days. Particularly it's the winter I miss. It reminds me of home."

"And where was that?" Jimmy asked from his place by the door. She held her breath, wondering how long they could string this nonsense out.

Borodin decided to oblige. "A little village in the Pale, a dot on the map. In spring it was ankle deep in mud. In summer, baked earth. In winter, frozen tundra."

"Sounds like Illinois," Jimmy agreed.

"Just like Illinois."

That seemed to be the end of it, so Rayna took the moment to tell him that Jimmy Sheean had graduated from the University of Chicago. As Borodin motioned the journalist in, Rayna excused herself, explaining she had work to do. Borodin walked her to the door, reminding her in a low voice of the time when she sat next to Mme. Sun. "She likes you," he added, seeming to mull over the implication of that.

Two days later he came down to the newspaper office and asked if she would help Mme. Sun with a project involving village girls. She flushed to the roots of her still-cropped hair. He nodded and was almost out the door before she called out, "Of course." And then, "You must be pleased to be out of your cast."

A week later he fractured the arm again moving boxes and was back in a sling.

CHAPTER 4

The next day Rayna received a message. She was to come to Mme. Sun's villa in the British Concession. The Borodin and Chen families were also housed in the same enclave, although most nights Borodin himself camped above his office. When the government car dropped her off, a Chinese servant opened the door and nodded as she passed between the two armed guards flanking the entrance. She was nervous and wearing her best dress, a fern green number with a dove colored band around the hem. She'd had only minimal success with her unruly hair, now a copper penumbra, but dug out from her jewelry box a clunky turquoise necklace. A Chinese girl with bobbed hair glided up with an outstretched arm to indicate she was to enter the sitting room.

Mme. Sun rose from her brocade settee and took up both Rayna's hands. "Welcome. I have been looking forward to continuing our acquaintance."

Rayna started to mumble a reply, then checked herself, stood upright and looked the Chinese window full in the face. "I am honored."

That seemed to suffice. Mme. Sun motioned for the Chinese girl to pour tea. That done, the Lady asked the girl to join them, but the girl chose to perch on a bench near the door. "Mei-hui is a ward of mine, the granddaughter of my father's oldest friend. She helps with my various education duties. As you know, having launched this momentous effort to modernize China, we have a grave responsibility to protect the women in their new freedom."

Rayna was about to say something about protection and freedom, but Mme. Sun caught the contradiction. "I know. Sometimes we run too fast and sometimes too slow." She nodded at the girl. "Mei-hui and her young colleagues are the ones at risk. They cut their hair and march as we direct them, but then, if they are unlucky—"

Rayna knew what she was referring to, an incident in Canton when a band of marching girls had been bayoneted and dragged through the streets by thugs hired by irate merchants. "But here we can protect them?" Rayna hoped this was true.

Mme. Sun sighed. "We must be brave. Communicate that braveness to others. It is all we have." She stopped. "How old are you?"

Rayna was startled by this question. "Thirty-three."

"Just a few months younger than I." She considered something and then added, "Dr. Sun and I married when I was twenty-two. We eloped. Scandalous that a Chinese girl should do such a thing."

"And now all Chinese girls should be free to do such things?" Rayna was thinking about her father, what he thought of the two men she'd chosen.

Mme. Sun bowed her head in a noncommittal way and then placed her untouched tea on the table. "Now we shall take a tour of the village education projects. Mei-hui will be our guide." The girl stood and with a grave look gathered her papers.

In the government car, Mme. Sun told Rayna how she had once been ambushed in Canton. It was a story Rayna had heard before, but to hear it from the Lady's own lips was a pleasure. She called her that now, the Lady, though not to her face.

"When word came that we would be attacked, Dr. Sun wanted me to accompany him to his gunboat. But I said

40

no, I would be a burden and that as a private citizen, a woman, I would be perfectly safe remaining. The Presidential home was a lovely villa, connected by a wooden bridge to the offices where Dr. Sun conducted his business. But the compound was not protected, and when wayward troops entered the city and began rampaging, I awoke to gunfire, bullets spraying through my windows. My personal guards rushed in and I dressed quickly and, along with my two maids, left the house accompanied by fifty soldiers Dr. Sun had providently left behind. We made our way onto the bridge, in the midst of gunfire, toward what we thought was the better protected office building.

"Midway across, when we were crawling on our hands and knees, they started hurling firebombs. Whenever one of our soldiers stood to fire back, he was picked off. It was a sorry state I had put myself in, I must say." She let out a tinkling laugh at her remembered foolishness. "You see, I should have listened to my husband."

Then her tone became somber. "Let me tell you, it was a long night. One of my maids was killed and I made the decision to take off her clothes and wear them."

Rayna tried to imagine the gruesome business of stripping bloody clothing off a dead woman's body. Mme. Sun continued in an oddly jocular voice. "No time for modesty, that's for sure. I had to dress in front of all my men. At dawn my remaining troops made a frontal assault, thus allowing me and my one remaining maid and last bodyguard to escape. We wandered the streets for hours trying to get some strangers to take us in, hide us from the marauding troops that were searching door-to-door. Finally we found one brave soul. Or greedy, I didn't care which at the time. I always carry gold for just such an emergency."

Rayna wondered where on that slender body the gold was now being carried. Whether something like this could happen in Hankow.

As they drove into the village in a cloud of dust, Mme. Sun summed up. "The next morning I was able to slip away and make it to the gunboat where my husband was waiting. A few days later loyal troops arrived from Shanghai and pushed the marauders back and that was that." She paused, then added, "None of my brave men on the bridge, the ones who opened fire to allow my escape, survived."

Rayna's work on the village project was mostly propaganda. News releases, tours for visitors, interviews with the cadre of girls Mei-hui was training to go out and coax other young women to join the cause. Three nights a week they worked on skits in the Lutheran Mission dining room, using white table cloths and cut up blue napkins to make banners announcing the scenes. There were two skits, the result of much discussion about what messages they wished to convey to the young women of the villages. Finally they settled on two: a lesson in speaking up that involved a girl pointing out the miscreants who fouled the village duck pond instead of using the communal latrine and a second skit on fairness, featuring different sized rice bowls and which children in the family got a fair share.

This on top of her job at *The People's Tribune* and arrangements for the upcoming Pan Asian Labor Conference. The fifteen hour days left her shaking with exhaustion as she made her way back each night to her penthouse apartment. Often as not, some journalists living downstairs would be there, drinking Chinese beer and keeping Bill up past his bedtime.

Bill was coughing blood but refused to go down to Shanghai for treatment. Also, he had laid down the law that the dog must go. Millie Bennett was on her way from Peking to help with the newspaper and Rayna had the idea that she could sleep in the extra bedroom and maybe take care of Dan, but hadn't any idea how they were going to pay her. Against her better judgment, she made an appointment with Borodin to lay out the whole financial mess.

The next afternoon, as she mounted the once-grand stairway to Bee's third floor apartment, she thought about Mme. Sun's ambush. The news from General Chiang's camp was not good. Both factions of the KMT were courting the northern warlords. By coming to Hankow, the legitimate government had more or less ceded the southern coastal cities to General Chiang. He had the bulk of the army but Moscow was still backing the Hankow regime. Surely the Russians could do more to turn the tide?

She resolved to ask Borodin that question, but first had to deal with the matter of Bill's health. After escorting her to the sitting area, three leather chairs around a low Chinese table, he asked about her work with Mme. Sun.

"The girls' cadre is mostly trained. We've printed up lesson books and I've been teaching them about petition drives and public speaking. They've developed skits, little performances they plan to put on for the villagers, the lessons, of course, having to do with giving their daughters the opportunity to do what they want."

Borodin grimaced. Was it how she had phrased that idea or had he just jostled his arm?

"Not do what *they* want, do what *we* want. What the revolution needs."

She thought about saying that young women need first to do something entirely personal, that only then will they have the courage to do more. But instead she nodded to acknowledge his reprimand, and then, in a backward way to make her point, found herself telling him about the dead baby depository. He listened with his head down as she described the red-tile roofs and the view of the bay, the steep climb to the cement bunker. She kept it objective, not dwelling on the men's scorn. "I kept being told there were no such things, that what I'd heard was an old wives' tale, that the revolution had wiped them out." She stopped. "You see the contradiction. It can't be an old wives' tale and also something the revolution wiped out.

Anyway, I saw it, the remains in that cement bunker. It was recent and it was true."

Her voice had taken on a plaintive note. She looked up from studying her white knuckles. "What Mme. Sun is doing is so important. That's why people have to respect — "

Borodin interrupted. "Men," he said. "You are speaking of men. Men in power."

She nodded.

He continued, turning around her frame of reference. "We communists believe there is a single point of the lance, and that is the proletariat, the industrial workers, both men and women. That is the thrusting instrument that will puncture the capitalist boil. But there are others, among them some of our Chinese comrades, who see the revolution as more of a pitchfork. Twin prongs of attack, workers and peasants. Then there are those, like Mme. Sun, who see the revolutionary movement in China as having three prongs."

"Women," Rayna said, deeply stirred by the possibility he had just articulated.

"Yes," he agreed. "It is not orthodox, but this Chinese caldron is bubbling so wildly, who can say what is orthodox."

With that he got up and looked out the window. "Forgive me, I am preoccupied. My wife is returning from Shanghai where she saw off our son Norman. She was due back three days ago." He readjusted the sling on his arm and returned to the sitting area but remained standing, an indication that she should go.

"Bill," she said as she began to rise. "He's not well. I've sent for Millie Bennett, who worked with us in Peking. We will have to pay her."

Borodin waved away this detail. "Fine. Talk to Chen."

She took a deep breath. "I would like to send Bill back. There are doctors in Shanghai. Mme. Sun has agreed to arrange treatment." She gathered up her thoughts and looked at him with the peculiar intensity she used when she wanted something. "Maybe there is something he could do there. So he won't feel so useless."

Borodin looked thoughtful, taking his time to examine her importuning expression. "Perhaps we could find something. Do you want me to ask Chen?"

"No." She hastened to block that idea. "Say to Chen that you would like someone to keep an eye on events there, an American who can travel freely. Let him come up with the idea of Bill." She took another deep breath. "And if that works out, if Bill has his own masthead, so to speak, then I can concentrate on things here."

Again he looked thoughtful, although she wasn't sure what he was considering, her proposal regarding Bill or the fate of his wife. But as he walked her to the door, she detected extra pressure on the inside of her arm.

Millie arrived and set about getting the newspaper in order. She took the maid's room opposite the pantry where Rayna had installed Dan. A week later, they waved Bill off to Shanghai. In addition to getting treatment from Mme. Sun's doctor, he was to take up an open-ended assignment to revive the news clipping agency that had been closed in Peking. Now more than ever, Rayna's apartment became a nightly collecting place. Millie loved to drink with Tom Mann, the London delegate to the Pan Asian Labor Conference, while his American counterpart, prim Kansas-born Earl Browder, looked on. The festivities lasted into the wee hours, and Rayna, who had hoped for time alone, instead found herself caught in a social whirl she came increasingly to dread.

Soon it was time to try out their skits in the villages. The first one went okay, the elders grumbling and the women and girls afraid to watch, but at least their banners weren't torn down. But in the second village an unfortunate incident occurred. A couple of girls came over to watch. Mei-hui was urging them to join in, to play the second and third girls in the family drama of the rice bowls, but then one of the fathers appeared and shook his herding stick and began to drag his daughter off. It was only when he began to beat the girl across the legs that Rayna's temper flared.

She strode over and grabbed the stick, pulled it out of his hand and smashed it against the corrugated tin side of the oxen shed. With the third whack she broke it. "Don't you ever do that to your daughter again," she hissed with barely controlled fury.

Mei-hui interceded to placate the father, and the guard who had driven them moved in to ward off any further violence. The father spat out something, an oath, which Rayna thought she recognized.

"What did he say?" she demanded.

"Nothing, he said nothing," Mei-hui hastened to explain.

"I know what he called me." Rayna felt saliva pooling in her mouth and had to choke back the urge to spit.

"He said nothing. Come, let us go."

The other girls gathered the banners and stools and hurried back to the truck.

With Fanya gone, Borodin had retreated to his office. The news about his wife was bad. She had been kidnapped at Nanking, tipped off no doubt by Chiang's people, then sold to the warlord in Peking. At least that was the rumor. But the Pan Asian Labor Conference was in full swing and attention must be paid. Mme. Sun's girls' cadre was on the agenda and they had to scramble to find the right village, assuage its village elders with cash and bring in some reliable extras to watch. The show was a big hit. On the special banner-bedecked train, the KMT girls' cadre served as hostesses. Rayna hadn't liked that idea, her young women serving tea, but Chen had ordered it and Mme. Sun had not objected.

Now the big finale, an outdoor rally. She was perched just below the podium, troubleshooting speakers' arrangements, trying without success to keep each man's remarks within the agreed-upon time limit. Her head was killing her, the afternoon heat beyond endurance. Her dress was caked with dried sweat but still she perspired, even though it felt as if the last ounce of water had been wrung from her.

The platform was set up at the far end of the racetrack. M.N. Roy, a newly arrived emissary from Moscow, was holding forth. He was Hindu, a Brahmin dressed in a fresh white tunic she suspected he'd donned just moments before. He was lifting an arm to command the sea of heat-stunned workers. His precise words were delivered with forceful frowns and well-practiced hand motions. Rayna let her eyes unfocus as she tried to take in this figure as he walked back and forth, tried to see him as the Chinese workers must — gangly, aristocratic, his long jaw working to bring forth well-rounded English vowels. Not that she sensed a lack of respect — the crowd didn't seem restive, but there wasn't much fight in them either.

They seemed dazed, as if a hidden drop in pressure presaged some imminent collapse.

She felt a touch on her arm. Mei-hui stood beside her, her thick black hair now shorn to a rough bristle. A warning, retaliation by village elders against the education cadre's efforts. Since that latest incident Mei-hui was always accompanied by a guard. "Mme. Sun wishes to see you." Rayna could barely hear the words above the echoing loudspeakers.

A soldier led them behind the crowd to the far edge of the grandstand fence where a square tent, sky blue, with a government flag painted on the side, served as shelter for Mme. Sun. Guards were stationed at all four corners. As they went inside, Mme. Sun took Rayna's arm and moved her to the center. She glanced at the guard, who took his cue and withdrew.

"You must speak to Commander Borodin for me," she began, the soft words suggesting great gravity. She kept her grip on Rayna's arm and looked around before continuing in a loud, formal voice. "And how did your husband find my humble arrangements?"

Rayna tried to match her tone, knowing that this polite conversation was intended to be overheard. "My husband is well settled, thanks to your kind efforts." Then, not sure that made sense, she dropped her voice. "What is it you want?"

Mme. Sun glanced at Mei-hui, who bowed and slipped out. Rayna supposed it was to check on the guards. Mme. Sun relaxed a fraction of an inch. "I am sorry to say, as the days pass, we are all at greater and greater risk." Her face displayed polite dismay. "And I have burdened you unforgivably with my confidences."

"No, you haven't." That didn't make sense either. Was Rayna implying that the Lady's confidences were no burden or that no confidences had been conveyed?

"My brother T.V. says my sister weighs the prospect of killing me." With a delicate hand Mme. Sun pushed that notion away. "I do not believe this, my brother is given to exaggeration. Still, it lends urgency to our need for a safe departure."

"Yours?" Even before the word came out Rayna knew it was impolite. But if Mme. Sun left Hankow, joined forces with General Chiang as her older sister had already done and her brother was reported to be on the brink of, the game was up. As Borodin had said of the KMT ministers in a moment of painful jest: "Mme. Sun is the only real man in the lot."

"No, I will not leave." Mme. Sun ignored Rayna's suggestion and gave her back a sad smile. "It is Commander Borodin who must leave. I have been told this is a condition of keeping our government ministers from going over to General Chiang." She hesitated. "After that, perhaps I can consider my own situation."

There was a message wrapped in these delicate words

but what was it? Rayna opened her hands in a kind of surrender. "What can I do?"

Mme. Sun cleared her throat. "Forgive me, but I must make a request. I ask only because the hour is so dangerously late. I do not know how to phrase this politely." Rayna watched her twist her hands in a small gesture of agony. "Commander Borodin." The next words came out quite clear. "Can he be trusted?"

Rayna's breath caught. Her mind raced. "Why is it you need to know?"

The Lady stared up at the tent roof. Rayna could hear the drone of loudspeakers, a new dignitary trying to whip up the crowd. "Because in times of deep turmoil," Mme. Sun continued in a kind of trance, "one must rely on one's inner voice. I must know if I can trust him with my life."

Rayna felt her nervous smile spreading. "Of course." Vague words that cut down the middle, suggesting either agreement with the wisdom of the question or a favorable response to it. Suddenly she became aware of the overwhelming heat. Her head dropped, her eyes looking through sweaty red curls in search of Mme. Sun's immobile face. She remembered Borodin's words about the point of attack being a one pronged lance or a two or even three-pronged pitchfork. Was one theory of revolution compatible with another? What was Mme. Sun asking? Was she probing to find out if Borodin's responsibilities to Moscow were consistent with loyalty to her?

There was no return to Rayna's questioning look.

Streamers stamped with revolutionary slogans lay tangled in the reeking stone gutters. In the gathering dark, Rayna picked her way down the littered street as the last speeches droned on. Some days it all seemed like just words. In Canton, she'd often had days like these, when her thoughts undermined her determination, left her adrift and wondering why she was in China. If only she could get to Hankow, she had thought, to the pure revolution, away from the rats in the ceiling, away from the huge empty rooms. If only she could be part of the vanguard. Being alone in Canton had made her do foolish things, wander for hours in a swirl of black and crimson and gold. Collect foolish things, silk wall hangings, temple urns, a dog. The urns broke in the steamer hold or were stolen. But she arrived with the wall hangings and Dan.

Now, on the street, she saw a boy holding a bird cage. He was about seven with arms and legs no thicker than bamboo. An electric surge ran through her, a warning. She had to fight off the urge to take him home. He wore pinstripe pants chopped off at the knee and held around his waist by a rope. She wondered where the coat was, the dress shirt, the silk necktie and felt fedora. Where was the man who had belonged to these clothes? In what field or alley did he lie; whose side was he on? In spite of the heat she felt cold, shivered as she hurried past the boy without answering his look, past his cries to buy his nightingale. She kept her head down so she could see nothing of what was around her and raced to the safety of Borodin's second floor quarters in the gray granite building along the quay.

She stopped at the ground floor newspaper office to pick up copy for the morning edition. Wang, who ran the night shift, looked up. He was tending a broken tie rod in the main press. The jagged steel quivered where the connecting piece had broken off. Wang whistled through his teeth as he considered how to fix the problem. She came up and stood behind. "Are you going to sing?" he asked without turning around. It was a game between them, her singing to keep up his spirits.

"The 'Internationale'?" He liked when she sang that, how tears came to her eyes. She didn't tell him the tears were mostly fatigue, self-pity more than pride in the revolution.

"No. Something funny. 'Pie in the Sky.'"

"Sorry, I haven't the energy."

Wang plunked the rod, frowning at her response. The broken piece gave off a flat note. He folded it up as best he could and patted the metal hood. "She needs a rest."

"We all do." She touched his shoulder and then moved off to collect her proofreading copy. She was thinking about Bill, how she should have written.

A note awaited her. "M.M. Borodin is available to see you at 9 p.m." She checked her watch, ten minutes, then grabbed the note and ran outside to the separate entrance and bolted up the stairs.

She was stopped, as usual, by the guard. She waved the handwritten note but he ignored her as she struggled to contain her breath. A second guard came up and studied the paper. Finally, he pushed down the handle and waved her on. Inside, she noticed, as if for the first time, the somber oil portrait of Sun Yat-sen placed in counterpoint to the tinted photo of Vladimir Illych Lenin.

Borodin came forward to greet her in a freshly pressed white suit. His arm was still wrapped in cloth but he looked more comfortable than he had in days. On his neck, where the sling chafed, she could see a red mark. "Hi," she said, still gulping for air. The way he came out from behind his desk always reminded her of the way her father greeted clients in his brokerage office. She held out the handwritten note. "I listened to your friend M.N. Roy. He's stirring the pot with the workers but is going to make the merchants very angry."

He looked at her sharply. Suddenly she felt foolish, shamefaced to be the one telling this next part. "I heard Chen talk about a letter, something Comrade Roy showed to the Prime Minister."

"Chen shouldn't have done that." He busied himself with his sling. "Is this common knowledge?"

She hesitated. "I don't think so. But there are rumors that the ministers are demanding the Russian contingent leave."

"The whole contingent?"

"Yes."

"Do you know what was in that letter that Comrade Roy supposedly showed around?"

Again she hesitated. "They said it came from Moscow's highest levels. That it directed the rearming of the peasants, something the KMT government thinks is not in their best interest."

A mirthless sound escaped him and he turned to the stacks on his desk, began moving paperweights around. "I didn't ask for this job. I had no plans to stay. I could long ago have gone to some other assignment. Ankara. Delhi."

"I should like Delhi," she breathed out before she knew what she was saying.

Once again he gave her a sharp look. "I thought you were going to save the women of China."

"There are also women—"

"Comrade Roy is from India. You would have to contend with him."

She smiled to show she accepted his jibe. "Actually, there is something else I need to tell you. Something Mme. Sun said to me at the rally."

He looked up from repositioning his paperweights. "Yes?"

"She said her sister may be trying to kill her. That her brother T.V. has decided to throw in his lot with Chiang."

He let out a long breath. "All that in one short conversation."

"She also asked if she could trust you."

He nodded, turned to look out at the gunboats. "Now that is interesting. I wonder what it means."

"I don't know."

"You know I can't leave until Fanya is released. We are trying bribes but so far they haven't taken."

"I didn't know that."

"Thank God there's something you don't know."

"I want to go with you."

"What?"

"To Moscow. When you evacuate, I want to go along."

"You want to go along."

"Yes."

"To do what?"

He was punishing her. Making her declare her intentions. She took a deep breath for courage. "I want to be part of what you do. I want to be with you. So you can help Mme. Sun. To prove she can trust you with her life."

He stared at her for a long minute. "You really are the most extraordinary creature. I'm never sure whether your vision is too shallow or too deep."

"Sometimes I think I have no vision at all. That I'm just stumbling my way."

"We all think that. Well, Mme. Sun confides in you. Chen blabs to you. In the long run neither is of any concern. But what Mme. Sun does is of vital importance. So, stay with her. Let me know if she says anything more. In the meantime, you have an additional assignment. Preparing for my getaway. We will go through the Gobi. I am negotiating now for safe passage. More bribes, you needn't get involved in that. What I need from you are cars, good reliable cars and trucks to carry the gasoline."

"Are there roads?"

"No. But I'm told the sands are hard packed. We'll need shovels, of course. At least one machine gun, better two, and hunting rifles, dried food, water, spare parts. Talk to whomever you need to sort it out."

"When will you leave?"

"After I hear word of Fanya. Before they tar and feather me."

She returned to her main theme. "I want to go with you."

"No women on this trip."

"I'll go separately. I want to be there. At the next stage, whatever it is."

Something in her voice conveyed the essence of what she was asking.

"Your husband? His plans?" He meant did her plans include Bill.

"I don't know. I haven't spoken with him."

Borodin returned to his desk. Back to the stacks and the paperweights. "As you wish."

CHAPTER 5

She and Millie were having an early dinner with Tom Mann and Earl Browder. Mann, missing his pubs, wanted some "real honest-to-God English beer" and the German Concession was the next best thing. Browder thought a drunken night in the company of the *Boche* was a mistake, but Mann dismissed his concerns. "Our last night here. Drink your Shirley Temple and polish off that last bit of nasty fish. I've got a bottle of Scotch we'll finish off at Rayna's." He heaved himself from the table, asking the sullen waiter where to find the Gents.

Rayna motioned for the check, wondering how on earth Chen was going to cough up the hard currency to pay for this. While Tom was gone she took the moment to ask Browder about a matter she'd been mulling over. As she began, she shot Millie a warning look.

"I wanted to ask about the Lenin School, the one for international students. I know you have say on who gets in."

Browder feigned surprise. "You interested? You'd be a fine candidate, of course—"

"Bee thinks it would be a good way to keep my hand in. A course of study along the lines of what I've been doing here with the girls' cadres."

"Indeed." Browder looked uncomfortable. He probably thought she was angling for a job later in Shanghai.

"I know the women's slots are harder to fill." She took a

deep breath. "I thought, since I'm going to be staying on in Moscow—"

He looked relieved. "By all means. When you're there, take it up with the director. I'll put in a word."

Tom, weaving his way back, asked what word, and when Rayna explained about the Lenin School he insisted Browder write a letter, right then, recommending her. "Least we can do," he concluded, "considering the lovely company." Rayna snatched up the check with the astronomical total marked in red while Browder composed his missive with Tom Mann giving him pointers. On the way out Millie whispered, "Does Bill know?"

Rayna shook her head. "It's a long shot. A whole list of credentials I don't have. Under thirty-five: I make that barely. Mass movement experience: got that. The big stumbling block is Party membership. I'd have to join more or less retroactively." She laughed and set her mind to finding them rickshaws.

During the ride Millie had more questions. "I hear that place is pretty hush-hush. Are you sure about joining?"

"The Party? If I get admitted, I will. And yes, it is a kind of walled-in existence. A new name, no outside contacts."

"Forever?"

"Just for the time you're enrolled. Then it depends on what your job is. There's a short course that's somewhat more relaxed."

"What about Bill? If he's left alone he'll curl up and die."

"I've got to find out if they'll make an exception. Take him even though he's way over age. Or create some kind of adjunct job." She shook her head. "It's just an idea. Don't say anything."

The party continued in the living room, a new batch of journalists joining in. By two in the morning she was trying to figure out how to get the men sprawled on her couches home to bed. Jimmy was trying to rouse them to a spirited chorus of "There'll be pie in the sky when you die!" but he wasn't having much luck. She fervently wished he'd take his pie and shove off.

As she made a display of emptying the ashtrays, Jimmy came over. "Another interview with the great man?"

"I suppose." She opened the windows to let the stifling air out into the equally stifling night.

"I hear strange things about Shanghai. Has Bill wired any news?"

She ignored that question, instead clapping her hands to get everyone's attention. "Time to go." The men grumbled but started to move. Tom Mann appropriated what was left of his Scotch while Earl Browder began putting the beer empties in the waste basket. Jimmy, however, was not distracted.

"Rumor is that General Chiang has underworld ties. That the reason the Shanghai Communists walked into a trap is that Moscow directed them to surrender their weapons stockpiles to Chiang."

She kept shooing the men out, a fixed smile on her face. What was Jimmy talking about? Was there any truth to what he was saying?

Tom Mann, who, if anyone, should know what the Russians were telling the Chinese Communists, overheard. "What are you saying about Shanghai?"

"Nothing, Tom." Rayna pushed him out the door, straightening his hat on his crown of flyaway white hair. "Jimmy is just blowing hot air."

"I am not." Jimmy took on an injured air. "You don't take me seriously. You should."

"I take you seriously." She was pushing him out the door as well.

"Do I get my interview?"

"Tomorrow," she promised, then shut the door.

The next day Jimmy opened his interview with a softball question. "Why did you choose the name Borodin?"

Borodin was spread out on his favorite leather chair, one

leg slung over the arm rest. He fiddled with a letter opener while he pondered. "It is a name," he said at last, "that connotes great accomplishment." He placed the letter opener in a clean ashtray, began staring at the ceiling. Jimmy was getting frustrated, Borodin dishing out this stock response. He had dozens of them.

Jimmy tried a different tack. "You lived a decade in Chicago."

Borodin nodded. "And you as well."

"And Rayna," Jimmy added.

"And Anna Louise, my good friend, the journalist, who is arriving from Moscow. She also lived there."

Jimmy did not like a new competitor brought into the mix.

"Yes, all from Chicago," Borodin summarized, as if that put an end to the discussion.

She could see Jimmy wondering where to go next. "All great minds from Chicago. It must be something in the water." Then his wicked reverse. "A lot easier there, I've found, to get a decent bath."

The great man looked up and burst out laughing. He unwrapped his leg from the chair arm and leaned forward. "Did you ever visit that bath house in Chicago? The Turkish one on Division Street with the blue tiles out front?"

Jimmy nodded as if he had.

Borodin continued. "Each Friday, without fail, I would take my little ones. Fanya would pack us off, soap, underwear, little towels." He squared his hands to show how little the towels had been. "'Come back clean—' she'd yell, as if we planned any different." His face had taken on a relaxed cast.

"Where are your sons now?" Jimmy put in.

Borodin seemed to count them in his mind. "Fred is in Moscow, Norman on his way." His face changed. He was thinking of Fanya, Rayna guessed, her capture after seeing Norman off.

"Which one is more like you?" Jimmy persisted.

Borodin pretended to think. "Fred. He likes parades, the clash of cymbals." He smiled at the word play, then stood. "You must excuse me. I am preoccupied, awaiting news of my wife."

Rayna shot Jimmy a glance to tell him that now was not the time to ask about Shanghai.

Jimmy nodded and then made one last stab. "Have you ever thought of escaping?"

Borodin looked startled, then, with some effort, amazed. "From what?" He held out his palms as if this were a mystery. Then, with a shrug, conceded the point. "Don't we all?" He cleared his throat to indicate the interview was closed.

Rayna stood and took up her sheaves of paper. As Borodin was escorting them to the door, Rayna said in a low voice, "If I could take a few minutes."

"Of course." Once Jimmy was well beyond the closed door, Borodin turned to her with a face that revealed all that he had struggled to hide.

"You must be exhausted," she said.

"Aren't we all?"

"I've heard some troubling things. Things I don't understand."

Borodin showed her to the chair Jimmy had vacated. "Yes?"

"About Shanghai. Jimmy said Chiang is in league with the underworld. That our Chinese cadres were led into a trap, ordered to disarm." She didn't tell him the other part, Jimmy's wild idea that the Russians were behind the order. Because if Moscow was behind the order, Commander Borodin was the one who gave it. "Do you trust General Chiang?" she asked instead.

A sour face. "Of course not. A scoundrel of the first rank. But the great Dr. Sun picked him." Another pained expression. "You see, I'm not omnipotent. I take orders like everyone."

"When do you leave? Mme. Sun says it must be soon."

"When I hear about Fanya."

"What if you don't?"

He shrugged. "When Moscow says I must."

"What happens to me?"

Now came a look that absolved him of responsibility. "You must make your own—"

"I want to go with you," she reminded him. "Tom Mann says I should apply to the Lenin School. Earl Browder has written a letter."

He studied her for a long time. "We will discuss this some other time. Now, I would like you to accompany Mme. Sun on a probably fruitless excursion to persuade General Feng to join our side. It seems I have not been invited."

Rayna went home to find the much heralded, large and very pink Anna Louse Strong awaiting her in the Lutheran Mission.

"They've given me a terrible room overlooking the alley and a mattress that's ripped. You're in charge here, I want you to fix it."

Rayna decided a course of flattery was in order. She told Anna Louise how much she admired her writing, mentioned her latest book on Soviet life which Bill had read in Peking but she hadn't opened. "I hear you are an old friend of Bee's."

Anna Louise looked confused and Rayna explained they had taken to calling him that.

"Yes," the famous journalist agreed, adjusting her corset which must have chafed in the unrelenting heat. "Mikhail and I have known each other for ages. I'm friends with his wife. Do you know Fanya?"

Rayna allowed as how she did.

"Terrible about her being kidnapped. The security here must be woefully lax."

There seemed to be no answer that didn't lead down a path to more unwanted criticism. "Bee tells me you are going to write an account of these last days. You're very lucky. I asked as well but was turned down."

This made Anna Louise perk up, to have something on a younger woman who was so much smaller.

"I'll do what I can about the mattress," Rayna conceded. "I can't change the room, we're full up. I'm going north tomorrow but if there is anything—"

"Are you going to see General Feng?"

Good lord, Rayna thought, had the woman been handed the keys to the kingdom?

"I'm going too." Anna Louise played this card in triumph, forgetting for the moment her ripped mattress and appalling view.

And so it was that Rayna spent the next day, six and a half long hours of it, next to Anna Louise in a train compartment churning ahead through a vast arid plain. In some ways it was a relief to get out of Hankow, to be free to drift.

Anna Louise had her face pressed to the filthy glass. "The land here looks like North Dakota." Then she went off about a hunting trip her father took her on when she was ten. Everything reminded her of something else. Rayna wished she would just shut up. "Look at those graves." She grabbed Rayna's arm to pull her close to the streaked window. "They're just like ones I saw in the Ukraine." Bones stuck up at odd angles in the packed yellow mud. Anna Louise then changed her mind and said it reminded her of Dagestan, then changed her mind again and said it was more like the stacked dead of the Finnish campaign. The grim list made the space behind Rayna's eyes throb. "They were stretched out in a line," Anna Louise recalled, moistening her lips to work up to a fuller description, but Rayna cut her off.

"My head," she announced, closing her eyes to contemplate the great shimmering waves that lit up like jagged fireworks.

Blessedly, Anna Louise fell silent, rummaged in her string bag for something to eat. But soon she started up again. "All that was left were the bodies themselves. Peasants moving over them like carrion, taking shirts, canteens, identification tags." She touched Rayna's arm, waiting for her eyes to open. "The Russian Civil War was hard, hard on the people. It drained some human quality from the stock."

Rayna watched as her companion's mouth worked, trying to say something better left unsaid.

"You see it most in the women," Anna Louise finally offered. "The difference between what they thought was theirs and what it turned out to be. It's bitter—"

The last note, a kind of warble, made Rayna sit up, focus on the thing she most wanted to ask. "Are you sorry you went to Moscow?"

"Good heavens, no!" Anna Louise's face brightened, took on a set expression. "It's a wonderful place, an honor to be a part of something so elemental. People work so hard, give so much..." Anna Louise was gauging the reason for the question. "Are you planning to go?"

Rayna said yes, then backtracked, "I've been thinking about it." She straightened in her seat and studied her hands. "If I can make a contribution." She did not like the sound of her voice, the tenor both hopeful and needy. She didn't want Anna Louise to know how thoughts of Bee filled her nights.

"It's difficult," Anna Louise agreed. "A strange place, you feel so alone. Of course, there are Americans, English, a few Aussies." She smiled, now on solid ground. "The Americans especially bend themselves into pretzels trying to make things work. I should know. I spent years organizing a farm for orphans. Now it's all sliding into the typical Russian morass. The Russian revolution got rid of all the impediments to utopia except the Russians themselves." She laughed, then thought better of it. Took both Rayna's hands and examined her with a fixed expression. "You really must go. It's the future."

For China? Rayna wanted to ask, but didn't.

Busying herself with her string bag, Anna Louise pulled out a lopsided pear, bit into it, then handed what was left to Rayna. "Here. Make sure you get enough water." Still chewing, she turned her attention to their mission. "I think Bee is fooling himself if he thinks Mme. Sun can keep her government from throwing in the towel. If not after this session, then soon."

They were coming into what looked like the outskirts of a good-sized village. Rayna took a deep breath and said what was on her mind.

"You've just come from Moscow. Can you explain why they are so skittish about the Chinese peasant armies? After all, we need all the support we can get."

Anna Louise took her time to answer. "I suppose it's explained in part by Soviet history. They don't trust them. I was in the Ukraine during the civil war. Peasant bands fought against the Red Army." She considered some more. "Then there's the theoretical problem. Marx insisting that the industrial proletariat would be the vanguard. But China, that may be a different story."

Rayna decided to touch on her one piece of forbidden knowledge. "They go back and forth, Moscow does, about whether to arm or disarm the peasant armies."

Anna Louise looked startled. "Oh, no. That is settled. They've been disarmed, once and for all. Of course the KMT ministers are delighted by this turn of events. They all own vast tracts of land, so land reform isn't on their agenda."

Rayna wondered what Anna Louise would say when news of Moscow's latest directive to rearm the peasant armies seeped out. Besides, the order to rearm would be nearly impossible to fulfill. As far as she knew, Hankow had no spare weapons.

The train was coming to the station, General Feng's honor guard striking up a lively rendition of "Onward Christian Soldiers." It was easy to let the awkward topic drop.

Immediately they were shown to the grand conclave which was well underway. Rayna sat in the back listening to the drone of Chinese, hearing the whisper of the interpreter and thinking about the stacked bodies she'd seen from the train window. Bodies from a war north of their war, a war between warlords, a war from another century. She looked at General Feng, the bursting ammunition belts strapped across his well-larded chest and the chests of his skinnier aides. They are waiting for chaos, she realized, waiting for the vacuum to emerge in Hankow. Then they will make their peace with Chiang and take back their hereditary territory. Alliance with Feng is an illusion.

The delegations sat in two half circles, with the KMT ministers on one side and General Feng and his aides on the other. None of the KMT's Communist ministers had been invited. But M.N. Roy had insisted on attending and Rayna was glad to see he'd been banished to a corner, alone by the tent opening.

They were discussing the terms under which General Feng might remain Hankow's eternally loyal ally. It all boiled down to cash. Feng, being a Christian, cast the demand in terms of maintaining his ministry with the troops. The KMT ministers, merchants for the most part, haggled relentlessly, pointing out that Feng's troops were mere riffraff, worth no more than a bowl of rice. M.N. Roy, ear cocked to his whisp-ering interpreter, occupied himself by fiddling with the tent cord. Mme. Sun sat in the middle of her delegation, eyes closed, hands twisting in her lap, seeking redemption. There was no redemption here.

Six hours later the delegates adjourned to a great banquet laid out by Feng from his Christian coffers supplied by Moscow. Ducks by the scores revolved on long spits, dripping and spurting into the flames. Hordes of black flies swarmed over honeyed fruits laid out on long tables. Rice steamed in great kettles, root vegetables spattered in giant woks tended by cooks wearing wooden crosses and army puttees. Smells of smoke and horse dung mingled with river muck, the setting sun vibrated red. A skim of perspiration that had coated Rayna's face all day broke into heavy sweat. She tried to swallow but her throat constricted.

"You don't look well." Anna Louise came over and pried open an eye, then took Rayna by the arm to lead her to a patch of shade. "Did you stay away from those egg things?"

"I'm fine. I'll sleep on the train."

Another seven hours on the train with Anna Louise. Just before dawn, they arrived back in Hankow to find the water system shut off. So, instead of going home for a soak in her tub, Rayna went directly to Borodin's apartment, still smarting from the news Anna Louise had dropped on the ride home that she had been invited to join Bee on the escape through the Gobi. When had that happened? Had she arrived from Moscow with the invitation in hand?

The night guard said Commander Borodin was sleeping, but Rayna flashed some papers and insisted she had to wake him. Standing over his bed, she ran through her report, the set speech she'd rehearsed on the train. Who was there, how Mme. Sun looked, Roy alone by the tent flap twisting the pull cord. She told Bee that Roy had shown the Stalin letter to at least two other ministers, Mme. Sun had whispered as much. Borodin kept reaching out to prop her up as she swayed.

"You've had a busy day. Go home."

"There is no water. No reason to go home."

He got out of bed. Wrapped a robe about himself and straightened the cover. "Here. Lie down. I'll sit in the chair while you sleep."

It sounded like heaven. To be close to the sleeping smell of him, to feel his warmth. She climbed in and let oblivion begin to take her. "Tell me how you and Mme. Sun met. Why she trusts you." As she murmured this from the edge of consciousness, she knew that that wasn't exactly the way Mme. Sun had put it.

"It was in Peking, in early 1925," he said. "Her husband was dying. All sorts of rogues were lining up to subvert Dr.

Sun's magnificent accomplishment. Mme. Sun was a young, very devoted wife. Everyone who ever saw the two of them together knew it was a partnership of love as well as politics."

She wanted to ask him about that, a partnership of love and politics, but was too far into sleep and could only listen to the low ripple of his voice.

"Of course I had my instructions, to make sure the alliance between Russia and Dr. Sun's government held. And I knew Mme. Sun was the key. So I spent many hours with her at her husband's bedside, explaining the situation as I saw it, how Dr. Sun's principles could best be accomplished by continuing the arrangement."

"A marriage of equals?" she heard herself asking.

A soft snort. "Not exactly, but we let that illusion stand. I made the case that Russia would always be at China's side, help Mme. Sun and her husband's chosen ministers continue their work all the way to its completion. Together the two of us drafted a manifesto, declaring Dr. Sun's desire to continue the relationship, expressing his belief that Soviet help was necessary to guide China to his goal of a unified, democratic nation. She read it aloud. He nodded his assent and she guided his hand."

"You owe her a lot."

"My best efforts, surely."

An hour later he shook her awake, thanked her and said she must go. As she was leaving, she let herself lean against the door, to feel the cool morning air on its surface. She was about to say something about the Gobi, how she wanted to come. But he was touching her hair, smoothing it with the tips of his fingers. A tremor passed through her, electricity, sparks from the carpet, most likely. Her hair, she really must get it cut.

Chapter 6

On the way home she got waylaid by Chen who wanted to talk about a garden party. Notwithstanding the fact that they were negotiating for Feng's support, Mme. Sun was planning to auction off goods confiscated from Feng's many Hankow storehouses. She planned to use the money for medical supplies, whereas Chen thought the proceeds should go to his Foreign Ministry account. What did Rayna think?

Rayna murmured that it was Mme. Sun's garden party, her friends who were buying.

"But don't you see?" Chen's voice was chipper, much too chipper given the sad state of Hankow's affairs. "It's just a matter of time. We need to take the long view."

Ah, the long view, Bee's answer to any question that had no answer. She promised Chen to talk to the great man.

Then Chen asked about Bill. "I hear he's coming back."

She hadn't heard. Maybe there was a telegram. She pretended to know all about Bill's plans and begged off, claiming she needed a bath.

When she got back to the apartment, Jimmy Sheean was waiting, picnic basket in hand, not at all pleased by the news that she had forgotten their date. She explained she'd had no sleep. "But you've got to come," he insisted. "It's my last day."

It had slipped her mind that he was leaving for Peking, claiming to have contacts that might help secure Mme.

Borodin's release. Bee had endorsed his efforts, the both of them clutching at straws, Rayna thought.

She asked if the water was back on. When he said yes, she grabbed a towel, said, "Hold the phone," and went off down the hall.

An hour later, when they were settled by the river on a red checked tablecloth, he filled her in on the official reason for his departure. "My editor thinks there is no adventure left in Hankow. So he's ordered me to Peking."

She liked that. "Maybe you can get captured along the way. Disemboweled, drawn and quartered."

He pointed out that being disemboweled and drawn were the same thing. One had to do with how they got at the entrails and the other how elaborately they presented them.

She felt sick and thought maybe it was the river smell and tried to steady herself by staring at the peanut butter and raisin canapes that Jimmy had so elaborately prepared.

With great effort she brought her mind back to the present. "You'll miss the end. What kind of reporter does that?" The idea that Hankow was coming to the end raised so many bleak questions that she could not go on. He asked about her next step.

"I don't know," she said, pulling at the last of the dying grass. "I may go to Moscow. Bee has mentioned the Lenin School, I can enroll there."

"The spy school? I don't think you'd be any good at that. You're much too sunny and upright for that. Besides, with that red hair you'd stand out like a sore thumb."

She resented his dismissal of her painfully felt plans. "It's for propaganda training, not spying. Like the work I've done for Mme. Sun." The girls' cadres had been suspended. The government could no longer patrol the villages and there had been atrocities. Rayna suspected the KMT ministers were happy Mme. Sun's program had failed.

She pulled harder at the grass. "I can't just turn my back and go home."

"Ah." He limited himself to that, then reached out to inspect the leather bound book she'd brought along. "The Letters of Engels and Marx." He turned it over. "Binding's no good." She gave him a sharp look. He raised his hands in surrender. "Sorry. The great man gave you this?"

She nodded, not looking at him.

"Ever read Marx? I never did."

"Me neither." She rolled on her side to look up close at the checkered table cloth. "I'm not good at political discourse. Though I did once make a stab at Nietzsche."

"Nietzsche?"

"My first husband. He thought I should know about the inner lives of talented men."

"Ah." But instead of encouraging her to go on about Raph, he took off on a new subject — the rise of fascists, how he planned to go back to Rome. Which was a mistake, because she wasn't interested in Rome or the rise of fascists. Eventually he worked back to where he'd veered off, the end of Hankow. He reminded her about the bathhouse on Division Street and the little square towels, how Borodin was caught between two worlds. Then he asked if she were really going to study at the Lenin Institute.

She was twirling a lock of her hair, propped on one elbow staring at the sluggish river. "School," she corrected him. "Nothing so lofty as an institute."

He asked if she planned to stay on in Moscow.

She sat up, brushed the crumbs from her skirt. "What do you mean?"

"I mean permanently, are you going to buy into the whole thing?"

Was she going to join the Party, that's what he meant. Become a pale shadow of what Borodin had become. "Yes," she said, deciding it just like that.

His irritation broke through. "And what brings on this revolutionary *tristesse*?"

She gave him a look of disgust, which might have come

69

from her stomach rebelling against the peanut butter. She stood and looked down at him still propped on his side on the checkered cloth.

To recover his ground, he tossed her a raisin. She made a halfhearted attempt at a catch but it bounced off her fingers. They watched it ricochet into the water.

"I've found out what I want to do with my life," she said. Her voice had an edge to it, a warning for him not to take this lightly.

"Study Marx?" His tone was neutral but she could hear that the deference was only on the surface.

"No, that's just the beginning." After that, things became unclear. The glare from the water was making her squint, or maybe it was the effort at thinking. "It has to do with China," she offered, not wanting or able to tell him more.

"But you're going to Moscow," he pointed out.

"I know." She could feel her expression asking him to accept this in all its incompleteness.

He took his cue and began packing up. "Do you know how things are in Moscow?"

"I know it will be different." She studied the plate with its last cracker, then handed it over and straightened her shoulders. "You can't hold back from life, can you?" A faint quaver to this last.

He didn't answer.

Then she remembered the telegram that must be waiting at home. The uncomfortable question of where Bill fit in.

"Come on," she said, grabbing up the tablecloth, stuffing it into his arms. "You've got to go to Peking and I've got to get some sleep."

He stood there, checkered cloth bunched in his arms, its tag end trailing. "I need to go where you're going."

She squinted while she tried to figure out what he meant.

A blush rose on his fair Irish skin. "I mean it. I need to understand this." His eyes closed in the effort to say it right. "All of it," he added. "You. Especially you."

When he opened them, she was caught scratching behind her knee, still trying to figure out the message. "You mean come to Moscow? Trace the revolution to its source?"

He blushed harder at her flippant reference to his 'Headwaters-of-the-Yangtze' speech, a last ditch effort one night to keep her from pushing him out the door. "Yes. I'm like the Yangtze's yellow mud, pulled out to sea, bound to go where you're going. That is, if you'll let me."

Suddenly she felt giddy, a rush of energy overtaking her. "Deal." She crossed both sets of fingers and punched them in the air. "High noon, Moscow." Already she was moving off to sleep or a haircut or maybe back to Bee's office. A few steps later she came back and planted a kiss on his cheek. "Moscow," she promised, "last one there is a rotten egg!"

When she got home, Bill was sitting on the big curved couch talking with Eugene Chen about Shanghai. They were drinking beer, which was worrisome since they'd agreed Bill needed to slack off. There was a hectic look about him which made her think this latest cure hadn't taken. She went into the kitchen for bottled water and returned to hear Chen expressing disbelief at Bill's suggestion that maybe Moscow had been the one behind the order to disarm the Communist cadres in Shanghai.

"Why would they do that?"

Bill was slumped in the chair looking into his bottle of beer. "I don't know. I'm just telling you what I hear."

Rayna went over and took the bottle from him. "Have you had anything to eat?"

He looked up as if surprised to see her. "Did you get my telegram?"

"No. I wonder if they're intercepting them."

He took the bottle back. "Possible. Likely, in fact. Hell of a revolution, can't tell your friends from your enemies."

"That's China," Chen announced with relish. He looked over his round glasses at Rayna. "I hear you plan to go to Moscow."

She was irritated Bee had seen fit to pass on this news. "I'm thinking about it."

Bill looked at her with his airy expression. "Planning to let me in on it?"

Now she was irritated at him. "I've just come back from a God-awful trip to meet Feng. Mme. Sun is having a garden party to auction off Ming vases. Anna Louise tells me she's been invited to go through the Gobi." She swallowed, hoping this blizzard of information would shut him up. "It's been a busy few weeks."

He pushed aside her complaints. "In Shanghai they've got heads on stakes. Our men. That busy enough for you?"

The dog padded in. Millie must have let her out of the pantry. Dan was mangy, with a brown swishy tail, and she jumped on Bill's lap.

"Dan!" Rayna took her by the neck and dragged her over to the kitchen door. "Sorry, she sleeps in the pantry now. There's no food so it seems like a good place." She didn't tell him she'd taken the extra pillow from their bed so Dan would have the scent of her for comfort.

"Dan?" Chen was confused. In her struggle to avoid banishment, Dan had rolled over on her back, revealing twin rows of well-used nipples.

"I named her before I found out. Dan seemed the name she wanted."

"You wanted," Bill put in. "You knew the agreement we had on pets."

She noticed the past tense. "I thought about Danielle, but it seemed too sissy."

Suddenly she was bone weary. "I've got to rest," she announced, turning away from the men, leaving them with the dog. "There's some cheese in the kitchen. You should eat."

The tea party the next day was for women only, although Chen arrived with his two gangly daughters. It was hot, but there was some thin shade under awnings set up on the lawn.

Rayna accepted a glass of warm punch and wandered around the display tables. Anna Louise came up from behind. "Find anything?"

Rayna showed off a gold-rimmed plate with a scene from Dickens, a false hilarity sweeping over her. "What are we to make of this?" She meant the garden party, the whole incredible mess.

"Bee tells me you are in charge of the Gobi trip. I want to go over my requirements."

Rayna stiffened. Bee hadn't told her she was dogsbody to Anna Louise.

"I understand you have cars. I would prefer a Buick. The whole back seat of one."

"The back seat. I'll have to find the front seat first."

Anna Louise was looking around at the wealthy Chinese ladies. The bidding was set to begin. "Then why aren't you out liberating cars? Why fiddle with tableware?"

Rayna tucked her head down, not bothering to answer.

"I hear Bill's back. I suppose you two will be returning home. I hear Millie has already booked passage."

Rayna could see Chen's two girls emerging dripping from the stagnant water in the unused swimming pool. "Chen is going to Moscow," she said to change the subject.

"That's what they say. Taking his girls. Chen wants his two boys to go with us."

Once again Rayna had no answer. Two more nonessential people taking up seats in cars she had not yet requisitioned. "Whatever I do, I shall have to figure out what to do with Dan."

Anna Louise nodded. "That's the way, isn't it? You make a home for yourself and then have to leave things behind. I suppose I should buy a plate so I can leave that as well."

Rayna thought about going straight back to Bee and having it out with him, about Chen's boys and the pest Anna Louise was making of herself. She got as far as his office door before the guard told her the Commander was meeting with Comrade Roy.

Then the door opened and Borodin was escorting Roy out. Their faces were grim, at least Bee's was. Roy's expression had a satisfied cast. They shook hands and then Borodin turned to Rayna, displeased at her sudden appearance.

"I just heard from Anna Louise. She wants your best getaway car."

His face broke out in a tense grin. "Just like in the movies. Anna Louise as my gun moll." Then he remembered Roy. "Comrade Roy is leaving shortly to report to our masters in Moscow."

She took a deep breath. "I want to go."

Borodin checked to see Roy's reaction. "Mrs. Prohme has asked if she could join our Gobi trek. I've told her we are full up."

To stop this side game, she added, "Anna Louise tells me she wants a Buick, the full back seat of one."

Borodin spread his hands. "Such complications to our ignominious end. Don't you agree, Comrade Roy?"

He was needling Roy, although Rayna couldn't figure out why. He turned back to her. "I need you tomorrow at seven. To go over provisioning. I'm sorry I didn't warn you about Anna Louise."

When she got home, after collecting the day's proofs, Rayna was on her last legs. She hoped Bill was asleep so she could put off any discussion until morning. But no such luck. He was waiting where she had left him, with Dan tied up in the pantry moaning to be taken for a walk. "Stupid dog," he said. "If I had a gun I'd shoot it."

"You're not in a good mood," she observed, putting her work on the coffee table and offering him the gold-rimmed plate. "Souvenir." Then she sank into the couch and began to cry.

The weeping brought Bill around to a somewhat better frame of mind.

He got up and brought her some water and said he'd eaten the last of the rat cheese. They sat in silence in their Lutheran living room and contemplated what to say next. "I've wired your father in Chicago," he began.

"You didn't." Tears began to flood again. "You promised you'd never—"

"I know. You're dead to them, at least this week."

They were silent again. "I wish you hadn't."

"We have no money. That is the hard truth. This revolution is over, the stragglers are heading for the hills, and we don't have the scratch to get home."

He made it sound like her fault. Another long silence. She rose and went to the kitchen, bringing back a chipped teapot. "Here is what we are going to do." She pulled out the last of her hard currency and shoved it at him. "Tomorrow you book a ticket back to Shanghai. Your doctor's there and I'll move heaven and earth to get you some kind of paying job. Maybe with Earl Browder, he's staying on."

He took the money and eyed her with some suspicion. "What makes you think you can scrabble together a paying job at this late stage? Why don't we go down together?"

"I can't. I need to stay with Mme. Sun. It's the only chance we've got to keep our connection."

"There is no connection. This great adventure is over."

She felt a simmer of anger but tried to keep it out of her voice. "No, we'll regroup."

"Who'll regroup? The great man? What kind of leverage has he got?"

Bill never used to speak this way. Time was when there had been only reverence for Bee. He's ill, she reminded herself. Ill and broke and afraid.

She forced an optimistic look on her face. "Don't worry. They'll need someone in Shanghai to keep track of things. It would be perfect for you."

"For us," he reminded her.

She stood up. "I have to go walk Dan," and went to the pantry to untie the creature that had become the most reliable thing in her life. She thought about loyalty, Borodin's obligations to Fanya, Mme. Sun's loyalty to her late husband. How alone Mme. Sun had looked at her garden party. Yet in all her solitude, she was the only one who seemed free.

CHAPTER 7

Bill was unwilling to leave things as they had been the night before, wanting to revisit his plan. "We don't have to go to Chicago," he coaxed her, "there's California, Hawaii."

"We can't just drop things, pretend this all never happened."

"No one needs us anymore."

She stifled the urge to correct him, to say that Bee needed her, Mme. Sun. Instead she told him she had to go to the office. He put a hand out to push her back into her seat. "We will decide this here and now. I am not going to Shanghai without you. That's final."

She could feel her face harden. "Then you'll have to stay. I can't go yet. I am responsible for the Gobi trip. The Buick and the Dodges. I have four but Bee says I need one more. And that's just automobiles." To make her point, she pulled out her list. "Five hundred ten-gallon gas cans, twelve canvas tarps, two hundred pounds rice." She turned puckish as she edged toward the door. "I'll let you in on a scoop: the war's not going well." Awful truth, but at least she could laugh about it.

Making her way to the office, she scribbled corrections as she dodged the morning night-soil carriers, laborers on their way to shuttered factories, food vendors with nothing to sell. How was she going to get Bill back to Shanghai? A job, paying something, any pittance would do. She decided the time had come to beg Chen and so made a right turn to his plush office on the top floor of the Foreign Ministry building. After waiting an hour, she was escorted to the inner sanctum. Chen had already guessed what she was calling about.

"Bill tells me he wants a job so you two can return to Shanghai. Sorry, I told him that's impossible. General Chiang won't let us publish."

She kept her face pleasant. "I was thinking of a newsletter, an internal report to Bee in Moscow. To help us plan our next step."

Chen looked interested and dismissive all at once. "You think the Russians have a next step? As soon as they get home the Russians are going to dump us once and for all."

"We can't let that happen."

His face acknowledged that she was right. "Have you explained this to the great man? That he has no choice but to keep his band of weary Hankow veterans afloat?"

Now she told a white lie. "Yes. And he likes the idea of Bill in Shanghai. Says Mme. Sun might be able to find the scratch."

"Her family's cut her off. She doesn't have a *sou*. But be my guest."

Just what Rayna was hoping to hear. But it was a week before she got in to see Mme. Sun. Things, by then, had become dire. All the nonessential Russians had left, going either north by rail under diplomatic cover, or south by boat in disguise. There was still no word on whether Fanya Borodin would be released. In Peking, Jimmy Sheean was doing his best to stir up a diplomatic hornets' nest, but she doubted that would persuade Peking's current warlord, who wanted the pleasure of a public beheading.

Bee was also too busy to see her. Every night more government troops disappeared into the countryside, at first a trickle, then a torrent. Gangs of boys roamed the streets. Flyers denouncing the Soviets and extolling the virtues of General Chiang appeared. The holdout government ministers met in secret without Mme. Sun, then emerged to announce that *The People's Tribune* would continue under new leadership. She would soon be out of a job. Since Millie had already booked tickets to leave, Rayna talked her in to taking Dan as far as Shanghai.

"But when are you coming?" Millie asked, not unreasonably. "I am not going to cart a forty pound half-German shepherd to Shanghai if you aren't there to take her off my hands."

"I'll be there," Rayna assured her, without being specific about when. "Find her a nice kennel. British, they know how to take care of dogs."

All the foreign journalists had faded away. There was less and less work for Rayna to do. A cable, forwarded from Shanghai, said that Rayna's father would prepay two return tickets to Chicago but nothing more. Bill took this as proof of the wisdom of his plan while Rayna thanked her stars she still had the secret money from her sister Grace.

Finally, word came that Mme. Sun would see her. The Lady had moved from her estate in the diplomatic compound to the safer confines of her brother's apartment over his bank in Hankow. As Rayna passed by a doubled contingent of bodyguards, the same servant showed her into a reception room. Mme. Sun rose to take her hand.

"I am sorry I was unable to meet earlier but, as you can imagine, there are many preparations to be made."

"Have you decided what you will do?"

"Return to Shanghai, certainly. After that—" She shrugged. "But this is no time to think of such things. Here." She took out three sheets of paper covered with precise English handwriting. "A statement I wish you to publish. Before they seize your paper. Can you arrange it for tonight?"

Rayna skimmed the careful sentences, the devastating critique of her government's failings. She opened with a denunciation of the Hankow government ministers, how their recent actions had repudiated her husband's great policies, judged them unfit to call themselves followers of Dr. Sun. Then she detailed the many times her husband had urged land reform and declared peasants the backbone of the revolution.

Next she moved on to the scandalous expulsion of the Soviet advisors and explained how cooperation with them and the Chinese Communist Party had been essential to making China's great revolutionary progress to date.

'But now all that is in ruins,' the declaration read. 'The National Government has sunk to the level of a semi-feudal remnant, despised by foes who used to blanch and flee at the sound of its armies on the march.'

She did not name General Chiang as the major culprit, but did something worse: lumped all the wayward Hankow government ministers in with Chiang in a blanket condemnation, a prophecy that they would fail. As for her own situation, her course was clear: 'It is necessary for the revolutionary wing of the Kuomintang – the group with which Sun would today be identified – to leave no doubt in the Soviet Union that there are those who will continue true and steadfast.'

"Wow," Rayna murmured, wondering if she should leave right away to begin setting type. But just then the servant reappeared and Mme. Sun went out into the hall. Rayna could see her speaking to General Teng, the KMT minister who led one of the few divisions remaining loyal to Mme. Sun's diminishing wing of the government. He looked exhausted. After a while Mme. Sun summoned her guard to escort her visitor somewhere to the back of the apartment.

"General Teng," Mme. Sun explained, as she returned, "has traveled some distance, having escaped Nanking." Teng was one of Mme. Sun's favorites, an early follower of Dr. Sun. From his filthy tunic it looked as if he had been traveling for days. "Say nothing of this," Mme. Sun cautioned. "If it becomes known he's here, Chiang will track him down."

"Does Bee know?"

"Say nothing to him either." Then she reconsidered her sharp tone. "I am sorry to have embroiled you in this."

"You haven't embroiled me. Are you in danger?"

"Of course." A tinkling laugh but the sound was hollow. "Anyone associated with me is in danger, more's the pity." Then she remembered Rayna had asked for the meeting. "My dear, forgive me, you had something you wished to discuss?"

"My husband. We've decided he should stay in Shanghai. To help, hopefully, in communicating the situation to Bee in Moscow."

Mme. Sun nodded politely to show she was listening. Not as great a reception as Rayna had hoped.

"Bee says that with the advantage of an American passport I could go back and forth." Mme. Sun didn't respond. Rayna could feel rising discomfort. She hated to beg. "Only we have no money. Bee can't provide any, at least until he gets established, and by tomorrow I won't have a job." She lifted the paper with Mme. Sun's declaration as proof.

Mme. Sun took her time answering, motioning in the direction of the tea pot to ask if Rayna wanted more. Finally she spoke. "I can see the advantages. At least in the interim. Mr. Chen says he will take on that task, keeping lines open, but it is always better to have more — what shall we say? — avenues." Her smile was sweet. Then she added, "And your husband, what does he think of your plan to go back and forth?"

That was a problem. Mme. Sun had very conventional views of a wife's responsibility. "The truth is Bill's not my husband, not legally. We are together, yes." She stopped, fighting down her embarrassment, then resumed. "China was a test, to see if we would find something that would seal us together."

Mme. Sun nodded, then came out with an oblique inquiry. "And have you found it?"

It took Rayna a moment to understand what she meant. "For myself, yes. With Bill, it's still an open question."

"And what is that something that you have found?" She was looking at Rayna with care.

In for a dime, in for a dollar. "You. Your cause, social change in China."

"I see." She indicated the hand written pages Rayna was holding. "Then you have your assignment. After it is printed I will become a target for retribution. I am planning to retreat to my well-guarded house in Shanghai. I may or may not be safe. It all depends."

"On what?"

"My family. Whether they protect me. Mr. Chen will be responsible for the next step, when and where I go from there." She thought some more. "Do you think, if I were to make arrangements, a stipend that would carry your husband for, say, three months, he would consent to escort Mr. Chen and his girls down to Shanghai?" She dimpled. "As you know I have much experience traveling in disguise. The time when I eloped, that other time when I was attacked by soldiers. My guards are loyal and well trained. But Mr. Chen and his girls are another matter. I would be grateful if your husband could disguise them as his servants."

Rayna, who'd always sensed that Eugene Chen and Mme. Sun were companions of necessity, knew how galling it would be for Chen to pretend he was Bill's servant. "I'm sure Bill will do anything to help." And how could Bill refuse a direct order from Mme. Sun?

She thanked her hostess and made her way back to the office and up the stairs to show Bee what Mme. Sun had entrusted her with. He nodded and said he'd been up all night helping to draft it. She told him about the stipend and the plan to have Bill escort Chen and his daughters down river.

"Excellent," he said, then motioned in an offhand way for her to leave. She was crestfallen at this new evidence of his disinterest but then straightened her back and went downstairs and spent the rest of the day setting type for Mme. Sun's elegant diatribe.

Bill and Millie were called in to help, and Rayna had some touchy moments explaining to Bill why she had been the one to come in possession of the piece since he had resumed the title of editor. But by five that afternoon they had put together the single page broadsheet. Mme. Sun's declaration covered the whole front and back while they filled the inside with a mix of international news. All but one of their Chinese helpers had slipped away so they used the hand press to crank out their small run. It was a race against time, as Millie had a six o'clock departure. Rayna left at five and raced back to the apartment and coaxed Dan in a trot down to the dock. Dan must have sensed something was wrong because she wouldn't go up the gangplank and Rayna and Millie struggled to carry her. Fortunately Rayna was holding up the rear when poor Dan wet herself.

"She'll be all right. They have a kennel in the baggage hold. That's what Dan doesn't like. Promise me you'll visit her every day."

The steward made it clear he expected a suitable reward for taking on this new burden. Rayna handed over the last of her Mexican silver. "I've got to get back. There's a kennel somewhere in Shanghai. I'll be there in a few days. Meanwhile, guard the copies with your life."

"You mean don't use them to line Dan's cage." Gallows humor, they all were so anxious to get Mme. Sun's declaration, with its implicit call for continued resistance by the CCP, to the world press.

There was a hurried good-bye and then Rayna raced back to the newspaper office and she and Bill continued cranking out copies until midnight, when the police arrived with three government ministers to confiscate the entire run. They were escorted from the building and it was padlocked. For the record, Rayna made loud protest, but the steamer with the twenty precious copies had departed on time.

They woke at dawn to learn that Chen had issued a statement congratulating the new figurehead editor of *The People's Tribune*. Then Bill and Chen retreated to huddle over their departure plans. Rayna went back to Borodin's office to find out where things stood.

Borodin was in a state of high excitement. "Fanya has been released!" He grabbed Rayna and hugged her before he remembered himself. "Money passed hands, of course, and we had to spirit away the judge who released her, but she is safe and now all we have to do is figure out how to get her out."

Rayna told him of their success in smuggling out copies of the last issue.

"Good, good."

She was disappointed to have no other news, knowing she was forbidden to say anything about General Teng. "About my plans—"

"No time for that. Later."

Just then a Chinese messenger was let in. "You must come. Mme. Sun has been presented with an atrocity." Outside, a motorcycle was waiting. Borodin motioned for his car and they hurtled down Han Chung Road, horns blaring to part the dense crowd of families making their way out of the city in cars and wagons and on foot.

They passed the Hanyang Iron Works, the huge padlocked gates and the massive idle smoke stacks. Beyond that, Serpent Hill, a long rocky ledge rooted in the surrounding plain. They drove up the ridge to a place that reminded Rayna of the village south of Canton. The same windowless bunker set in a clearing, a cement enclosure with a locked door and small caged opening.

Mme. Sun was standing alone by the tree line. Beside her, hanging by a rope with a sign around her neck, was Mei-hui. The girl's head, which had been shorn as a warning in the last outing of the propaganda cadre, was now scalped. A square section of flesh, bristled with half-inch hair, lay on the ground.

Her arms had been pulled back and tied, her mouth gagged with a length of black cloth. Her pajama top had been ripped open, the trousers missing. Down the inside of her legs, blood. But Mme. Sun's eyes were fixed on the girl's waist, to the spot where the entrails had been arranged in a neat girdle. Rayna was taken back to the moment in the village, when she had snapped the herding stick, flaunting her powers as a Red Hair. Mei-hui had paid the price. A flush of shame too painful to bear overcame her and so she turned her attention to Bee.

"My God," he was saying, the words coming out as a low moan. He went up and touched the face, tried, fruitlessly, to pull together the ripped pajama top, his mouth working to no avail. Finally, he motioned for her to be cut down. As the guard began to saw at the rope, Borodin took up the body and held it so she would not fall. Then steadied himself and, with an arm under her knees and another supporting her neck, carried Mei-hui to open ground. His face, as he lowered her, was a shifting sea that Rayna could not begin to decipher.

With his free hand he held her loosened entrails, took off his jacket and placed it as cover, then hid his face in his hands. "I am so sorry," he said to no one in particular.

The three of them stood vigil while the undertaker was summoned and the body removed for proper burial. Mme. Sun insisted on accompanying her charge and so they spent several hours in making arrangements. Much later, when there was nothing left to be done, they returned to Borodin's apartment and turned to the question of meaning.

Mme. Sun had ascended to another plane. "They will not have me," she said in a steely hushed voice. "General Chiang will not bend me to his will. He is a butcher, corrupt to the marrow. I am the widow of Dr. Sun Yat-sen."

"What can my government do?" Borodin was leaning forward. Rayna could tell he was feeling his way.

Mme. Sun shook her head. She did not know.

"Come to Moscow," Rayna heard herself saying. "Come with me. We can carry on there."

Mme. Sun did not seem to hear but Borodin cautioned Rayna with a look. "At least think about it," she added.

Borodin then tried his own way to rouse Mme. Sun. "Now is a dreadful moment. But events move quickly. Time does not allow us much chance to reflect. First we must secure your safety. Get you out of Hankow." There seemed a flicker of willingness to accept this, so with a nod to Rayna, Borodin extended the thought. "Sweden, Switzerland, the United States, these are all possible places from which to gain perspective. The issue is not place, but what can, what must be accomplished. Your husband regrouped after each of his many setbacks. So must you. For China." He squatted on his heels so he could look into the Lady's eyes. "I, too, love this revolution." Mme. Sun nodded, seeming to give consent to the plan he was laying out.

New possibilities started flooding Rayna's brain. But before she could sort them out, Borodin took to pacing the room. "We must think beyond the present. This phase is over, there is the urgent need, now, to lay the groundwork for the next."

He saw in Rayna's eyes that he was moving too fast, that Mme. Sun was still caught up in her grief. So he dropped back and went out to order more tea, put on a record, and the three of them sat watching the sun rise, listening to the tinny sound of the Leningrad Symphony play the *"Pathetique."*

Shortly thereafter, Borodin dispatched Rayna with an armed escort to gather the necessary things from Mme. Sun's apartment. They had jointly made the decision that Mme. Sun must leave, in disguise, as soon as possible.

"Arrange passage for yourself and a servant," Borodin told Rayna, meaning the servant would be Mme. Sun.

Rayna started to object that she was needed here, but he waved that away. "Book a second stateroom for a Mr. Lee in Kuling. Then, when the boat stops, get off. Mr. Lee will provide protection the rest of the way."

Kuling, a day's journey down the Yangtze, was where Borodin was planning a last conclave ahead of the Gobi trip. Rayna was not supposed to know about it. She wanted to ask more, but confined herself to asking about transportation back. Her mind was racing. There were no tickets to be had. The only possibility was to persuade Bill to postpone his trip.

Borodin nodded and went to his desk to pull out a box of silver and counted out what she needed for the passage. She whispered her idea about Bill's two rooms on the steamer leaving in two days. He nodded and said he'd speak to Chen.

She rushed home to persuade a skeptical Bill he needed to go down to the wharf to rebook his tickets in her name. He wanted to know what she was doing.

"I'm supposed to escort Mme. Sun down to Shanghai and then I'll come back." She left out the part about Kuling, that instead of being gone for two weeks, she'd be gone overnight, though she didn't quite grasp the part about the mysterious Mr. Lee. She supposed there would be a bribe involved, but decided the best way was to keep the second room booked as if the Chen girls were still coming. Instead of Mr. Prohme and the manservant and his two girls, it would be Mrs. Prohme and the maid and her two girls. She and Bill went down to the German steamer office and spent two hours haggling with the clerk; more money passed hands, and then it was done. She left Bill and went back to Borodin's office to explain what she had been able to accomplish.

"I will take care of Kuling," he assured her, "and make sure her guards will be housed with the crew." She was so relieved she wanted to hug him, but was afraid to, feeling guilty that the part of her that wanted to stay with him outweighed the part that had pledged undying loyalty to Mme. Sun.

CHAPTER 8

When Rayna got down to the wharf, Mme. Sun had already closed herself away in the cabin. Rayna counted off eight doors along a narrow galley, the bronze fittings pitted with sea air and neglect. The door handle would not turn. "It is mistress," she called out, using the signal they had agreed upon.

"No one here." Creaking hinges opened to reveal a stoop-shouldered woman in rags. Mme. Sun had perhaps overdone the disguise. Without a further word, she returned to her lower bunk and drew the bed curtains around her. She had also closed the porthole with its deep green curtain and left the room stifling. Rayna realized this was probably best, but felt let down at getting no thanks for arranging the escape and no companionship to calm her own nerves. Still, she decided to follow suit and climbed onto the top bunk, not bothering to draw her bed curtains and lay there sweating on the moldy mattress until the ship's twin horn blasts signaled departure. The first danger point passed.

That night Rayna had a lot of time to think and not much willingness to do so. Instead, she chastised herself: the whole China excursion was no more than a childish adventure, a way to dispel her morbid fear of an ordinary life. When things became their most desperate, when all was in dire peril, that was when she felt the most cheerful. That was Bill's real attraction, that he tolerated this in her. Of course now he was jealous. Why wouldn't he be? Borodin, in her imaginings, inhabited the heroic realm without the tarnishing of the domestic. Though Bee had his own domestic drama.

From there her thoughts turned to Mme. Sun and her ethereal marriage with Dr. Sun. Rayna guessed the heroic had been the attraction there as well. And so Borodin's bet that Mme. Sun was unwilling to abandon her husband's memory was a good one. The trick was to persuade the Lady that Moscow was the place to keep that memory alive. But first, they had to get her to Shanghai and keep her safe from General Chiang.

Rayna fell into a fitful sleep only to be awakened by the blast of the ship's horn as it nosed into the rickety landing at Kiukiang. The British resort of Kuling was above them, high in the misty hills. This was the second danger point. Who would be there to meet them? Had Borodin arranged the bribes?

The sheer cliff was an imposing sight ahead of her as she stumbled up the gangway. A zigzag trail no more than three feet wide traced up the steep mountainside. Sedan chairs waited at a taxi stand for phantom guests who would never arrive. Outside the pagoda-roofed ticket shed, she could see a Russian she knew by the name of Comrade Reuben standing with a hard-faced blonde woman. Reuben was short but powerfully built and the woman towered over him, but they moved forward as a pair.

"Mrs. Prohme, meet my wife Virginia." The woman nodded but did not speak. Reuben, who had lived in Brooklyn, undoubtedly carried an American passport. "The arrangements are taken care of." He looked at his tickets. "My wife will sleep in your cabin and I will bunk next door with the extra man." He meant Mme. Sun's bodyguard.

Rayna nodded and then said she had to go back and get her bag.

"No need. It will be kept for you in Shanghai. As soon as we depart, a launch will come by to pick you up. You'll be home for dinner." His crooked teeth flashed with this heavy humor.

"I need to say good-bye."

"No need. It is all taken care of." He took the blonde woman's arm and walked up the gangway without looking back. She never saw the Chinese bodyguard.

Rayna spent the next twenty minutes feeling completely exposed. The sedan bearers crowded around her, looking for a fare, but she waved them away and finally took refuge in the ticket office. Then the horn blasted and the steamer began to nose its way out to the channel. She watched as it gathered speed on the trip downstream. They had to get Mme. Sun past Nanking, the site where Mme. Borodin had been kidnapped. Why did Bee think the bribes would hold? She reassured herself that safe passage, if there were such a thing, would come from the Soong family, not the Russians. With that thought, a small launch appeared. A Chinese sailor helped her to the deck and the sole Russian on board advised her there was tea and bread in the hold. By late afternoon she was back in Hankow.

On her way to report to Bee she passed the heavily guarded rail yard. The fruits of her labor were on display: spiffy Dodges and a lone black Buick sat decked out with KMT flags, camouflage nets to the side. Gasoline cans were arrayed in glinting pyramids next to the three trucks that would haul them. In her fanciful moments she imagined Bee's path through the Gobi marked by a trail of discarded red cans all emblazoned with the message, 'Rayna did this.' Inside the fence Borodin was touring the site, kicking tires and pinging jerry cans. She came up behind him and stood, waiting to be recognized, "We're ready," he said by way of acknowledgment. "You have done well."

On the way back to the newspaper building she gave him a report, Mme. Sun's state of mind, the addition of Mr. and Mrs. Lee. The once elegant office was now torn apart, his desk empty, cleared of its usual stacks of papers and paperweights. Boxes were everywhere. He motioned her to a chair and resumed the task of packing his books. "I have just heard from Fanya. Thank God she's in good health."

Rayna felt a tightness where there should have been relief. "So, that's it." She meant Hankow, that there was now no reason for her to stay.

He looked up, motioning with a hand around the room. "Help me with my books."

But she made no move, watching as he took down a volume, wiped its spine and cover.

"Did you read the book I gave you?"

She thought about the yellowed pages, the small print, the way Jimmy had sniffed at the binding. "I tried."

He did not take offense. "You are in for an extended journey. You'll need books." He examined the one in his hand. "Gibbons? No, a small Marxist-Leninist library." He said this with satisfaction, whistling as he peered at titles in the various stacks he'd made, selecting from one pile, then another, weighing each volume, assessing. He took his time, replacing one for another, re-dusting each volume and then squaring away the small final assortment. He rummaged for newspaper from a pile set aside for packing, took up a ball of twine and began constructing an elaborate package of newspaper, twine, then more newspaper, finally a piece of watertight tarpaulin and then bound once more with heavy cord.

All this took several minutes. When he was done, Borodin formally presented the gift. Then he drew two glasses of tea, and they sat, in the Russian tradition, for luck.

"Your arrangements to return to Shanghai are complete?"

She shook her head no. The priority had been to get Bill and the Chens rebooked.

He nodded. "You have told him of your wish to go to Moscow?"

"Not exactly." She lowered her head. "Nothing is settled."

He thought for a minute. "That is often the way." Then

cleared his throat. "Do you have any indication from Mme. Sun?"

"About Moscow? No."

"Then I think it is important that you go to Shanghai, stay close, be there if she waivers."

"It would help if she knew I was going with her."

With that he stood, looked around the dismantled room and instead of giving her an answer, announced that it might be best if he did not see her again.

The breath went out of her. Her beleaguered expression caused him to soften his tone. "Why is it that you want to become a Bolshevik?"

She heard a gentle mocking in the question and struggled to contain her humiliation. "Don't tease. I can't stand it."

He nodded, then lifted a hand in apology. "You remind me of Norman, the crumpled look on your face. It doesn't do to tease him either."

She tried to smile but couldn't. She could barely breathe.

"I need to know," he said, referring to his original question. "I will be held accountable."

"I can be relied on." Her voice was thin, at odds with the stubborn anger she felt. "Just tell me what my job is and I'll do it."

"Ah, if only it were that simple. A matter of fetching the Holy Grail."

"You're still teasing."

"No." Then, accepting the criticism, he said, "Take care of Mme. Sun. Get her to come to Moscow. That is your assignment."

Moscow, all that she wanted. They both stood. He walked her to the door. She leaned against the dark mahogany, taking in her last sense of the cool wood. A moment passed. Rayna found herself looking across the room, hearing the passage of her breath, the sound of it moving inside her. His hand hovered near her hair.

"Don't."

He drew back his hand. "You've cut it again."

"Yes. For the journey."

He pushed down the door handle and she felt the sharp click as the lock disengaged.

In a faraway voice, not looking at her, he said, "I am leaving tomorrow for Kuling. Before dawn." Then, on a brisk note, "A planned disappearance, to keep my head on my shoulders until the final debacle."

She understood, at least she thought she did. He was saying good-bye. She thought of the steep cliffs, what lay beyond them, the fabled English spa retreat of Kuling where he was going. She nodded to give the appearance of understanding. But she didn't, really. He was leaving and that was all she could take in.

He sensed this, and something more, because this time, when he touched her face, she let him. Gravely, he cupped her chin, the fingers of his other hand running through her damp hair. She let her head tilt back, fixed her eyes on the buttery mote-filled light that was streaming through the window.

"Do you want to come?" he asked in a husky voice. "With me, to Kuling, for a last day or two?" His voice, the question it held, brought her back.

Yes, she nodded, but could not speak.

She dawdled on the way home, standing outside the newspaper office, trying to see past the padlocked shutters. Then she went down to the dock, this time to the Japanese ticket office and put down her last remaining hard currency for a single passage to Shanghai eight days hence. She would have some explaining to do when she got home and having a ticket that fixed her arrival in Shanghai would make it easier.

Bill was out when she got there, so she had little to do until he returned. Her luggage would be taken off ship by Mr. and Mrs. Lee. But she would need some clothes for this second journey, so she busied herself with packing odds and ends, a box of stationery she hadn't used, old underwear she'd never quite thrown out. She missed Dan, didn't want to think of her cooped up in some kennel. What was she going to do about Dan? Bill would have to take her, that was that.

When Bill did come home she explained about Mme. Sun's escape. There was much they couldn't share these days, the details of Bill's arrangement with Chen, her own next steps. She said only that she was taking off again in the morning, a few days only, something to do with wrapping up Mme. Sun's work. Bill looked at her with wounded eyes that reminded her of Dan.

At dawn, another departure on the same high speed launch, a half dozen Russians drinking tea and eating black bread. Bee was locked in the small stateroom reviewing plans. He ignored her, for show she decided, and she responded in kind, finding a quiet corner, ready to claim a headache in case anyone asked. By mid-afternoon they all clambered out, piles of luggage were lashed on the backs of leathery-skinned carriers for the trek up the cliff. The Russians got ushered to a waiting row of sedan chairs, carriers stationed two to a side, front and rear, a total of four Chinese bearing a single foreign passenger. Borodin waved the rest of the party on, designating his personal guard to protect the rear. Then gave Rayna pride of place just ahead of him and they followed the now strung out line of sedan chairs in their slow passage up the mountain.

Rayna marveled that all the westerners had to be transported in this laborious way, not to speak of luggage and the town's provisioning. "Yes," Borodin agreed, "in a way it is a metaphor for China. The tortured way this civilization accommodates to extremes of wealth and backwardness. I shall miss it."

They were silent after that, jogging and pitching as the sedan chairs moved single file, higher and higher up a stone path cut into the mountain. Gingko trees crowded down upon her, and when Rayna lay back she could see bits of the village above. The air was blessedly cool.

Behind her, Borodin winced as his carriers hit a rough spot, jarring the newly mended elbow.

"Tell me about your childhood," she said, to distract him, to break her own discomfort caused by the rolling sensation of being carried up and around hairpin turns.

"My childhood," he said, as if that were a most peculiar request. "What is it you want to know?"

She lolled her head back, brushing her hand against the lacework of leaves, her fingertips running over hard red berries. "I don't know. How you became a Bolshevik."

He thought, or seemed to think. "I don't usually speak about such things."

"Yes," she said, keeping her voice grave, in imitation of his own. "But I need to know. It's part of my job."

"Ah," he said, as if that explained it. "Well, let me see. As a boy I lived in Vitebsk, a little village in the Pale. My father was a big strapping man, a wheelwright, a good enough fellow who provided for his family as best he could. My mother was a terrier. She stood every day outside our hut, in sunshine or in snow, knuckles dug in her hips, and yapped. Yapped at everyone, at me, the neighbors, the whole world. I loved her very much. I had a brother five years older and a sister, two years behind. She was deaf. I never knew whether she was slow because she couldn't hear or there was something else." He leaned forward in his seat. "Are you sure you want to hear this?"

She nodded in a contented way and he sat back, his voice low so the others would not hear. "One day, when I was ten, the Cossacks came. A pogrom. It was right after the killing of the Tsar, there were a lot of pogroms at that time." Rayna nodded, though he didn't seek any confirmation of her attention. "My father and older brother were away at the time, and there must have been some warning, because the rabbi gathered all the small boys and took us into his cellar."

A change came into his voice. "The women were left to fend for themselves."

Now he leaned forward again. "It came up fast. We had barely gathered before the hoofs came thundering over and the screaming began. Before the door to the cellar was pulled tight I heard my sister scream. Her voice had a special sound, that high animal cry of someone who can't hear."

His voice became clogged. "That moment I felt the most profound sense of shame. There I was, safe in a cellar, with my poor sister was out there being — God knows what.

"I flew at the rabbi, who was an old, feeble man, went at him like an animal, tearing his beard, kicking him, demanding to be let out. He resisted, so I shoved him down, pushed open the door and wriggled out. The village was in shambles, horsemen careening about, burning thatch, driving away goats, breaking down doors to see what they could find.

"I raced to my house and found the door smashed open, and in the shadows I could hear gasping, the cries of my sister. As I tumbled across the threshold, a great hand reached out and pulled me up by the scruff of my neck. A big lout – God, how he smelled! He held me close against his face, laughing and breathing all over me while my feet dangled helplessly."

Again he glanced toward her. "She wasn't hurt, they hadn't gotten that far. The commotion of my arrival upset things. And my mother, God bless her, was quick-witted enough to seize on the one thing that could be done." His voice rose triumphant.

"She had been cooking kishke in a great sizzling pot of oil. She took a straw, lit it, and set the whole pot on fire, then seized the handles with her bare hands and flung it across the floor. Flames everywhere, it was magnificent. The Cossacks froze, and my sister, whose arm got splashed, screamed louder, so they dropped everything and fled. Our house was burned to the ground and my mother's hands were never the same, but my sister was not seriously hurt and I was unharmed. After that, well, that day I swore I would fight them, fight them all, the rabbis who locked me in the cellar, the Tsar, the Cossacks, them all." He settled back in his litter, comfortable in the cool mountain air, pleased with himself.

"After that I became a troublemaker. The rabbis decided I was unfit for further education. So when my brother began running timber down the Dvina, I ran away and joined him. I was thirteen. After a while I found my way to Riga where I worked as a stevedore, became radicalized and joined the Jewish Bund. And undertook a bit of robbery here and there, some smuggling for the cause." He eyed her, to see how she was taking this last. "One day I found myself in Finland, it was in 1903, a delegate to the world socialist conference and there I met one Vladimir Ilyich Lenin who was creating his group of Bolsheviks, and I told him I would join his cause." He touched his hat. "And that's how I became a Bolshevik."

She tried not to smile. "And how much of that is true?"

He shrugged. "Enough."

Reaching the village, they paraded single file along the almost empty square. It occurred to her that their secret retreat couldn't possibly be so secret.

"No matter," Borodin decided when she voiced the thought. "The town's empty of all Europeans and Chinese are not allowed." He meant the merchant class, Chiang's allies. Of course, there were servants who could spy or even poison. How odd that a deserted British enclave should become the hiding place for the Bolsheviks, that they should think themselves safe because it was peopled only by Chinese servants.

"Besides," he added, seeming to read her thoughts, "we are well guarded."

As they passed up the final hill, a secluded lane framed by shale outcroppings and massive boulders, his mood changed. He called forward to his men to dismount and indicated that Rayna and the baggage should go ahead. Left to parade on, she felt isolated, borne aloft in a way that made her feel vulnerable. Her sedan chair rounded a bend. Below was the river and overlapping blue hills and beyond that the brown endless plain. Mist rolled off the canopy of trees. There was the sound of a creek, a waterfall. Where had the world disappeared to?

The hotel was set in lush private grounds, three stories of stone behind wide wooden verandahs. A great rock fortress shielded by walls and sentry posts, a cluster of guest houses hidden in the foliage. At the hotel's front entrance she was let down, returned bows to the house servants, and was led up a grand stairway to a second floor room. Double doors opened onto a balcony with narrow bed frames hung by chains to allow guests to catch the evening breeze. Inside, a larger western-style bed sat square in the middle with Chinese side tables, rattan mats and a washstand completing the spare furnishings.

She decided to set about a systematic scrub. Arms, shoulders, ankles, thighs. Then she slipped off her sandals to take a crack at her feet. She rubbed without much success all the while longing for a full immersion bath, the soaking kind she drew for herself each night at the Lutheran Mission.

A servant arrived with her small suitcase and she began to unpack – two changes of underwear, a second dress, a jacket in the mad hope it would get cold. Bee had said a few days, she had told Bill three. He was leaving in less than a week and she'd promised to be back for his departure. In unpacking she came across a slim volume of Marx, his ruminations on Hegel. She sat on the bed, trying once again to make sense of a section she'd marked. *The socialist principle itself represents, on the whole, only one side, affecting the reality of the true human essence.*

Now what did that mean?

We have to concern ourselves just as much with the other side, the theoretical existence of man.

What theoretical existence?

In other words, make religion, science, etc., the objects of our criticism.

She was stumped. How on earth was she going to get through the Lenin School if she couldn't make heads or tails of Marx? Everyday human existence, is that what good Marxists hankered for? Or was it the opposite, some kind of vague theoretical existence? The distinction was fundamental, she knew, essential to the proper ordering of objective and subjective reality. Whatever that meant. Bill with his well-worn claim that objective reality superseded subjective.

But she herself was a hopelessly subjective creature, able only to verify reality by touching it, the only loyalty she could trust within herself was the personal. She closed the book, walked out on the balcony, looked at the blue hills and beyond that the distant brown flatlands. The light seemed to shimmer. A trick, she supposed, of the swirl of mist and dry air. Maybe she was just tired, worn out by the constant work, the long days and driven pace that real revolutions seemed to consist of. What did Marx, in his study nattering on about theoretical existence, know about wanting a bath?

So she lay down and slept, in the middle of the day, for the first time in months without the excuse of a high fever or blinding headache. She simply slept, put the past out of mind and turned, unconsciously, to the demands of the future.

After two hours, she awoke, slipped on her sandals and padded down the curved staircase past a closed library door. There was shouting inside. She could hear Borodin and Comrade Roy going at it, something about what to tell the Chinese. Then Bee's voice rose louder. "Moscow must give instructions that do not rely on blind loyalty, ones that are capable of being explained!" A brief silence, then the rumbling began again.

She summoned a servant and wrote a short note, saying she needed to speak to him and would be waiting out back, then found a door through the sun room and followed a path up terraced gardens. Back and forth up the hillside, crossing a small bridge, pushing aside tangles of lacy red maple, she made her way. Up, higher and higher, until she came out on a hidden pavilion, a secret pond surrounded by flagstones of green slate. Goldfish darted among the lily pads, dragonflies hovering above. A worn rattan lounge sat in an area of dappled sunlight. Rayna lay down, an arm flung over her forehead, her face turned to breathe in the smell of her humid skin. Feeling drugged, she listened to the leaves, the whine of insects.

An hour later, Borodin found her, his hand pushing aside her feet to make room for himself. She struggled to come awake.

"You look resplendent," he observed. "You have been thinking about — what?"

"Nothing." Her voice was thick. "I've been thinking about nothing."

"A good topic," he agreed, then took up her hand, turning it over to examine it. "Have you been thinking about your journey?"

"No," she said. "I'll think about that when it comes. Now, I want to think about nothing." A realization broke through. "I don't want to think."

"For the moment, I've had enough of that, too." He was still holding her hand, a peculiar quiet expression on his face. Suddenly she sat up, swung her feet to the ground, rose and tried to pull him up with her. He resisted, disengaging his fingers, letting his hand drop as he watched her lurch toward the lily pond.

Aware his eyes were following her, she bent to slip off her sandals. Then stood and pressed her hands into the small of her back. "I've been dreaming about a bath," she announced, face tilted toward the sky. "About being submerged." Then she turned. "Now is as good a time as any, don't you think?" With that she bent, braced a hand on the slate, dropped down and slipped in.

Muck was heavy on the bottom, she hadn't expected that, and had a moment of panic as her feet sunk deep into the ooze. Her toes gripped for purchase, she stuck out a hand for balance and sent up swirls of greenish sediment. But she plunged on, step after step, up to her thighs in the murky water. A step more and she would be wet to her waist. Fish darted toward her, zigzagged away. She lowered a hand to grab at something just beneath the surface and set the nearby lily pads to trembling. "Are you coming?"

He stood, not knowing what to make of this. "Here, let me help," he decided, moving a step closer, then another until he stood at the edge of the pond. He held out a hand.

She shook her head, rejecting the offer. "I want you to come in." And to prove it, she took a step backward, sending up new swirls of green muck. "It's our last opportunity," she countered, stubbornly, illogically.

"You'll ruin your dress," he observed, his voice low, his eyes fixed on a spot where the trees canopied just over her head.

"Yes," she said, as if he'd finally gotten the point, and bent to submerge herself, soaking herself up to her shoulders, then rose. Cascading water pulled at the thin fabric, revealing the outline of her small breasts, and she wondered why she'd done that. Of course she knew. And could see by the way his eyes searched her face and then dropped lower, that he knew as well. "Come in," she prompted.

"I have a meeting," he replied, tilting his head in the direction of the hotel. "Comrade Roy has more to discuss."

"Tell them I fell in and that you had to rescue me." Still he said nothing. "There isn't much time," she reminded him.

He hesitated a moment longer, then began to take off his jacket. Folded it and set it on dry slate. She caught sight of circles of yellow rime on his shirt as he pulled down his suspenders. He took off his shirt and she marveled at the black hair on his chest, how it dipped like a heart in the middle. Smiled at his awkward attempt at grace as he stooped to unlace his shoes and, at the last moment, remove his watch. It was almost comical, the way he struggled to appear calm, balancing on one braced hand, a sort of grunt as he swung his legs into the pond, drenching his spotless white trousers. Something, a concession to parity perhaps, made her dip down again and unbutton the top of her dress. Then she rose, having shrugged off the unwanted fabric down to her waist.

Her skirt flowed around her, a wide circle in the lily pads, swaying and dipping as he waded toward her. She swallowed hard, blinked and tried to smile. His eyes fixed on hers. She dropped her gaze, noted her abundant freckles, the unexpected goose bumps. He followed her gaze. As he approached, she reached the flat of her fingers out to touch the brown nipples in their nest of shining black hair.

"Skin," she said, as if that were all there was to it.

CHAPTER 9

Saffron yellow light cast long shadows through the fringe of high waving branches. Mud from her dress caked on the rattan lounge; her fingers brushed sprung seeds that coated the green slate. Her other arm was nestled under Borodin's clean white jacket that lay atop her. He had settled her in the lounge chair after escorting her from the pond, then went back to retrieve his coat to place over her bare upper body.

Now he sat on the ground beside her, his trousers ruined, his hand resting under the linen jacket on her damp stomach. She watched the tree canopy sway in the late afternoon sky. His expression was distant. "I should go back. Chinese are expected. To hear our instructions, assuming they will listen."

"Right now Hankow seems so far away."

"Yes."

Her voice was thick. "Do you ever feel you are living the past, present and future all at once? I do. Almost all the time." She turned on her side to look at him, adjusting herself so that his hand slid away. "Sorry." She turned back so that his hand could rest once more on her bare skin.

He was looking at the lily pond.

She didn't know what he was thinking, whether his mind was on touching her or on the Chinese he was due to instruct. To bring him back she slipped her arm out from under his jacket and took up his hand, examined its five fingers. "Tom Thumb, Peter Pointer, Toby Tall, Ruby Ring and Little

Finger." She counted them off in all seriousness, then licked her finger and ran it through the hills and valleys she had counted off.

"Stop." Anger rose in his eyes. "You are not in a nursery."

"Sorry."

He relented. "I used to play that game with Fred, when he was sick with scarlet fever." And then, "Now is not a good time for such things."

She dropped his hand, rearranged his jacket over her and then stretched both arms out behind her head. He waited and then put his hand back where it had been. "I ought to go."

She did not answer. Instead, she closed her eyes, attending to her breath, the weight of his hand. "Sometimes I feel I am an angel. Because of my Sephardic mother."

He said nothing but she thought she felt his hand press down a bit more. "It came from my getting the words mixed up," she said, "seraphic and Sephardic. She was dead and had red hair and I never got to know her."

His fingers slipped down, searched for the curve of her belly, but got stopped at the waistband. "An angel," he murmured. "We don't see many of those in the Bolsheviks."

"No," she agreed, settling her hips so that his fingers could slide down a fraction more. "That must be why I want to be one, a Bolshevik." She cast her eyes at him with a droll expression. "An angel-Bolshevik. Someone has to be."

"Ah." His attention was only fractionally with her. He was looking down the hill, trying to see if anyone was searching for him.

"She died in a fire, downstate, when I was twelve. I never knew. All the time I was growing up I thought she was dead, and then I found out she wasn't. My father never told me. My brother did one day years later when he was mad."

He still wasn't paying attention. She turned sideways and sat up, peeling her wet dress top off the muddle around her waist, seeking a way to thread her arms through the collapsed sleeves.

"Here, let me help you." He stood, sounding grave, formal, as if this were part of his ministry.

"My father kept this from me because my Sephardic mother was locked away in an institution." A dead space where she expected murmured sympathy but there wasn't any. "He put her in an asylum and annulled the marriage and never told me she was alive. That's why I won't go back to Chicago."

"I'm sorry."

She bent over to strap on her sandals. "Me too." She looked up. "It's as if I'm living her life as well as mine. Do you think I'm crazy?"

He bushed the seeds and pollen from his pants, buttoned up his wet shirt, took the now damp jacket and placed it once more on her shoulders. "No, I don't think so," then started them both down the steep path, taking the moment before they emerged from the trees to comb his hand through her tangled hair. "Perhaps you are an angel."

Just as she thought they might make it back to the house unseen, they ran into M.N. Roy who was waiting for them in the kitchen garden. "Ah, Mikhail! I see you and Mrs. Prohme have been taking your leisure." She felt Roy's eyes scan her top to bottom, taking in the muddy legs and ruined skirt, the fact that she was wearing Commander Borodin's jacket. His lip raised in a canine display of interest.

"I slipped," she announced, looking him straight in the face. "I fell in the lily pond and fortunately Commander Borodin was there to rescue me."

"Yes, fortunate." Roy savored this thought, turned it over for its various meanings, then announced, "Feng has let General Chiang's troops through to Hankow."

Borodin cursed something in Russian.

Roy snorted.

Another flicker of anger from Bee. "You think that is cause for levity?"

Roy's sly smile still held. "No, merely an occasion to reflect. On the multitude of errors."

"Which errors were you thinking of?"

Roy shrugged. "The Chinese position on hegemony." He turned to Rayna. "Young lady, I hear you are undertaking Marxist instruction from our esteemed comrade. Lucky girl." The yellow teeth flashed. "Tell me, have you formed an opinion on the matter of hegemony?" Before she had a chance to respond he gave her a hint. "As it applies to China?"

Rayna pulled in her breath. What was it Bill always nattered on about? "Do you mean the matter of joint hegemony or whether the proletariat is the only historically correct vehicle of leadership?"

Roy rewarded her with a sour smile. "Nice," then turned to Borodin, all the while letting his fingers brush down Rayna's arm. "She's coming along nicely. She even dissembles like you." He grinned as he walked toward the kitchen. Without a further glance at her, Borodin growled, "Go upstairs, stay out of the way." Then he left, circling around the house to head in from the front.

She sat in the back garden for a while just because she'd been told not to. Then tried to look at things from his point of view. She could see that being intercepted by Roy was not for the best, that she'd been the one responsible for the predicament in the first place. But he'd invited her to Kuling, and there was an implication in that of something. So they were both responsible for getting caught by Roy, although she'd been the one to get them all muddy. Reluctantly, she decided to obey his instructions and stay out of the way, which she did, taking a nice sponge bath from a basin of hot water she requested from one of the Chinese servants. The bed was delicious, the afternoon almost cool, and she slipped easily into a deep sleep that was past and future, somewhere blissful and green that was not the present.

She slept through dinner, and when she woke a meal had been sent up. The next morning she rose with the sun, hugely energized, and determined to be businesslike for the remainder of the visit, seeking out Borodin at his breakfast table with a clipboard of papers and asking him in her assistant's voice what she was expected to do.

"Chen's coming up for a couple of days," he said, not looking up from his porridge.

He took a sip of tea. "The boys are coming too, a last minute surprise, so you should find some place to put them."

She nodded and asked who handled accommodations and then was on her way. Chen arrived at the landing around two, and she was there to greet him, having been trundled down the cliff at break neck speed like so much freight. Reading was impossible, so she had time to think, and mostly what she thought about was Bill, and what Chen's visit meant, and what, if anything Chen had told Bill about her being in Kuling. She needn't have worried. Chen was surprised to see her and didn't hide his annoyance. Nevertheless, he put on a good face with the boys and the trip up the cliff face was a distraction.

Chen found the guest house she had requisitioned to his satisfaction. She asked how long he would stay. He asked the same question of her. She said, "As long as Bee wants me to," which was the truth. She didn't know if she was staying two days or six. That seemed to satisfy Chen, and he confided that his reason for coming was to make sure that Borodin understood his requirements, as he was the sole representative of the KMT government traveling to Moscow. He also requested that his sons, Percy and Jack, be accommodated on the trip across the Gobi. Rayna blanched at that bit of gall, but then remembered Mr. and Mrs. Lee. They had been scheduled for the Gobi and pulled off at the last minute, so there were two open slots. She might as well stay on the good side of Chen and murmured that she would take it up with Bee.

"See that you do," he commanded her, "and I would like to start my Moscow discussions tomorrow at nine." He pulled out a big briefcase to demonstrate the importance of this upcoming event.

When she cornered Bee at dinner she filled him in on Chen's boys and her idea about the two vacant slots. "Let him bring it up directly with me," Borodin said and then told her he didn't have time to meet with Chen, that she should conduct the meetings herself and turn whatever Chen had on his mind into a memo for his review with the goal of getting Chen out of Kuling and back to Hankow as quickly as possible.

"Bill's new tickets are for three days from now."

"Good. That should light a fire under Chen."

Rayna was glad she had a specific task, an important one, that would help to repair any misimpression of her role in Borodin's entourage. Nevertheless, her meetings with Chen dragged into a second day. She could see that he was furious at being fobbed off, and resisted any suggestion that she might be useful in Moscow. "The KMT government is Chinese. Even more so since the split with the Chinese Communists and the forced departure of the Soviets. Yes, we are traveling to Moscow to meet with the Soviet leadership, but it is to explain our Chinese path going forward, how we may collaborate in the next stage."

She hardly knew where to begin. She tried suggesting that Mme. Sun should be consulted before he drew up his plans. He dismissed that. "She is important to our government, yes, but was never a member of the inner cabinet. Therefore it is I, the Foreign Minister and Acting Treasurer, who must carry the burden."

She gave up, simply took down what he said, let him draw his charts and lay out his plans for meeting with this high Soviet official or that. He asked about his accommodations in Moscow. She said she didn't know, but would raise it with Bee. He asked if she had inquired about taking Percy and Jack on the Gobi trip. She said she had but that Bee wanted to discuss the matter with Chen himself. By the end of the second day she had put together a five page memorandum with his handwritten attachments which she promised to convey to Bee prior to a full discussion arranged for the next morning. As she headed out, she advised him that his villa was booked for other guests and that he would have to take the afternoon launch back to Hankow.

The next morning Borodin was frank. Chen's fantasy of a Moscow reception as the acting KMT head of state was not in the cards. "They are going to deal with General Chiang from now on. Nasty business, but there it is. Our little band will be on the periphery, trying to nudge things back into the channel. Blame will be assigned. Be prepared for some of the shit to land on you."

Chen didn't like that. In an effort to diffuse the tension, Rayna brought up the matter of Mme. Sun. Chen bristled again, but in a different way.

"You dismiss official receptions. But let me tell you, if she decides to come, that kind of welcome will be expected."

"We Russians are not barbarians," Borodin put in smoothly. "Of course the widow of the esteemed Chinese leader will be accorded full protocol."

That seemed to mollify Chen and he returned to the matter of translators, suitable offices, housing for his large family. Bee gave bland assurances. Rayna was aware that the matter of whether Mme. Sun would actually elect to make the journey was being sidestepped. Before she could bring that up, Bee switched to the question of Percy and Jack joining him on the Gobi trip. "I think that is a good idea. We have a couple of spots that have come vacant. Mrs. Prohme is in charge of these matters so when she gets back to Hankow later this week she can make the arrangements." He stood. The meeting was over. Rayna stood as well. She had grown skeptical not only of Chen's talents but his motives. One more reason to stay close to Mme. Sun.

She saw them off later that day and escorted a new band of visitors up the cliff. Among the new arrivals was General Teng. The Communist ministers in the KMT had been pushed out at the same time as the Russians were ordered to depart. The rest of the cabinet was going over in twos and threes to Chiang. General Teng was now the only hold out still aligned with Mme. Sun. Rayna had first met him at Whampoa Academy where he was Borodin's propaganda officer. Later he led the march to clear the way for the government to move to Hankow. Rewarded with a position in the cabinet, and then dispatched to Nanking to negotiate with General Chiang, his recent whereabouts had become unclear. Rayna remembered the visit to Mme. Sun's apartment. Now he was arriving on the Russian launch, dressed in full military uniform. On the way up the cliff, Teng told her he had been educated in Germany, so they conversed in a combination of her bad German and his bad English. She stuck to the weather but then asked whether he had ever visited Kuling.

"No, I have not had the honor. Tell me, is Commander Borodin soon to depart?"

She said that it would happen any day now.

"Good. I must go too. How do you say? The window is closing?"

The next two days she did not see Bee at all. Nor did she have any work to do or any distractions now that Jack and Percy Chen had gone. The meetings seemed to have been transferred to another place, somewhere in the countryside with the remaining CCP leaders, commanders heading up ragtag peasant armies, cadre organizers from the cities. But she didn't ask. Teng, whom she supposed was Mme. Sun's emissary, had disappeared along with the rest. She was restless, ashamed of her behavior in the lily pond, yet felt it had been somehow necessary. Now that she resolved to go, a need came upon her: to touch him, to feel his beating heart. She began to hover in the hall to intercept him on the way to meals. During one dinner break, when he arrived with a phalanx of Russians, she steadied her nerves and pushed forward.

"Excuse me, Commander." Her use of military rank, unofficial as it was, caught him off guard. He motioned for the others to go forward.

"Yes?"

"I believe it is time for me to leave. I've booked space on tomorrow's launch."

He nodded.

"I must ask instructions for what I do in Shanghai. And after." She looked at him, willing him to understand. "Later tonight, or tomorrow morning would be fine."

Borodin was looking past her, to the men at the table. A flicker of irritation when he returned his gaze. "Yes," he said, in a low voice that might have been for her benefit or just to keep the sound from spreading, "Tonight or tomorrow."

"Or both," she suggested, hoping her meaning was clear, then turned to go so that their conversation would not attract further attention.

She went up the huge staircase back to her room, stripped off her dress, washed for the third time that day and tried to retreat into fitful sleep. If Bee was going to join her it would be hours before he came. She could not plan on it, could not plan on anything. But she did have to get things clear. How forceful was she to be with Mme. Sun? Would she accompany the Chinese widow and, if so, in what capacity? What of once she got to Moscow? Those were the formal questions she would put to him. The personal ones were just as stark. What had happened between them? Would it continue in Moscow? What of her obligation to Bill, his to his wife? Those thoughts swirled as she struggled to sleep. Her last memory was of Bill telling her he'd asked for tickets from her father. She was not going back to Chicago. Much was unclear but that was not.

She woke to the sound of loud voices. The Chinese must have gone, otherwise Bee wouldn't be shouting. "They will all be deposed," she heard him yell. "Six weeks and the peasant army will turn on our handpicked leaders." She could imagine exhausted Russians sitting at the felt-covered library table littered by overflowing ashtrays.

Maybe it had been a dream, because she awoke to silence and the moon shining in her window. She rose and padded out to the balcony, wishing she had taken up smoking because this was the perfect time for a cigarette. She pondered slipping down the hall and camping out by his bedroom door, but decided she had disgraced herself enough and must wait until the morning to make her last plea for his attentions.

But that wasn't necessary. Because close to dawn, when she had finally sunk into a dreamless sleep, there was the creak of her door, a shadow above her bed. She knew, without opening her eyes, that it was Borodin.

His body slipped in beside her. As he lifted the covers she heard him murmur a few words. "Do you mind?"

In a thick voice she had said no. She did not mind. In her half sleep, she was open to all that came next, the play of his hand, the other things. Content to record its many sensations, while on a separate track, in a separate part of her, meaning engraved itself. She did not allow herself to anticipate. Tomorrow was another time, she would be another person.

When dawn began to lighten the room, she found him looking at her, a finger tracing down her cheek. He touched her lower lip. "What are you thinking?"

"Nothing," she replied. "I'm thinking nothing."

His finger trailed down her chin to the curve of her collar bone. "You enchant me," he said. "I am baffled by it. Now what do you make of that?"

"Nothing," she said, her voice still detached from both mind and body. She patted his arm. "We're just two people." Then she closed her eyes, lolling her head back and forth. "History of the world won't be affected." With a sudden smile, she slid back to sleep, leaving him, she hoped, to wonder what he had done.

Two hours later she reached for him and found an empty space where he had been. But later he sent word that they should meet on the back patio. As they sat over mid-morning tea, he became explicit. "Moscow," he told her, "is a swamp. It was a swamp when I left and now the smell is stronger than ever."

"That bad?" she murmured, her finger playing with bits of tea leaf floating on the surface of her cup.

He cast about for a way to make his warning more concrete. "You know Chicago, those bare knuckle politics." She looked up, smiled. "It's a hundred times worse."

"A hundred times," she said. "Well." Then tipped back her head to drink the last of her tea.

"You don't understand."

"Apparently not," she agreed. "But if it's that bad, why are you so ready to go back? Do you have some secret plan to save the Russians from themselves?"

"I doubt they would let me. My family is there. I have cast my lot. You know, it is not the first time I've lapsed into heresy. In Chicago, I was found guilty of consorting with moderates." She pursed her lips in mock horror. "Just as I am accused now of so doing. This time, though, I was acting under orders, but that doesn't seem to matter."

"Ah."

"Just so," he agreed. "We make choices. Chicago, two sons, a loyal wife, a nice business. Who would have thought Ilyich could have pulled it off?"

"How well did you know him?" She was still absorbed with the bit of jasmine that lay plastered against the side of her cup.

"I was one of his boys. In the inner circle. An anomaly, a real, honest-to-God proletarian. What's more, I could read."

"And smuggle," she added.

"And smuggle." His leg was giving in to nerves, going up and down like a piston.

"What about your wife?" she asked. "Was she happy you went back?"

"No." That was all he said for a while. Then he added, "I was young, without prospects. She knew English, bookkeeping. But ten years later..." His expression became distant. "By then I had made a name." He put a hand out to stop his leg hammering and looked at her. "Deep down, Fanya was not pleased at this change in our circumstances."

She shrugged, then came out with a question. "And a normal life in Chicago was not enough? You had to go back?"

He let out his breath, the whooshing sound that was becoming a permanent part of his vocabulary. "No, it was not enough. Once Ilyich stormed the Winter Palace, I had to go. I had to have more."

"Like me." She closed her eyes in embarrassment at comparing her situation to his.

He stood, forgiving her for her grandiosity. "Let's walk."

As they climbed through the terraced gardens, he spoke to her about her trip down the Yangtze, the contacts she was to make in Shanghai, how she was to approach Mme. Sun.

"Can I accompany her to Moscow? Stay there with you?"

He made the decision. "At least for a while. Then we shall see."

He returned to mechanics, how the most dangerous part would be getting out of the Shanghai harbor. A Soviet trawler would take them to Vladivostok, then a train to Moscow.

"What happens when we arrive?"

He frowned. "Don't be like Chen, thinking too far ahead. If you get there first, ask to see Bukharin, he'll take care of you."

"The head of Comintern?" She was doubtful.

"Or Litvanov. If you can't get in to see him, contact Joffe. He knows Mme. Sun. It's important she be comfortable in Moscow, that she knows we are doing everything to help."

"What about the Lenin School?" She was throwing stones over the wall that banked the terrace, watching them bounce against a lower wall. He stopped, unwilling to consent to this new demand. She threw another stone. "Do you want me to wait or go right in and talk to them?" She knew by his silence the answer. "I want to be part of this. I want to join the Party."

"Things aren't that simple," he replied, caution blanketing some deeper concern. "Take care of Mme. Sun, that is your charge. The rest can wait. When I arrive we will take up the matter of you becoming a Bolshevik. When the moment is right."

She did not like the sound of that. So she bent down and picked up a larger stone, hefted it, threw it as far as she could. Only the stone broke apart, it was only dried earth, and pieces flew in all directions, one chunk dislodging a bird's next tucked in the wall, rolling the new born chicks over and over down the steep hillside to their death.

Chapter 10

Later, after he'd bid her good-bye with a formal handshake, waved from the verandah as the bearers lifted her up to poke their way down the mountain, she had time to reflect, once again, on what she was going to tell Bill. In Hankow she would make final arrangements for Borodin's departure, then take the Japanese steamer down to Shanghai. A car from the Soviet Embassy would meet her and drive her to the Rue Moliere, Mme. Sun's residence in the French Concession. All the while she was to keep up the pretense she was remaining with Bill, keep up that fiction until the last minute, when she and Mme. Sun would make their getaway in the dead of night. It all sounded very dramatic.

But as the heat and dust of the flatlands came back to greet her, she asked herself what lay ahead. Bill in Shanghai. The escape. The reception Mme. Sun would get in Moscow. Once landed in Hankow, she drifted back to the granite building that housed her newspaper. A shiny-booted officer, one of General Chiang's men, was being allowed an inspection and, for a moment, she could see the smashed machines and overturned composition tables. Her revolution felt similarly demolished.

For the next two days she checked and rechecked arrangements. A last inquiry to make sure the bribes were in place, the final squeeze for the turncoat Feng, through whose territory Borodin's party had to pass. She was there to witness the Russians' departure. A five-car train festooned with government banners, the Dodges and the lone Buick lashed down on their flatbeds, another holding the trucks and jerry cans, a boxcar for provisions, salted pork, melons, sacks of rice, and a corner reserved for the all-important machine guns. In the passenger car, in a concealed compartment, a store box filled with gold bars to be ladled out according to a schedule drawn up by T.V. Soong, a space for initials by each bribe so as to reconcile the accounts.

She watched the ritual expressions of regret by the few remaining government ministers, their plea that he stay on, Borodin's somber regret that his country called him home. She held a glass of warm punch for the endless toasts, declined the sticky rice cakes. She would have laughed, had she been able to, at the final comic note. As the train pulled out, Anna Louise waving to the crowd like Queen Victoria, Borodin sitting beside her in a sullen lump, the military band broke into a ragged version of Dr. Sun's national anthem, his Three Principles set to song. The Chinese revolution marched not to the "Internationale" but to "Frere Jacques." Ding, dang, dong. She let out a painful laugh. History repeats itself, Borodin liked to tell her, the first time as tragedy, the second time as farce.

So Rayna was there when the curtain came down, with its silent boos and invisible hurled cabbages, as Hankow bid good-bye to its Russian Commander. Utterly depleted, she went back to her room to collect her small bag. Then on to the Japanese steamer that was just like the German one except it was dirtier and the cabin curtains were red instead of green. She had brought enough food for a week and proposed to stay in her cabin, only going on deck at night, when it was cooler and she did not have to talk with the few other passengers.

The first night she slept like the dead, and in the morning resolved to write long overdue letters to pass the time. "I am plying down the Yangtze on a Japanese steamer, the last to leave Hankow before the opposition takes full control," she began her letter to Raph, three pages now, the ink furry with humidity. "I am leaving Hankow, where the government has fallen to Chiang's right-wing army, a hard fight with much treachery that makes me bitter with disappointment. Not only Americans kicked out, but all the Russians as well. Our commander, Mikhail Borodin, whom I have come to regard as a very great man, has been called back to Moscow."

She examined the candy pink stationery, the box she had carried with her from Peking to Canton to Hankow. Only this morning had she slit the creamy band holding its envelopes. Last night, listening to the stuttering engines, she thought about her marriage to Raph, the wedding an elaborate affair orchestrated to cover the fact that the two families detested each other. Back then her young husband Raph had been lit by the fierce glow of literary ambition. But soon it turned to morose fear of failure. Now he had a hit play on Broadway and, in her roundabout way, she was trying to tell him that she, too, had achieved her moment of success. "I am about to embark on a mission, an escape involving an important Chinese figure. We will board a Russian trawler and then take the Trans-Siberian Express, which is no longer an express, eight days it now takes, twelve in bad weather. But at least we will be fed and have a cushion to curl up on, so it will be heaven compared with what will happen if we are betrayed."

She stopped, thought about what she couldn't write: Borodin's lovemaking, the mission he had so grudgingly agreed to. She was to protect the widow of the esteemed Chinese leader, escort Mme. Sun to Moscow. What could she tell Raph without giving away those twin secrets? "My hope is to join him there," she wrote, "or wherever he goes next. He knows my geographic desires."

Rayna looked at her hands, freckled like the rest of her body from so much time in the Chinese sun. The bones on her wrists stood out. Her dress, once apple green, now faded to lichen. She looked at the curling pink paper, her scrawled writing, her body remembering the lovemaking, its fierce need stoked by fear of being left behind. Whatever she had once felt for Raph, and later for Bill, was mild compared with what had happened in Kuling. That night was of a different order. It defined, remade her. A Russian had made love to her body, given her an assignment, assured her that they would meet again. If they both made it to Moscow alive. That, too, had traced through their lovemaking, danger bound up with the certainty of loss. She frowned, put the letter aside. She didn't know why she was writing Ralph now, except to make sense of her situation.

The trip was uneventful, two days longer than scheduled. By then she'd written a packet of letters, three more to Raph, one to her sister Grace, a couple to her best friend Helen, and, on impulse, a last one to Dorothy, her old college roommate. She had no stamps, so she shoved a couple in her skirt pocket for mailing when she got on Russian soil. The rest she tore up.

As the steamer began its docking maneuvers she tossed the letter scraps overboard and watched them float away. On the wharf she could see Bill's rumpled outline, his outsized wave. She looked down at her dress, its belt drilled with extra holes she'd added with a kitchen knife. She smelled of smoke and river muck. Decide, she told herself, how much will you tell?

Behind Bill was the Russian car and driver. Poor Bill, she thought as she stepped off the gangplank, tugging at her belt as Bill folded her into his arms.

"Rough trip?"

"Smelly. Hot." The driver from the embassy was making his way toward her.

"You're tired," he decided, releasing her and guiding her toward the street.

"Disoriented," she said. "At the end, heartbreaking."

"You waited too long," he said in a voice sure of its facts.

"Heartbreaking," she repeated as she motioned for the embassy driver to wait. She pulled Bill over to the shade of a warehouse. "I have a message for Mme. Sun. I must go there first, then I'll meet you."

"I'll go with you."

"You can't."

And so it began, the last excruciating interval, where she spent her days and nights in the villa of Mme. Sun, running errands, visiting the Soviet Consulate to check travel arrangements, squeezing in time with Bill, letting him down slowly, telling him Chen was in hiding but working on a Shanghai assignment for him, as yet unspecified. She'd withdrawn more of her money from the bank account replenished by her sister Grace, and gave Bill twenty British pounds. "It's from Chen. He's working on getting more." A white lie, but a lie nonetheless.

She told him she would be out of the country for a while. She didn't say Moscow but he could figure that out. He wanted to know about Dan, what he was supposed to do with the dog.

"Visit her," she said. "She's lonely."

"It's your dog."

"I know, but I haven't a spare moment." She gave him her best smile, feeling guilty about Dan and the lies she was telling, but reminding herself it was for the greater good. "You should look for a place," she said, "with space enough for Dan." Left unsaid was that she was abandoning them both, at least for a while. He took it the opposite way, that she would be returning soon, and she let him think that.

On the wharf in Shanghai she had kissed him and then left in the embassy car. On arriving at Mme. Sun's villa that first time, she'd been distressed to see Comrade Reuben, the mysterious Mr. Lee with the Brooklyn accent who had taken over escort duty at Kuling.

He'd stood on the steps at the Rue Moliere to block her access, a sour expression masking his evident satisfaction. "I've informed Mme. Sun that your services will no longer be needed. Eugene Chen and I will manage from here on out."

"You informed her."

"Yes"

"She doesn't make her own decisions?"

Reuben's expression implied this didn't deserve an answer.

She tried again. "That's not what Commander Borodin instructed me."

"He is no longer in command."

"Nevertheless, if there is a change in plans I need to hear it from Mme. Sun."

She waited him out. Stood on the doorstep in the blazing hot sun until she felt like fainting. At last one of Mme. Sun's maids came with a message that Rayna was to be shown in. The house was small, European feeling, set close on the street, but in the back there was a deep garden with high walls. The house of a widow, almost a museum, memorabilia of her husband everywhere.

In the sitting room, Rayna was offered tea, then some cakes and finally, after an hour, shown to a room on the second floor. A bathrobe and towels were laid out and the maid in halting English suggested she freshen up. "I have no clean clothes," Rayna pointed out, and the maid motioned to her small suitcase, explaining that her clothes would be washed and ironed. So Rayna surrendered the dress she was wearing and most of her suitcase and retired to a large tiled bathroom with a ceramic tub full of hot water and scented with sandalwood oil.

Dinner was sent up on a tray while Rayna waited for her newly washed clothes. At nine she was summoned for a conference with the Lady. "Rayna, how nice to see you," Mme. Sun said as she rose to greet her.

"That man outside, Comrade Lee? I must say I don't like him. He said my services are no longer required."

Mme. Sun was unperturbed. "Yes, these days we find ourselves with strange companions. Of course your services are required. We have gone from the frying pan into the fire and now must escape the kitchen." She took Rayna out to see the garden in the last daylight, whispering that it would be a week, maybe longer, before the Russian trawler arrived, that the Soviets were waiting to see if Russians scattered here and there could make their way to Shanghai. In the countryside, she said, it was a bloodbath.

Rayna did not want to hear about that. Her own assignment was tenuous enough. "Bill is waiting for me at the Bristol Hotel. Not the best, but the best we can afford."

Mme. Sun glanced away at this mention of the promised money. "I have spoken with Mr. Chen. He claims our cupboard is bare."

Rayna was not surprised the offer was being withdrawn. "Don't worry. We'll figure something out."

"Nonsense. I will speak to my brother."

"No, he's done enough." T.V. Soong had arranged the bribes with Feng, paid for the gold out of his own pocket so Bee and his party could pass through. All for the honor of his sister even though General Chiang would have gleefully shot the lot. Then another thought. "Does your brother know of your plans?"

"No. I would not want him so burdened." Borodin had told Rayna that pressure from Mme. Sun's family was intense. By then it was past curfew, so she spent the night, worrying about what Bill would think, and only managed to catch up with him at noon the next day.

To make it up to him, she went to the Pan Pacific Trade Union and pleaded with Earl Browder, made the case that her husband was committed to staying in China. She trusted that Browder could read between the lines about her own plans for Moscow. To make sure, she took out his letter, the one he'd written in the German restaurant in Hankow. "I'm going to use this."

He nodded.

"It's Bill I'm asking for. I'll be fine, but he needs to keep occupied."

Browder was noncommittal, said he'd get back. She knew he would check with the higher-ups, but wondered if Chen had already decided to shuck Bill.

She had to be careful. There were spies everywhere, Chinese spies, European spies. Mme. Sun was unable to leave her residence; virtual house arrest a condition of the French agreeing to let her occupy her own dwelling. Her brother came and went, bearing messages from the family.

Each day Rayna would go to the Soviet Consulate, across from the Astor House hotel, to gather information for Bill's nonexistent newspaper. She paid particular attention to reports from Moscow and gathered what information she could about Russians trying to escape the countryside roundup. She kept up the fiction with Bill about the clipping service, and Bill began pasting together a sample issue, whistling as he sorted through the reams of material she brought back each day. Most nights she stayed at the Rue Moliere, but every few evenings she made a point of staying in Bill's hotel room, to keep up the pretense that their separation was only work related. At times she believed this, but convinced herself not to think about where all this was headed, about Dan in her kennel that she still had not had the courage to visit, the fact that Bill showed no interest in finding a place to keep her beloved dog. Rayna's secret bank account was down to the last few hundred dollars, and she transferred half to her joint account with Bill. He didn't ask where the money came from and she didn't volunteer.

Meanwhile, Mme. Sun decided to give her a going-away present, a Chongsam, the Mandarin-style dress that was high fashion in Shanghai. Mme. Sun wore it in black, but Rayna's was to be deep gold with a black stand-up collar and embroidered side closing. "I don't know where I can wear this," Rayna protested as she stood for the fittings.

"You'll need it for ceremonial occasions," Mme. Sun told her. They never spoke the word Moscow. "This will make you a warrior. You know about Chinese women warriors, do you not?"

Secretly, Rayna was thrilled at this show of affection, of confidence in her powers. It could have been just good manners, but Rayna took it as a deepening of their alliance. After thanking her hostess for the fourth time, Rayna changed the subject. "We are really going, then? No turning back?"

Mme. Sun said she had no choice. That many times her husband had retreated to a foreign shore to regroup, and she must do the same. When Rayna asked if her destination was unchanged, the Lady was quick to nod yes. "I will begin there, gauge the tenor of my reception." Rayna recalled the tenor of her own reception with Comrade Reuben, how distrustful she had become of Chen, how confused she was by the reports drifting in from Moscow of the escalating struggle between Trotsky and Stalin. But she couldn't let any of that stop her. She must take her own first step.

Finally, word came that the trawler was on its way. In two nights they must be ready to depart. She left most of her clothes at Rue Moliere and returned to Bill's hotel with only a few things in a woven string bag. Better not call attention by any change in routine. She sat down and explained they needed to talk. "My work with the Lady is taking a critical turn," she said, adopting the shorthand that had become second nature. "For a while, at least, you will need to carry on the newsletter alone." It was better this way, leaving it open-ended as to when she would be back. He suggested dinner, in celebration of her speedy return and the newfound money from Chen. She accepted.

Before making their way to his favorite Japanese restaurant, Bill steered her into an outdoor market. "I want to buy you something." She protested that she was traveling light, but he seized upon a pair of rattan slippers to go with the summer dress she was wearing. She wanted to tell him that the slippers would be useless, that summer in Moscow would be over in a blink, that her plans were to stay several months. But she didn't. When they got to the restaurant and were seated near a water fountain that blotted out sound, he said, "Now tell me what this is all about."

"What?"

"Did Borodin decree you should join him?"

She flushed. "We had a discussion. About how important it is for the Lady to go."

"When was this?"

"Just before your departure. We were in the mountains. At Kuling."

"Just the two of you?"

"No. There were meetings. Last instructions for the Chinese."

"And you were at these meetings?"

"Of course not. I arranged logistics." She didn't tell him Chen was there. Apparently Chen hadn't either.

He was chewing on some pickled cabbage. "Are you in love with him? Has he convinced you of his undying ardor?"

"Of course not. Why would you say that?"

He put down his chopsticks. "Let's just say I know you. And am aware that I have become an inconvenience."

She hastened to deny this, all the while feeling that was exactly the situation. Then she blurted out, "I know, I'm awful. That's what Raph used to say." Once there had been a time when Bill had rescued her from this relentless self-reproach, the feeling of unworthiness that Raph was so skilled at evoking. "What kind of person am I to leave Dan? Put her in a kennel and then forget about her? Oh, Bill, you have to take care of her! I shall die if I have to worry—" The dinner ended when she was unable to contain her tears.

When they got back to the hotel she said she needed to take a bath. The facilities weren't nearly so nice as those at the Rue Moliere but as she soaped herself in the rusty bathwater she distracted herself by remembering Kuling's moonlit lovemaking. It seemed so far away, dangerous to bring to mind. One more secret she must keep in a storehouse of secrets. Bill's jibe about Bee's persuasive powers had struck home. She must not think things would be the same when she arrived in Moscow. Instead, she must concentrate on the tasks at hand. Insuring Mme. Sun's warm reception, her own plans to enroll in the Lenin School. If it took months, or even longer, for things to reestablish themselves with Bee, she could wait. And Bill would wait, too, like faithful Dan, in Shanghai. She would find him some work and write him every day. When she finished with what she'd set out to do, she would call for him to come to Moscow, or join him somewhere else. She couldn't stand the notion that she was abandoning him. She promised herself she wouldn't and then promised herself she wouldn't think about it anymore.

The next day Bill again brought up the subject of joining her. To placate him she allowed him to come on her errand for the day, to check on the launching site for the sampan that would take them to the trawler far out in the harbor. They took the trolley along Bubbling Well Road and then transferred to a shabbier line that took them out to the go-downs that lined the Whangpoo. She was to meet the fellow in charge of smuggling them aboard the Soviet trawler.

Bill was still of two minds about Moscow. "Why do you want to go there? Did Borodin put you up to it?"

"Actually, I suggested it."

He slouched in the rattan seat, the trolley rattle making it hard to hear. "How long has this been cooking? Since you got rid of me by sending me down to Shanghai?"

"Bill. That's not fair. It came up at the last minute. Anyway, it's more or less settled. We're waiting for news of the trawler."

He gave her a long look, the pain leaking through the stifled anger. Then he shrugged. "Go ahead, do what you want, you always do."

A new flood of guilt. "It's just for a couple of months, until the Lady gets settled."

"Settled. When has that ever been a condition of our lives?"

"Look," she said, "I'll get paid. We'll pool our resources, and in a few weeks, a month, two at the most—" She let that thought run out. "Besides, I can't take you. Winter is coming. You couldn't stand the climate."

He had no answer to that. The trolley was pulling up to the stop near a ramshackle shed. Her contact was a Harbin fur dealer, a Comrade Skolnik, who was not pleased to see them. Mongolian pony skins, smelling of their former lives, were piled high on rough pallets. With a grunt, Skolnik heaved a batch of rough-scraped skins off a crate for them to sit. "I don't sell to tourists," he growled. "Go back to the city." That concession to a cover made, he took them outside to inspect the ungraded skins that stank even more. As he grumbled in a loud drone, Rayna whispered the set speech she'd agreed upon with Bill, that her husband wished to come, that she was asking permission.

"*Nyet.*" Skolnik had no such authority, he claimed, he was just an intermediary. He glared at Bill to drive home the point. Bill lifted his hands in retreat. And that, Rayna hoped, was that.

The countdown clock was ticking and from that point on she saw little of Bill. Mme. Sun was in a state of high nerves and demanded Rayna's constant presence. Then a handwritten note on embossed paper arrived, an invitation to dinner with a certain British journalist. That was the signal. She pressed the cold and shaking hands of Mme. Sun, returned to Bill's hotel for a last few hours, running her fingers through his thinning hair. "We'll get through this," she promised. "Have faith."

"Faith," he said. "That's a little in short supply."

She let that pass. "Dan," she prompted, "you've got to take care of her."

"Why should I? You're not taking care of me."

It was then she decided she would have to take Dan with her to Moscow. It was the only way.

Part II
Waiting for Borodin

CHAPTER 11

The invitation from the British journalist said to meet him at the Astor House for tea dancing. Around two in the afternoon, Rayna left Bill and bought some black slippers from a street vendor, then took a trolley to the hotel where she left the gold dress in the cloak room. Out on Bubbling Well Road she tipped the doorman to hail a rickshaw that took her to the edge of the British Concession and the kennel where Dan was incarcerated. She could hear the yelps of the dogs in the exercise yard as she approached.

Mrs. Withers, the proprietor, was one of those types kinder to dogs than to people. "I have to say. Mrs. Prohme, that I am disappointed you have not come sooner. I was led to believe—"

Rayna fumbled in her purse and produced the necessary cash to satisfy the bill. "Do you have her leash? Millie must have brought it."

"I do." Mrs. Withers took out her keys and unlocked a large cabinet to extract the tagged lanyard. Rayna found herself trembling with the need to see Dan.

She was led back through a long row of cages to find Dan curled up in the far corner, looking very thin. The dog raised her eyes and examined the visitors without interest, then saw, or smelled, Rayna. A sharp quiver ran through her and she rose on unsteady legs to make her way over.

"She hasn't eaten much," Mrs. Withers hastened to add. "Doesn't make friends with the other dogs in the yard. So it's good you are here."

Rayna brushed away the implied criticism, and stooped down as Mrs. Withers opened the cage's gate. "I've come for you, my lovely." Dan nestled her snout in Rayna's crouching knees. "We've got a hard journey ahead of us but I'm sure we'll make it." With that she snapped Dan onto her leash and walked her, for the last part carried her, to the waiting rickshaw.

The next step was less clear. Rayna told the driver to take her to the Rue Moliere, and then, when she'd paid him, she held the leash tight by Dan's neck and marched up to the front door. The guards waved the dog off but finally allowed Rayna to take Dan through the side gate to the walled rear yard. She tied Dan up by the kitchen and went in to ask the cook, Mrs. Ma, for a bowl of water. Then she returned to the front and asked to see Mme. Sun.

The answer was the Lady was in seclusion.

"I'm sorry, but I must see her or at least get her a message. It's about Dan."

There was a long wait in the lower parlor until Rayna was called up to the second floor. In the sitting room, the Lady wore a strained expression. "I understand you brought Dan, that she is in the yard."

Rayna delivered a breathless explanation about Millie and the kennel and Bill. She said she had no other options, either Mme. Sun would agree to keep her at the Rue Moliere until Rayna could get back, or she would have to take Dan along. She didn't say anything about their closely guarded plans that night, knowing this was upsetting the arrangements the Soviet embassy had put in place.

Mme. Sun blinked while she considered. "It is not wise to leave her here. The house may be shut up, or ransacked." Then she added, "The Chinese are not kind to dogs."

The other alternative sat there between them.

Finally, the Lady sighed. "I'll ask Mrs. Ma to take charge. At least that way poor Dan will get food."

Rayna breathed out in relief. Mrs. Ma was scheduled to meet them at the Russian trawler. She was going along as Mme. Sun's cook.

Then she rushed back to the Astor House, going into the ladies' room to change into her gold dress. The dancing had started at five and by the time she got there it was after six and the party was roaring. That was good, because she could sip ginger ale and chat with the group at her table and fox trot with a couple of the men. The Astor overlooked the Whangpoo and she used the excuse of the heat to go out on the balcony and look down the embankment to see the wharf where the sampan would ferry them out to the trawler. Just after midnight her British journalist looked at his watch and said it was time to escort her home.

He made a pass in the back seat of the taxi but she didn't mind. She thought maybe it was for show, in case the driver got asked what his passengers had been doing. But to be on the safe side, she said, "Do that again, I'll throw up on your fine white dinner jacket." He minded his manners after that, but at the Bristol Hotel she had to repeat the performance, only getting rid of him by promising to meet him the next day for lunch. Then she was free to embark on the next part of the plan, which was to ride the rickety elevator to the third floor and race down the back stairway and out the emergency exit to the alley where a dusty black Citroen was waiting. She felt guilty she hadn't been able to wake Bill and say good-bye.

The car drove around for what seemed like an hour, then dropped her at a street corner deep in the Chinese city, where she transferred to a rickshaw and was told to hide under the seat. After some wending around, the coolie stopped, laid down his traces and helped her out. Her gold dress was filthy by then and she prayed it would come clean in some future washday that she couldn't even imagine. As she picked her way through muddy ruts to the pony skin shed, she could see Mme. Sun dressed in greasy work clothes, her face covered with a fine coating of ash.

"I brought you some rags." The Lady held out a filthy carryall, then said in dismay, "That beautiful dress."

"I know. I didn't have time to change." Rayna stepped behind the pony skins and stripped off the dress, rolled it up and put it in the carryall, then pulled on a gray tunic and overlarge trousers. A padded black coat, one shoulder with the stuffing showing, completed the outfit. She pointed at her muddy black slippers. "At least they belong."

Mme. Sun surveyed the transformation. "Your hair," she said. Curly and red wouldn't do.

"I'll slick it down with sea water." Rayna pointed to the greasy slosh that lapped against the skid where the sampan was hauled up.

"Hardly necessary." Mme. Sun shook her head with distaste, then changed her mind. "Actually, smell is a good defense." Rayna was about to tell her that smell would have been helpful in the taxi but by then the waiting boatman was lowering a rope and bringing up a wooden bucket of sea foam.

Rayna eyed the bucket. "Just the thing," she agreed, bracing her hands on her knees while he poured the foul mixture over her head. When she stood, the rancid foam slid onto her face and neck. She made a good show of rubbing it in and then slicked back her curls. "Will this go with the dress?"

"Where we are going, who knows what the fashion will be?"

The gold wrinkled bunched-up mess she carried for dear life as the sampan sloshed through rotting fruit and dead sea creatures, was clutched tightly as they slipped past fishing barques lashed together and bearing silent sleeping families. Farther out, they edged between military vessels bristling with guns and huge green idling tankers. Keyed up by the danger, Rayna could sense she was on her way. Good-bye old self, she wanted to shout. If I die tomorrow, so be it.

An hour later, where the river opened up to the ocean, they were hauled over the side of the Russian trawler like so much baggage and told to wait on the deck for the rest of the arrivals. First came the sampan with Chen and the two girls. They were similarly transferred to a lifeboat and winched up, Comrade Reuben standing there to greet them. Then the whole party waited on slippery deck lockers for another half hour for Mme. Sun's entourage. Finally that sampan came into view. The process was repeated while Rayna looked in vain for Dan. Maybe the instructions had gone wrong, maybe – but then she saw Mrs. Ma wrestling with a long black duffle bag, one she wouldn't let the sailors help her with, and Rayna could see the outline of a back leg pressed against the canvas.

Mrs. Ma struggled over the rail winded but triumphant. She stood at attention and placed the duffle at Rayna's feet, then bowed. The duffle bag twitched. Comrade Reuben came over and nudged the lumpy package with his foot.

"Don't!"

Reuben looked at her with surprise. Then with suspicion.

"It's my dog. I couldn't leave her behind."

By now one of the sailors had unzipped the bag to reveal Dan's groggy face. Rayna stooped down to touch her dog's muzzle and spoke up to Comrade Reuben with defensive certainty. "I'm not leaving her."

"Useless fool," he said, meaning them both. He motioned to a waiting seaman. "Throw the dog over."

"No!" Rayna hadn't thought of this. She must do or say something to divert this command. "If you do I'll throw myself over. Mme. Sun, what kind of example would that be for her?

It was at this juncture that Mme. Sun stepped forward. "I suggested this course of action. Mrs. Prohme and the dog are part of my party. I expect them to be well treated."

With that Comrade Reuben gave up, and with a disgusted air told Rayna that she was not to let the dog out of her cabin. Only after they were out in the Yellow Sea were they escorted below deck. Mme. Sun had a cabin alone with her maid while Rayna got a four-bunk stateroom with Yolanda, Sylvia Chen and Mrs. Ma.

Dan crawled under the bed and would not come out for hours. Rayna washed her hair as best she could in the stateroom sink, donned fresh blue coveralls and a long sleeved shirt provided and handed the rags out the door to a grinning Russian seaman. Then she pulled her one rough blanket over her head and tried to blot out the chatter of the Chen girls. She slept for twelve hours. When she woke Dan was hunched up against the wall by her side.

The next afternoon Comrade Reuben assembled them all in the wardroom. After a brief welcome and a few ground rules about not engaging with the crew, he dismissed the Chen girls and Mme. Sun's staff, though he consented to her bodyguards standing outside the door. The boat was starting to pitch in swells off a coming storm and Rayna concentrated most of her energy on not getting seasick.

"Very well," Reuben began. "Our expected time of passage is three days. Because of rough seas there will be little opportunity to discuss our arrival on Soviet soil." Rayna noticed his odd rubbery lips that contorted when he emphasized certain vowels. He told them he had been in China for five years, spoke the language, a point he emphasized to demonstrate his sweeping command of the political situation. His analysis of the Hankow government was not flattering; his explanation of the wisdom of Soviet instructions to the KMT fullsome. Rayna kept her eyes fixed beyond his left ear, to the hardware around the porthole, and tried not to think about what impression this lecture was making on Mme. Sun. To Rayna's surprise, or maybe not, Chen leapt in with a fervid statement of agreement. With a motion of her hand, Mme. Sun cut him off.

"Thank you Comrade Reuben for making these arrangements." Then the Lady rose. "Your suggestion that we retire to our cabins because of choppy seas is a good one. I, for one, am in need of rest." With that she bowed before the Russian with the Brooklyn accent and slipped out of the room.

Reuben struggled to disguise his anger that the star pupil had waltzed out of his class. The ship lurched and Rayna also rose, thinking she might use the same excuse, but Reuben stopped her with a tight grip on her arm.

Chen, however, showed no sign of wishing to leave. "Well," he said, "we should begin making our plans."

"Certainly," Rayna agreed, sitting back down, not having much choice and wanting to block Chen from making any promises on Mme. Sun's behalf. "What I would like to discuss is my husband's job in Shanghai. The newsletter you promised. Comrade Reuben, do you have authority to move that forward?"

"There is no money," Chen put in. "I told you that."

"Others have told me otherwise. After all, every bit of the money you spent, on newsprint and banquets and bribes, every *sou* came from the Soviet Union."

Reuben rewarded her with a sardonic smile. "Mrs. Prohme is right. We will decide what happens to Bill Prohme and his project."

Chen felt the need to straighten his waistcoat. "Of course. Once we get to Moscow there will be time—"

Again Reuben cut him off. "A new team has been formed. You are to report to me."

"Excuse me," Rayna said, "our understanding is that Commander Borodin will lead that team and we are to wait for his arrival."

A new unpleasant smile. "One team replaces another."

She tried to look willfully ignorant, a stubborn sound creeping into her voice. This was the man who had wanted to throw Dan overboard. "This new team you are referring to, is it the one that sent you and Comrade Roy to Hankow?"

His eyes drilled into her. A staring match until once again Chen declared his allegiance. "As you wish. I shall convey the new instructions to the Lady."

Then, as if on cue, the trawler fell into a deep pitch that lifted everyone out of their seats. Rayna was thrown against a light sconce and cut her scalp. That provided a welcome end to the meeting.

During the next two days she kept to her cabin, or escaped to the wardroom when the dance acrobatics of Sylvia and Yolanda made her headache unbearable. Sylvia fancied herself a ballerina but her mode of expression was borrowed from the cabaret. They practiced over and over, Yolanda playing the male part, Dan watching from under the bed, but in the tight cabin, the poor girl kept having to climb up the bunks to execute her steps. As the ship pitched, the two would fall together and collapse on the floor in helpless laughter. Mrs. Ma was at least smart enough to report to the galley each morning and smoke with the crew while she prepared Mme. Sun's meals. Rayna doubted the Lady ate more than a few bites because Dan got the rest.

Rayna scribbled short letters to Bill describing the scene, omitting any mention of Dan, calling Reuben 'the fellow from Brooklyn', and Chen 'Uncle.' Anything she sent would go through Soviet mails, as well as Chinese, and then either French or British depending on where Bill was staying. She felt guilty about the separation, guilty she was still angry with him about Dan, reminding herself that he was ill, that she had known that when she agreed to make a life together. She didn't intend to ditch him, leave him alone and stranded. So she wrote that she loved him, which was more or less true. She didn't write that she needed a respite, a time to herself, didn't crow about the important work waiting for her in Moscow.

And then there was the matter of Borodin himself, what would happen between them. In the month since Kuling, the ache had diminished and in its place came a sturdy resolve, a conviction that she would do whatever was required to stay in his company. She would keep her connection with Bill, remain in the role of his wife, as long as she didn't have to live with him. At least not now.

On the last day the weather improved. Approaching Vladivostok, Comrade Reuben called them all back to the wardroom and explained about security, being reunited with their luggage, how they would have an opportunity to wash and rest before they were escorted to a special traveling car hooked onto a troop train. "So you will be well guarded," Reuben joked in his heavy manner. Mme. Sun ignored him, staring out the porthole. Chen, on the other hand, was anxious to know details.

"Ten or twelve days, depending on track conditions," Reuben said. "There will be welcoming parties at each rail stop. You, as Foreign Minister, and Mme. Sun as nominal head of state, will be expected to greet the populace."

He handed out a script, one to each. "Memorize this. If there are questions, I will answer them."

Mme. Sun folded her piece of paper and slipped it unread into her black leather case. Chen read his twice. "It doesn't say anything about the KMT," he protested. "It's all about the Chinese Communist Party."

"We are now in the Soviet Union," Reuben answered with deliberate emphasis. "The CCP is our brother organization. The KMT is no longer a factor."

Mme. Sun did not express an opinion, but remembering what the Lady had written in her last declaration, Rayna doubted that was the case.

CHAPTER 12

When they walked down the gangplank in Vladivostok they were trundled on the back of a small flatbed truck to an army barracks along with their hand luggage. Each passenger was given a towel and sliver of soap. The communal shower was filthy and Mme. Sun refused to enter it, having her maid bring a bucket of water for a sponge bath behind a hastily erected curtain.

Rayna used the facilities to give her dog a good shower, watching Dan shake herself dry with more energy than she had shown to date. Mrs. Ma had fattened her up well during the short sea voyage so Rayna was cautiously optimistic that from here on out all would be well.

An hour later they were called outside. One four-seat carriage replaced the flatbed truck, so Mme. Sun and her staff were transported to the train first, then the Chens, leaving Rayna, Dan and the luggage for last. By the time Rayna got to the concourse, the others had entered the waiting train.

Now Comrade Reuben appeared. "Mrs. Prohme, I am sorry to inform you that Soviet authorities will not allow a Chinese dog onto our territory. Health regulations."

Rayna bent down to clutch the rising fur on Dan's neck. "But she has been with me for three days, she's not ill, she'll die if she's quarantined—"

Reuben answered with a set expression that seemed malicious. "No quarantine." Then he waved at two armed guards standing by the warming shed. "Take it away."

Rayna stood to confront him and, in doing so, lost her grip on Dan as she was pulled away by the men. "You can't do this, I am a guest, part of an official— From the corner of her eye she could see Dan being dragged off the cement concourse and around the corner of the shed.

Comrade Reuben stood with his arms crossed, ignoring her, enjoying this spectacle. "You are a guest of the Soviet Union, yes. It is time you learned how to be a good guest."

Rayna could hear a commotion, four sharp barks, then a single shot.

The train trip was endless but Rayna found it a balm to her grief, watching the dark and silent Taiga roll by. They were housed in an Imperial carriage, heavy gilt and purple drapes, electrified wall sconces that flickered every time the brakes engaged. The women slept in two compartments, Mme. Sun with her maid in the imperial one, the four others together in servants' quarters. At the back end of the car, Chen had a cubbyhole to himself, as did Comrade Reuben. The Chinese guards were housed with the Russians, in the regular troop carriages, which Mme. Sun objected to but was unable to reverse. Nevertheless, she insisted that Mrs. Ma make separate meals and one of her guards stand outside her sleeping quarters at all times. Once or twice a day the train would pull into a hamlet to be greeted by its few inhabitants. Mme. Sun would emerge looking pale and clutching her script, which she read in a low voice with no inflection, much to Comrade Reuben's consternation. Rayna wondered whether this performance was due to her dislike of the man, or to a script that made no mention of her husband's legacy, or if the resistance came from something deeper. For her own part, Rayna avoided Comrade Reuben, refused to look at him at all.

The first evening, in the corridor outside their sleeping rooms, Mme. Sun whispered her condolences, but Rayna felt ashamed at accepting them, realizing how much more dreadful was the fate of Mei-hui. At least Dan had died quickly. And there were those last three days together before the end.

On the eighth day, after a major whistle stop with more than a thousand people turning out, Mme. Sun sent word that she wanted to see Rayna and Chen alone. Once settled in her compartment, Chen pointed out that Comrade Reuben was not present, that if he should find out there would be hell to pay.

Mme. Sun dismissed this objection. "I am sure our conversations are being overheard, so in a sense he is with us anyway." Rayna felt a prickle of alarm. Was she concerned that the Lady would be caught out? That this meeting was sure evidence of a gulf opening up? Or was it a sign that Mme. Sun expected she would be afforded only provisional hospitality from here on out?

As always when under duress, Mme. Sun twisted her handkerchief into a tight knot. "It is time to determine what the nature of our visit will be. Who shall be considered part of our team?" She looked at Rayna. "I am assuming, for the moment, that we three constitute the core." Rayna flushed with pride and avoided looking at Chen. "Others who are traveling separately, Commander Borodin and General Teng, will join us in due course." She spent a few more seconds twisting her lace. "These are the essential parties to our mission. I will speak now of the mission itself."

Chen interrupted. "The mission is quite clear. We are guests of the Soviet Union, here to make clear our opposition to General Chiang and his assault on our legitimate KMT government." He rattled on for several minutes in praise of the expected hospitality of their hosts.

When he wound down, Mme. Sun continued. "A demonstration of our opposition to General Chiang is all well and good. The matter at hand, however, is how to go forward. Commander Borodin will be studying this from the Soviet perspective and I am sure Mrs. Prohme will be assisting him in that." Something about this last announcement, gracious as it was, sounded a second alarm. Mme. Sun glanced at Rayna, then at Chen. "It is the other half of this assessment, the next step in my husband's great undertaking, that requires our attention. General Teng will lead in that effort. Mr. Chen, as Foreign Minister, you shall be part of that team. Mrs. Prohme, I would like you to help me keep the two efforts coordinated, to be the bridge, as it were."

Rayna let out a jagged breath, not aware she had been holding it. "Yes, of course. Whatever you wish." Chen then asked the question Rayna had been afraid to.

"What about the CCP? We've been reading these scripts at every stop about how Soviet support is full bore for the Chinese Communists. This is the beginning of civil war, the Communist Party remnants against Chiang. The question is, where does the KMT fit in? Are there two sides to this battle or three?"

A flicker of irritation from Mme. Sun. "We will hear all thoughts on this subject at a later time. I, for one, shall prepare myself through a deep spiritual inventory, seek the guidance of my late husband." With that, the interview was closed.

By the tenth day Rayna's heart had half healed and she was well enough to perk up at the Soviet welcome of flag-waving school children and ribbon-bedecked Moscow generals. Much like the crowds at the whistle stops but weightier. A man in a dark suit stepped forward and introduced himself to Mme. Sun.

"I am Maxim Litvinoff, and this is my wife, Ivy."

Mrs. Litvinoff spoke with an upper class English accent. "So pleased to meet you." She gave a tight smile and took Mme. Sun's hand, pumped it once, then turned to Chen. "Eugene Chen? These are your daughters? Which one is Sylvia?"

Sylvia bobbed in a curtsy fit for a queen.

"I hear you are a dancer. Sometime you must show me." Another tight smile.

Off to the side, Maxim Litvinoff was conferring with Comrade Reuben. After the school girls presented their flowers and the photographers took their pictures, Litvinoff spoke briefly to the scrum of reporters, then his aide hustled everyone to black cars. Chen, the girls and Reuben were seated in one car and Livinoff, his wife and Mme. Sun in the other. A third older vehicle appeared to take Mme. Sun's personal staff. No one gave any indication where Rayna was to sit. After the engines started, there was a long interval while Mme. Sun conferred with Litvinoff. At last he opened the door and with a motion invited Rayna to join them. She was to sit next to the driver. As they sped off, Litvinoff leaned forward. "I'm afraid there's been a mix-up. No accommodations were arranged for you. The Chens and Comrade Reuben have rooms at the Metropole. An office, typewriter, secretary, that sort of thing."

Ivy Litvinoff took over. "Mme. Sun is staying with us at the Sugar Palace. Not our house, actually, but we are in residence. It's not a palace either, it's just a big old house. Very grand, lots of marble and *bric-a-brac*, reminds me of my family's place in Surrey, unfortunately, but there you have it."

There was a silence while Rayna waited for more.

"I've asked to have you stay with me," Mme. Sun added. "You are part of my party."

Rayna supposed she should be grateful, and she was, and she guessed the mix-up was Reuben's doing. She smiled and had a moment wondering how things were going with Bill in Shanghai. "Thank you."

The Sugar Palace was as grand and awful as Ivy Litvinoff had promised. Light bulbs seemed to be rationed, and the gloom of the baronial rooms magnified Rayna's sense of being inside a mausoleum. Mme. Sun, reunited with her staff, refused the refreshments laid out and retired to her room. Rayna ate a few damp canapes and drank a glass of fruit nectar to make up for the slight. As she sat alone on a dusty sofa in the vast reception room and pretended to marvel at the dirt-encrusted portraits that adorned the silk-covered walls, Ivy Litvinoff returned and told her that her room was ready. A chamber maid took her up three flights of back stairs to a cubbyhole under the roof. She was given a towel and washcloth and directions in halting English about times for food and how to use the lavatory.

She sat down on her single bed. Next to her was the small valise that carried everything she'd brought in the way of clothes. Not a sweater or jacket in the lot. It was the second week in September. Autumn had arrived.

She took the thin blanket off the bed and draped it around her shoulders and looked out the window at the gray sky and almost leafless trees. Maxim Litvinoff — Bee had mentioned him but said no more. She must find out what his assignment was. Was he taking over the task of hospitality from Comrade Reuben? She certainly hoped so, but didn't want to ask. Maybe there was a way to find out from his odd English wife.

Then there was the question of Bill, whether his half-promised job would materialize. Maybe she should ask Litvinoff where jobs stood for them both. She took out the Browder letter. Egged on by Tom Mann, he'd written the usual dutiful phrases. Good organizational skills. Considerable field experience. Eager to study all aspects of theoretical Marxism.

Tom Mann had told her the short course came with a stipend and housing. Her plan, which she only half-admitted to herself, was to take the short course and then see where things stood. She had enough money to last two months if she didn't have to pay for a room. But she'd given more to Bill than she'd planned and her welcome so far had not been effusive. She had no idea whether there would be a paying job even after Bee arrived. She doubted

Comrade Reuben would put her on any payroll before then. That left the option of waiting for Bee or taking the Browder letter and trying to get herself enrolled in the Lenin School, that or falling on the mercy of Mme. Sun and asking her to get money out of Chen.

Rayna shivered under the thin blanket. First step was to get some sleep. Second was to find an English/Russian map so she could navigate her way through the Cyrillic street signs. Third was to get some warm clothes.

The next morning, after a scant breakfast of stale rolls and cold tea, she intercepted Mrs. Litvinoff, got a snooty English look before the cool smile appeared. "Yes? Your room is to your satisfaction?"

Rayna struggled to sort through her several questions. "I have a couple of letters to my husband. Where can I mail them? Where should he send mail back?"

"I'll take them." Her hostess placed them on a brass tray on a massive table that took up half the marbled entry. Rayna wasn't sure she wanted to leave her letters out like that, but decided not to protest.

"Bill said he'd write care of *Tass*. It was the only place we could think of."

Her hostess nodded. "As you like. *Tass* is not far from here. I'll have the door attendant give you directions." There was a pause. "You'll need a pass."

A pass? Was she in elementary school?

Ivy Litvinoff must have seen something in her expression. "It is to make sure our foreign visitors don't get lost. We host any number of special guests here, heads of state, distinguished artists. Normally we assign guides, cars to take them to events. You, of course, are in a different category." She let that thought linger, then brightened. "I shall check with my husband, perhaps we can declare you a journalist, give you more or less free reign. In the meantime—" She pointed to the burly guard who controlled the double front doors. Rayna took the moment to scoop up her letters. "I'm sure you'll find what you need at *Tass*."

So Rayna spent the morning trying to find the newspaper office using a map scrawled by the door attendant. He had written *Tass* in large English and Cyrillic letters so she could show people as she stopped. They would frown and then smile and point her around this corner or that.

At *Tass* she found a man named Rykoff who spoke English and was willing to root around the dead letter file to fish out two letters from Bill. She gave him her two letters, descriptions of the Sugar Palace and optimism about his job prospects. If Bill's next letter didn't say anything positive, she'd pin Chen down. When she thanked Comrade Rykoff and told him about *The People's Tribune*, her coming to Moscow with Mme. Sun, indicating that she'd be available to write an account, he waved her off. "We only deal with official dispatches." She'd never heard of a newspaper that didn't want firsthand information.

To read Bill's letters, she stopped at a coffee stall, ordering tea and getting a fierce frown when she paid with a large denomination note. She scooped up all the coins and paper change the waitress splashed on the table and put them in her purse, then tore open the two envelopes. The tone was bleak. Pleading and accusatory. She had left him high and dry. His tuberculosis was worse. He had no money, no official position. Government bureaucrats and journalists avoided him. He'd moved to a cheaper hotel. Was thinking of using his last funds to book passage to Moscow.

That settled it. She had to confront Chen, remind him that Mme. Sun had promised Bill three months wages. She had passed the Hotel Metropole on one of her twists and turns getting to *Tass*. By retracing her steps, and only stopping two Dutch tourists, she arrived at the granite six-story wedding cake. The red carpet that covered the entry steps was worn but serviceable, the lobby well-lit and clean, the registration desk untended. She rang a bell and waited. Rang again. Eventually a woman in a peacock blue suit came out adjusting her undergarment.

"I am looking for the office of Eugene Chen. He is the Foreign Minister of the Kuomintang." The woman gave her a blank stare. "He's Chinese," Rayna added. "With a moustache, round glasses." She made circles around her eyes to indicate. "He has two daughters."

"*Da!*" The woman waved her hands in a dreamy dancelike motion, then added in English, "Ballerina."

"Yes."

With that, the woman took a small piece of paper and wrote down the room number, then motioned for Rayna to wait while she spoke on the telephone. Rayna was sure it was Comrade Reuben she was consulting. Finally the woman called for a guard who escorted Rayna up to Room 407.

Chen was relaxing on a divan drinking coffee, the remains of a large breakfast in front of him. He put down his copy of *The London Times* and gave her a bright smile. "Yes? How is the Lady doing in her sumptuous quarters?"

Rayna wished their sumptuous quarters were as warm as the Metropole. Instead she blurted out, "Bill is in Shanghai. He's in terrible shape. I want to know when his assignment begins."

Chen blinked. "Assignment?"

"Mme. Sun promised me that Bill would have three months of work to do, drafting reports about what Chiang is doing."

"My dear, Mme. Sun is too kind. We have plenty of Chinese to provide us with such information."

The jab was deliberate. She and Bill were Americans who worked for the Russians. Why did Chen need them now?

She tried a different tack. "About my stipend. Commander Borodin said I was to begin on a collation of his papers, an assessment of the Russian contribution—" She stopped. What had been the Russian contribution? What were the results of all their money and men and training?

Chen recognized her confusion and it made him smile. "My dear, you will just have to wait for the great man to arrive. I have no money to give you." With that Sylvia and Yolanda burst in to demand rubles so they could go shopping at the GUM department store down the street.

CHAPTER 13

It seemed such a simple idea, an excursion she was entitled to. After all, no one had forbidden her to go out, it was just the impression she was given, that it was best to stay and wait. That, and the fact that the gate was locked and guarded. But hadn't Mrs. Litvinoff said she would speak to her husband about getting Rayna journalist's credentials? No one had said she couldn't buy a coat. With exception of an occasional word from Ivy Litvinoff, no one had spoken to her at all. She proposed her idea to Chen when he came by to collect his girls, who had moved from apache dancing to banging on the out-of-tune Sugar Palace piano, but he advised against it, pointing out that she could order a coat, that they were guests of the Soviet Government. Easy for him to say in his warm suite at the Hotel Metropole, he and Reuben thick as thieves doing God-knows-what.

She hadn't seen the sun in days, the garden outside her window was a clotted mass of wet leaves and broken stalks. Inside, the interminable piano medley, "Heart and Soul" interspaced with "Chopsticks." So to hell with Chen and Reuben and Ivy Litvinoff. She marched out hoping no one was watching, smiled at the guard, rubbed her hands up and down her arms, held out her fingers so he could inspect the blue crescents. She needed to buy a coat, she explained. To emphasize her point, she brushed her hands down her bony chest and smiled again.

Finally, after checking that no one was looking, he opened the gate, pointed in the direction of Red Square, drummed on his watch, instructing her to be back by dark. She promised, holding up a hand like she was swearing on a Bible. "Honest Injun."

The cold soon got to her, so she made a bee line for the Metropole, knowing that someone there would speak English. She announced to the blue-clad desk clerk with the tight corset that she needed to buy a coat. The woman looked Rayna over, then went back to collect the manager who spoke somewhat better English. He asked what she wanted. She told him she needed to buy a coat and also a sweater.

"Yes, yes." He started to move away. She leaned over the counter to explain that the coat was for her and the sweater for Mme. Sun. Or maybe the other way around. He cut her off, pointing to the tea buffet. "Americans. Go there."

Twenty men were crowded around a serving table laden with sandwiches and fruit drinks. A meeting was breaking up. She was about to resume her efforts with the manager when a figure caught her eye, a head that looked familiar. Something about the shoulders, the way the hair coiled behind the ears. She circled to examine this compact fellow who was waving a spoon at a colleague.

"Mike Gold!" He turned, his face hardening. "We met a long time ago in New York. At Dorothy's." She stuck out her hand. "Rayna Prohme. You knew me as Simons."

He put down the spoon, excused himself from his friend, and, not looking at her, began to drift away. Taking his cue, she followed him to a place near the elevators and pretended to study the framed instructions posted behind a pair of battered Louis IVX chairs. Finally Mike approached with a half-smile, trying to sort through who she was. When he got close, her name broke through. "Rayna Simons!" He cuffed his head with the heel of his hand, grinned and pulled her into a scratchy hug. "How long has it been?"

She held on to this man she'd met no more than twice in what seemed a lifetime ago. Her voice flooded with joy. "Ten years!" She broke apart to look at his face. "What have you been doing?"

"Being careful," he said. And then, "Come sit where we can talk." He motioned her into the open elevator past the out-of-order sign in both Russian and English, pulling in the two gold chairs. He sat her on one and waved off the hotel attendant who wanted to reposition everything in the order it belonged. "What was it we argued about, that night so long ago?" He was leaning forward on his spindly chair, hands locked between his knees, looking sideways to monitor the lobby.

"Nietzsche!" As she dredged up this bit of history it seemed very funny, memories of that long-ago dinner party, discussing this same thing with Jimmy just weeks before, the coincidence of meeting Mike Gold in Moscow, his three-sided reflection in the mirrored elevator walls.

"That fellow you were with that night, what was his name?"

"Samson Raphaelson, he became my husband. He was the Neitzche fan, I was just mouthing words."

"So what became of him, did he become a big-time fascist?"

"No, a big-time playwright. But he's not my husband now, I have a new husband. Well, not so new." She paused. "Not really my husband, either. We just say that. He's in Shanghai. I've just come from there." That didn't seem very coherent, so she tried again. "Do you know where I can get a coat?"

"One thing at a time." He pulled out a cigarette. "So, what are you doing in this famous city?" His voice became mocking, a little guarded. "Touring?"

"No." She took her time to answer, trying to anticipate his reaction. "I've been in Hankow. I'm here with Mme. Sun, at the Sugar Palace." His face proved impossible to read. She took in a breath and switched topics. "It's freezing there, I don't think the furnace works. I'm trying to find a coat."

He took up her hands, inspected the nails. When he spoke his voice was low. "You were with Borodin?"

"Yes."

He deposited her hands back in her lap, reached into his pocket. "I'm a delegate to the Comintern, here for the current plenum." He pulled out a battered red card case and flipped it open to show the embossed Cyrillic and blurry photo.

Now it was Rayna's turn to be surprised, but she wasn't. His politics at that long ago dinner and now were of a piece.

"And my name isn't Mike Gold, it's Irving Granik." She shrugged, apologizing for the *faux pas.* "But you can call me Mike, that's the way you knew me."

She understood what he meant, that they should keep their connection casual — old friends, an accidental meeting. But she was unwilling to let it rest there, and returned to the problem of the coat. She held his eyes, fixed the same gaze on him that she had used that night in New York, the one that always made men remember her.

He said he'd do what he could.

"Great," she said, then clapped her hands, accepting his offer to introduce her to the delegates around the tea table. It was the kind of group she had entertained often in Hankow. She knew what was expected, how to laugh, pump hands, and she felt for a blessed moment as if nothing had changed.

"I want you to meet Rayna Prohme." Mike grabbed the dark-haired fellow he'd been talking to earlier. "Manny Gomez, also a pal of Dorothy's." Mike flashed a conspiratorial grin. "And guess who else Rayna knows? Our old friend Borodin!"

"No!" Manny slapped his forehead, the signal of some private joke. Their laughter was caustic. It made Rayna wary.

Mike read her look. "We knew him a long time ago, right

after that dinner party. In Mexico, for God's sake." He turned to Manny, still with the funny smile on his face. "What a crazy world. Here in Moscow I meet Rayna, who used to be my old girlfriend's roommate, and I come to find out she's been in China, doing deeds with the great Borodin."

Manny nodded and took up the story. "Who, unbeknownst to her, used to recruit spies and smuggle jewels in Mexico with her old roommate's boyfriend!" He saluted Mike with his glass, they both threw back their heads and laughed. Rayna did her best to join in.

They decided to get her a sweater and a coat. Mike was staying at the Metropole so he went up to his room and brought down his spare cardigan, a brown cable knit with stretched-out arms. The coat was more complicated. Manny took three small bills from her diminishing wad of rubles and went off to the hotel cloak room and emerged a few minutes later with a man's trench coat sporting a matted sheepskin liner. They packed her in both garments so tight she could hardly move, then pleaded urgent business to their group and guided her out to the street. There Manny told her to check the pockets and clapped his hands when she pulled out a bottle of vodka from one and a tin of Norwegian sardines from the other.

They were going to have a party and strode three abreast down the Tverskaya toward Manny's hotel. "You've got to meet Mme. Sun," Rayna announced, warm, happy, wrapped in her layers of wool and canvas. "As soon as Borodin arrives, I'm enrolling in the Lenin School." Mike put a hand on her sleeve. Rayna felt the warning but ignored it. "He's setting up a China unit and told me I need theoretical grounding."

"Don't get too far ahead," Mike said. She felt a moment's anger; it was just the kind of placating remark Bee had made. "This is Moscow," he continued. "The land of Might-Have-Been. And don't go yapping about China." He put a finger to his mouth. "Loose lips, sink ships."

They piled into Manny's room, a top floor garret in a small

hotel near the telegraph exchange. Mike motioned for her to take the only chair. He sat on the bed while Manny perched on the radiator. The sun was setting. She remembered her promise to the guard to be back by dark. In the awkward pause while Manny worked the bottle cap, Rayna tried to start up the conversation. "Tell me about Mexico. How you came to know Bee."

"Well." Manny set aside the opened bottle and began inserting the key into the edge of the sardine tin. "He was young. Mike and I were really young, but Bee, as you call him, had this young buck sense about him even though he was — what? Thirty-five?"

Mike nodded.

"Anyway, to us he was old, but to himself he was young, a man on the cusp of great deeds. And the other thing was, he always spoke in whispers."

"Whispers?"

"Yeah, whispers. Always looking over his shoulder. We were in Mexico, for God's sake, no one knew what we did, no one cared." Manny took a swig and handed the vodka to Mike, then took out his pocket knife. "Except for maybe the rich Mexican who was bankrolling our newspaper, he might have cared we were running a revolution on the side. Borodin arrives on the scene with orders to form a Mexican Communist Party, finds us and decides we are manna from heaven." He dug the knife into the sardine can, speared an oily fish, lifted and dropped it into his mouth. "He didn't even know Spanish." Manny chewed, grinned and produced a sharp belch.

Rayna ignored it. One of her brother's favorite tricks. "He doesn't know Chinese either. Or need to. All the KMT ministers spoke English."

Manny caught a look from Mike. "Yeah, right. Well, back then we were just two guys avoiding the draft, happy not to be in some stateside jail." Mike cleared his throat. Manny sipped his vodka and let go of the point. "M.N. Roy was there too, you know him? That was the big coup, Borodin recruiting him." He stripped an imaginary headline in the air. "Ace Bolshevik Bags Brown Brahmin." Even Mike had to laugh. Then Manny turned modest on Borodin's behalf. "A piece of luck, actually, Borodin's finding Roy. Almost made up for the jewels."

"The jewels." In Hankow Rayna had heard those sly asides between Russians.

"The story was never clear." Manny offered the sardines around but had no takers. "The Comintern had given him a lot of Romanov jewels to hock in New York, to pay for start-up expenses. Anyway, the plan was not well worked out. Borodin was on a ship in the Havana harbor, a customs official boarded, he panicked and gave away the jewels, which were in a false-bottomed suitcase, to some German guy who was cleared to land. Or maybe he didn't and only said he did. Anyway, the jewels never got to the right people in New York. A few years later, suspicion was raised that maybe Borodin had taken them himself." Manny waved off Rayna's protest. "I know, the great man would never do such a thing."

Mike took up the story on a more reflective note. "You have to remember, those were tense times. It was 1922, Lenin was dying. Zinoviev, Borodin's boss, was aligned with Lenin's wife, Krupskaya, in a faction against Trotsky. That same fellow who is now giving Stalin such grief. Your man, then and now, was caught in the middle. But back then—" He made a sideways wiggle of his hand. "Stalin was keeping his powder dry, waiting to see who came out on top. Nowadays, of course, Zinoviev is on the outs, aligned with his old enemy, Trotsky, who is also on the way out."

"Dead man walking," Manny offered up while finishing off the last of the vodka. Mike raised a finger. Manny acknowledged and flicked his eyes heavenward.

"Anyway," Mike resumed, "in 1922, Krupskaya and Stalin were going at each other hammer and tongs. Zinoviev, in a typical move, cut a deal with Stalin. Getting tough with Borodin was just part of the show."

Manny glanced at Mike and then added another layer of analysis. "It was the grieving widow business, her supporting first one side then the other. Truth was, Krupskaya couldn't bear to see anybody succeed her husband. It wasn't personal with Stalin. They patched it up. But it was in that context that the matter of the jewels presented itself. See, Borodin was Zinoviev's subordinate, and Zinoviev had to prove himself. Just bureaucratic jousting, but our man became the goat."

"You mean they actually accused him?"

"Not exactly, but there was a hearing, very formal, testimony taken, they dragged out the whole bolt of cloth." Manny was cleaning his knife on a scrap of paper and got up to set the empty tin in the hall. "For my neighbor lady's cat. So, maybe the fact that he kept looking over his shoulder in Mexico meant something."

"Yeah." Mike motioned for them all to get up. He handed Rayna her coat. "And on that note, it's back to the salt mines."

As she hurried home clutching the lapels of her newly purloined coat, Rayna thought about Mike's voice, the weary tone. Had she heard that years ago or was it new, something to do with the here and now? There was so much she didn't understand. The looks between Mike and Manny, the oblique way they gave out information, what was said and not said. The Comintern, for example. In China, mention of it could cause any number of reactions — laughter, a roll of the eyes, anger or silence. Here, too, it seemed. It depended on the circumstances, circumstances she had yet to decipher.

It was not simple, not simple at all. Borodin had said she was to speak to Comintern's head, his good friend Nikolai Bukharin, explain about the China unit they were going to set up. But how was she to get an appointment? She didn't even have use of a telephone. And what was she to say? Why did she hesitate to speak of this to Mike Gold? And why did she always prickle at the mention of Chairman Stalin, the man who had sent the letter carried by M.N. Roy that had caused such havoc in Hankow?

The next evening she found herself staring at the gilded ceiling of a huge reception hall. Crystal chandeliers, the tinkling sound of drinks being served, *hors d'oeuvres* being consumed by a horde of formally dressed people she didn't know. She stood, holding something made of egg and radish, watching Chen out of the corner of her eye trying to break into conversation with people who looked aside. Mme. Sun stood alone, trying her best to disappear into the woodwork.

After days of being ignored, someone had signed an order. A long car had arrived and she and Mme. Sun were taken to a vast warehouse and outfitted with evening clothes, daytime attire, touring clothes, all selected from crowded racks monitored by women in black suits. Once back at the Sugar Palace with bags of costumes, as if they were members of a provincial theater troupe, they were told to be ready at the gate by six. Now they were here, set down in a sea of strangers at some important function no one had explained. Rayna tried to work up some enthusiasm for the deviled egg, then focused on a figure standing in a pocket of empty space across the room. An old woman with a dewlapped chin and large protruding eyes. It was the eyes, a feature famous from the photo. Krupskaya, Lenin's widow. She was standing, hands clasped together, at the far end of the canape table, dressed in black crepe, ignored.

Rayna had a moment's hesitation, then put down her cracker, slipped over to Mme. Sun and took her arm. "There is someone I want you to meet." Before any second thoughts, Rayna marched her charge over. "Mme. Krupskaya? I'd like you to meet Mme. Sun."

Mme. Sun closed her eyes and went into a deep Chinese bow. Krupskaya looked startled, blinked and then nodded.

"And you are—?" Krupskaya spoke in French-accented English as she took Rayna's hand.

"Rayna Prohme. I've come with Mme Sun. Worked with someone you probably know, Mikhail Borodin."

"Ah yes. Lovely man. My husband thought highly of him."

Rayna wanted to get the conversation back to the present. "Mme. Sun is, of course, a widow, married to the late Dr. Sun."

Krupskaya smiled and turned to Mme. Sun. "You are so very young. Too young to be a widow. Tell me, how are you finding your visit to Moscow?"

Mme. Sun murmured a few words about being honored to be a guest of the Soviet Union.

Krupskaya appeared to be unimpressed. "No seriously, how are they treating you? Are they listening? You have been through trying times and surely you are struggling to find a path forward."

Mme. Sun recited her husband's Three Principles: unity with an end to foreign domination, democratic government, ample livelihood for all people.

"Well, those are certainly worth fighting for."

Rayna could see a functionary who reminded her of Comrade Reuben making his way over to interrupt the conversation.

Krupskaya saw it too and her response was flawless. "We must meet again," she murmured to Rayna while she took Mme. Sun's arm and raised a hand to point out some feature of the crystal chandelier. Then, in earshot of the functionary, she moved Mme. Sun around the room, speaking of this old painting, the history of that beveled mirror. Rayna slipped back, feeling she'd done her job for the first time since she'd arrived in Moscow.

The next day, as punishment, the head housekeeper knocked on her door and announced she was being moved. "Pack, hurry!" The woman jabbed a finger in the direction of the bed. Rayna gathered up her sheets, wondering if she was expected to wash them or bring them along. The woman glanced at the underwear draped on the chair, Rayna's comb and brush on the dresser, the stack of newspapers. Rayna wondered how she was supposed to carry it all. For a long moment the woman's eyes held hers in disgust, then the matron took up the sheets and announced, "Downstairs, ten minutes, breakfast," and marched away, leaving Rayna to wonder if she should eat first and then pack, or the other way around.

She opted to pack first and leave her luggage by her bed before going down to breakfast, explaining to the guard where she would be in case whoever it was came and did not find her standing at attention in the hall by her bag. In the dining room she was surprised to find Chen barking orders at his daughters, who were engaged in a contest of balancing forks on the edges of their water glasses. After a short while, Mme. Sun drifted in, her maid, Mrs. Ma and two bodyguards behind. It seemed that Chen and Mme. Sun were being sent to the Crimea. For a rest, Chen told Rayna, and to inspect collective farms. Chen joked that he'd go to Hades itself if only they would provide him a competent interpreter.

Rayna bit into her poppy seed bun, stared at the black swirl of seeds, a tiny nebula that made her think of mold. Chen seemed cheered by all the forward motion. Mme. Sun treated this new event as part of the same continuing bad dream. "When is Commander Borodin expected?" she asked in a plaintive voice, as she did several times each day.

"Soon." Rayna tried to be encouraging, though she wondered herself how long they could keep up the pretense that they were honored guests of the Soviet Union, without Borodin to give it some weight.

Now, at least, they were going on a trip, a time filler before the next stage when the serious work would begin. At least she tried to tell herself that as she went back to her room to collect her belongings, the gold dress and the other evening gown in one traveling bag and the sturdier clothing that she'd been assigned in the valise. Would it be warm or cold where they were going? No one said.

When she got downstairs, the first car carrying Mme. Sun and her staff had gone. There were two other cars, and Comrade Reuben was now directing things. He didn't look at Rayna or her luggage, instead helping the Chen daughters into one car while Eugene Chen was sitting, along with two Russians, in the other.

She went up to Reuben, spoke to him for the first time since Vladivostok. "Excuse me, no one has told me, where we are going?"

He was directing the stowing of baggage, and motioned the guard to take Rayna's luggage to the car where the Chen girls sat. "They are going to the Crimea."

"They?"

"You are going to the Metropole with the two Chen daughters."

She had been cut from the herd. "Why? I'm supposed to—"

"Mme. Sun is our responsibility. You are assigned to the daughters of the Foreign Minister."

They were leaving her behind. A nanny to the Chen girls. In a black mood, she let herself be taken to the Metropole. At the desk she asked about Irving Granik, remembering to use Mike Gold's Party name.

"He is unavailable," a new desk clerk responded

Rayna asked about Mr. Gomez and got the same answer. Did that mean they were busy? Out of town? Been instructed not to talk to her? She was afraid to ask.

For the next four days she sat in her blue wallpapered hotel room, prowling the once elegant corridors, counting out scrip she had been assigned for meals at the stand-up buffet. She took long walks in her sheep-lined coat, Manny's prize catch obtained in a manner she did not care to think of. She joined lines of tourists at the tomb of Lenin, went to museums, visited churches turned revolutionary showcases.

She walked down the Tverskaya to the building that housed the Lenin School, a brick building set back from a square, and tried to collect her courage to go in. She would ask for the director, explain about Borodin and China, show him the Browder letter. But she couldn't compose a suitable opening. Hello, I'm Rayna Prohme. My husband and I worked for Borodin in China. Now that I'm here, I need a place to live and, of course, a stipend. No, that wouldn't do. She tried again. Excuse me, but what forms do I need to enroll? No, I don't speak Russian, but I've heard there is an English language section.

It was hopeless. She scrutinized the windows, deciding that fourth floor left was the English section, trying to imagine what was going on inside, what it was that she wanted to be part of. What was her plan? Leave her husband? Enroll so as not to have to think anymore? She looked at the gray sky reflected in the windows, the outline of bare trees. Why did she feel so wide open, open to everything, so unmoored?

It was getting dark and starting to rain. The door to the building was locked. Relieved, she turned to go back to her hotel, promising herself she would write Bill tonight without fail. She had a stack of newspapers in her room, and the books Borodin had given her which were still in their watertight packet. Tonight she would open them, begin the task she had set for herself.

As she pushed open the Metropole's brass door and looked across the red carpet that led up a half flight to the main lobby, she was thinking of envelopes, the stamps on her dresser. Dripping water, she stood on one foot wondering how much to tell Bill, in what order. Then something made her tuck her head down. She knew that voice. When she straightened, needles and pins ran down her neck, the shock of the sudden movement making her eyes lose focus. The blurry outline of a familiar head and shoulders was emerging from the hard-currency bar.

"Jimmy!" In rising excitement, she opened the canvas flaps that were dripping on the marble floor "You've followed me to Moscow!"

Stripping off her wet overcoat, leaving it in a sodden pile, she ran. He met her, scooped her up, his whole body trembling as he buried his face in her hair. He squeezed the breath out of her and she felt herself safe, safe for the first time since she'd landed on Soviet soil.

CHAPTER 14

From Sylvia Chen, Rayna found out that Borodin had arrived in Ulan Bator. There was no mention of it in the newspapers, no confirmation from any one in Moscow, but Eugene Chen had remarked on it in a family letter. These days Rayna was reduced to taking the Chen girls to dancing classes and their daily Russian lesson. Just that and the company of Jimmy Sheean, who folded her into his whirlwind of activities without a second thought.

After the good news about Bee's safe arrival came an unexpected blow. Hotel Metropole management informed her that her room had been assigned elsewhere, they were full up and she needed to vacate the next day. In a panic she called Jimmy and met him in his hotel's opulent dining room.

"I don't like eating here," she said, picking up and putting down the heavy silverware. "It's too pretentious." She was nervous and didn't want to be asking him for help.

"I'm pretentious," Jimmy replied, motioning for the waiter to bring them menus.

"I'd rather eat at the canteen."

"I wouldn't." Jimmy pointed to something in Cyrillic half way down. "I ate this yesterday, a French fried hockey puck, but tasty."

"I'll just have water," she told the waiter.

"Nonsense." Jimmy announced that the lady would also have the hockey puck and please bring two bottles of your best Russian beer. "Now what's the latest crisis?" he asked as he flipped open the white starched napkin.

"I'm being evicted." Then the whole story piled out. The tragedy of Dan, how she had been ignored, humiliated, by Chen and their Russian minder, Comrade Reuben. "That's not his name, it's one of those Party names the Russians are so fond of. Bill and I used to call him Fang, I don't know why."

The waiter brought the beer and poured for them both. Rayna, too anxious to protest, took a long gulp. "I'm still thinking of enrolling at the Lenin School. It may be my only way to get a stipend and housing."

"Jail and a work crew will get you a stipend and housing." Then he softened. "But you see how things are. What makes you think this Lenin School would make things any better? What do you know about it anyway? Really know?"

"I know I'd have to join the Party."

"Huh."

"It's only for six months. It would give me something to do while Bee puts together his China unit."

"Have you told Bill?"

She made a face. Just then the waiter arrived with the medallions of meat swimming in cream sauce. The carrots looked palatable so she started on those. "Mme. Sun hasn't responded to my letters. I don't know what that means. If she thinks I can't be trusted or what. Maybe because I'm an American she doesn't care to have me that close."

"Or because you're devoted to Borodin and all things Russian."

She gave him a hard look and he held up his hands in surrender. "Only speculating."

"I don't know where I'm going to find a place to stay. As of tomorrow, I'm out on the street."

"I can fix that. There's always a correspondent off on assignment who can spare a bed for a few days."

She hated to ask but felt a surge of hope. "Would you ask? I'm sure when Bee—"

But he cut her off. "I'm tired of talking about Bee. Let's talk about me. Or better yet, you and me."

She laughed and asked more about who might have a temporary room. He ran through a list, Lloyd from the *Daily Harold*, off in Geneva. Knapf from *United Press*, just leaving for Leningrad. "I'm sure we'll find something."

They walked around the city in the thin afternoon sunshine. He began probing about her family. She didn't want to go into it, but found herself telling him about her father, how much he was like her first husband, Raph. "I married a young man determined to make something of himself. He and my father clashed terribly."

"Not surprised."

"You know how it is. When men don't feel they're measuring up."

"If you say so."

"Anyway, at one point I just snapped. Raph was in New York, trying to make it on Broadway and had a play that just wouldn't jell. He ordered me to take dictation."

"There must have been more to it than that."

She didn't tell him the other part, that she'd already taken up with Bill, who was older, more interested in her for her own sake. "I suppose. Anyway, I struck out on my own. Moved to California. Got into journalism. Went to China."

"And here you are."

"No, that was earlier, in 1923. I was interested in Eastern religions. A subject very modish on the West Coast."

"How'd it go?"

"The whole trip was a bust. My stepmother cabled that she was dying so I had to come home. She wasn't. That's the last time I fell for that trick."

She didn't tell him about Bill, how she'd left California to get away from a man who was clinging and morose. But once in China she discovered just how insignificant a human being could be, was secretly glad of the excuse to come back. In Berkeley, she pretended the trip had been wonderful and

168

blamed her return on her family. But Bill was nowhere to be found, having gone off somewhere to sulk. Friends tracked him down in the Sierras and coaxed him back. Then he began his pursuit in earnest. Said he couldn't live without her, that he would go anywhere to be with her, earn a living for them both in whatever far-off place she would choose. She'd mistaken that declaration for both love and a painless way to get back to China.

"After Bill and I were married—" (A lie, but one that by now was almost official.) "—we returned to China, this time with a mission. To join the revolution. And so we have."

So much left out. Something made her want to say more. "Bill's not well, you know. Chen is supposed to fix him up with work but so far he hasn't. I write but get no letters back. Yesterday I cabled. Maybe I'll get a response today. Did I tell you my letters to Mme. Sun aren't getting through? Sylvia and Yolanda are getting mail from their father, so I think it's just a black cloud hanging over me. "

He'd slipped his arm around her, a comforting feeling given all that beer. "I have an idea, two ideas," he said. "To help Mme. Sun, and get you a place to stay."

The first part of the plan, as he laid it out over another beer at a worker's cafe (she'd insisted on that and just ordered tea) was for him to go back to London and round up paid work to finance a winter in Moscow. While there, he would contact his booking agent to arrange an American tour for Mme. Sun. "That way she can promote her husband's platform free from distortions. The KMT is a nationalist revolution, not the kind your Comintern people are promoting."

"So far their aims have been compatible," Rayna said, knowing this was not true.

"So far," he conceded. "But if she's going to keep her husband's legacy front and center she needs to stay in the public eye. Just like he did for all those years."

She couldn't argue with that.

"There is the problem that the booking agent will ask what she is going to say. American audiences are notoriously allergic to ambiguity. Is she going to come out for Soviet-style confiscation of the means of production, land reform for the peasants, or is she going to take her husband's tack and speak of democracy and an end to foreign domination as a mean to attract Western support?"

That did seem to be the crux of the matter.

"And then there is the question of what's left of the KMT," Jimmy continued. "General Chiang has stolen the mantle of the Three Principles for his counterrevolution. How is she going to get it back?"

Rayna didn't want to think about this. She pushed away the carrots. "What about my housing? Longer term, I mean."

Jimmy pulled out a roll of rubles from his coat pocket. "When I come back, which I will, with a big fat paying assignment, I'll need a place to live. So go rent me something." He peeled of a batch and gave them to her. "Three weeks, I'll be back, promise."

She started to protest but he silenced her.

"A suite would be best, two rooms so I have a place to write. You can use it in the meantime." He held up his hands to ward off further objections. "All on the up and up. Companions in the cause."

"What cause?" She asked this with some suspicion, still confused by the succinct parsing he'd done of Mme. Sun's dilemma.

"Why, Mme. Sun's cause," he replied, finishing his beer and pulling her up to continue their stroll.

He left her at the Metropole about nine. The next afternoon she gathered her bags, leaving the requisitioned clothes in the luggage room where Manny had light-fingered her coat, and made her way on the trolley to the apartment out past the Garden Ring where one of Jimmy's correspondent friends lived with his wife, their infant daughter and Russian maid. The Russian maid was sleeping on the floor. The baby was screaming. The apartment turned out to be one room. Rayna offered to pay for her accommodations, whatever they were, but was turned down. The wife spoke only Russian but smiled in a nervous way. In the morning, as the correspondent was leaving for Leningrad, he said he would be gone three days. "Feel free to stay in my absence," meaning be gone when I come back.

"Thank you," she said. There was nothing else she could do.

The next morning she went to the *Tass* office and found a cable from Bill. Still no work. He was thinking of Manila. She cabled back: *Pursue Manila. Will contact Browder, though no guarantees. Complicated here.* Ten words, the telegraph minimum, outrageously expensive. She couldn't afford that much longer.

She resolved to find a way to Browder, though she was not even sure where he was, in Moscow or China or back in the States. Comintern would know, and she had other business there as well. So, full of false courage, she marched up to the Comintern headquarters and showed the Browder letter to the man at reception. He examined it and rang for an English speaking officer who escorted her into a small cubicle.

He offered her a smoke. She didn't smoke, it gave her headaches, but didn't feel she could point that out.

"My name is Rayna Prohme. Here are my travel papers." She shoved the documents at him, holding back the passport which had the complication of her last name being Raphaelson. "My husband and I were on the staff of *The People's Tribune*, first in Peking, then Canton, last in Hankow." He studied her, then the documents. "I was the editor," she couldn't help but add.

He waited for more.

"I came with Mme. Sun to Moscow. She is now visiting the Crimea with Eugene Chen, the Foreign Minister. I am waiting for Commander Borodin, who I hear has arrived in Ulan Bator."

Still more silence as he sucked on his long Russian cigarette.

"I am here for two reasons," she continued. "First, to find Earl Browder or his deputy, Harrison George, whom my husband knows from the States. We are hopeful that Bill can find employment with the Pan Pacific Trade Union in Shanghai. Any help you can give would be appreciated."

The man didn't look as if the help he gave often led people to speak in terms of appreciation. She moved on to the second point. "You have the letter from Mr. Browder, written while he was in Hankow, that recommends me as a candidate for the Lenin School. I understand that there are slots reserved for Americans, and that the women's slots are under-subscribed. I would like to apply."

He collected the travel documents and the Browder letter and disappeared. After what seemed like a long interval, when the smoke began to dissipate along with her headache, an older man appeared. He extended his hand. "Mrs. Prohme."

She extended her hand, feeling like she was finally getting somewhere. He sat down and placed her papers in neat rows in front of him. "I am Victor Mushkin, an intake officer for the Lenin School. I am afraid there is nothing I can do about locating Comrade Browder, he is en route to China. I suggest your husband try to contact him there."

She would have to cable Bill. Advise him the Manila connection seemed the best bet. Browder was unlikely to offer anything unless pushed.

Comrade Mushkin, tall, white-haired, with a deeply creased face, was lighting another one of those endless Russian cigarettes. "How much do you know about the Lenin School?" he asked as he blew out a long stream of blue smoke.

She took a deep breath, off to the side where the air might be clearer. "I have some idea of the areas of study. My goal is to be trained for propaganda work back in China. Or elsewhere, if you should so choose. But my heart is in China. Mme. Sun and I worked together organizing women's brigades. They were very successful. For a time." She didn't speak of the girls who were killed, Mei-hui's eviscerated body. "I feel very strongly about this."

The man dipped his head in a kind of acknowledgment. Was he taking her seriously or just tolerating these effusions? "There are many steps," he replied. "The vetting is thorough. Several interviews, background checks. Also psychological testing, medical work-ups, to make sure you are fit."

She felt a rush of elation. They were taking her seriously. "I have one question though. If I pass muster, how soon could I enter?" Further explanation was required, but even as she spoke it felt like bad form. "My husband and I need to make plans. And there has been some confusion as to my housing arrangements."

"I see." Comrade Mushkin was standing and gathering the papers, giving her back her travel documents and holding aloft the Browder letter. "May I keep this? We will be in contact."

"At the moment I have no permanent address."

"Ah. Then give us an address where you will check in daily. You will get a message that says to contact a Mr. Herbert, and then you call this number and an appointment will be set up." He handed her a slip of paper with a phone number on it.

She gave him the contact name of Comrade Rykoff at *Tass*, wondering if that were a smart thing to do.

"Oh," he added as he offered a good-bye handshake, "and speak of this to no one."

CHAPTER 15

On September 25, Jimmy departed on the Leningrad Express. It was a near miss at the station, what with his good-bye festivities and the haphazard last minute packing. "Make sure you find those rooms," he'd repeated several times the evening before. "Prohme and Sheean, what a team!"

She was getting tired of the endless hilarity but didn't let on. Instead, she gave him two British pounds she'd squirreled away and asked him to buy her some good wool stockings. He pushed the money back but she pressed it on him. "I'm keeping accounts. If I find you a place and use it before you return, I'll pay you my share."

He took the money and didn't say anything, which she took as a good sign. But then, as they raced for the train, baggage banging against their legs, after he tossed the two suitcases to the conductor, he turned for a last, fervid kiss. She made a decision then and there to press on with the Lenin School so as not to rely any more on Jimmy's complex generosity.

Three days with Knapf's wife and then a stint with the roommate of Rachael Lloyd, the reporter from the *Daily Harold*. The roommate turned out to be Russian, some relative of Tolstoy, and unbelievably messy. In the middle of that short stay, the Chen girls announced that their brother Jack was arriving with Borodin on the noon train, so she rushed to meet them, only to be told by the station officials that the train would be delayed. They went out for lunch and when they got back Borodin had already come and gone, leaving Jack Chen to collect his sisters. The three Chens went off chattering, leaving her without an invitation to join them.

Two days later, Rayna went to see Borodin in his room located one floor above where Chen had his outpost. She knocked and heard a shuffling sound.

"It's Rayna."

He opened the door a crack and she wedged in a plate of kippers prized from a tin and arranged on old crackers. It was the best she could do.

He examined the plate and turned to make his way back into the room. Deep shadows made half moons below his eyes, there was an exhausted set to his shoulders. The condition of the room did nothing to improve her impression. The area by the window was set up as an office, boxes standing open but unemptied, a bathrobe thrown over the unmade bed. But the desk was spotless. Worse than spotless, bare.

"I've been waiting," she said. "We all have." Then regretted it because she feared putting too much pressure on him. She and the rest would have to solve their own problems by the look of it. "Mme. Sun is with Chen in the south. I hear from the girls that they are on their way back." To see you, she wanted to add, to have you solve their problems. She wanted to ask about General Teng, whether the plan for him to join the Gobi escape had come off, but felt that was not wise. "I wanted to meet you at the train, but there was a mix-up. I hear Jack was the only one who came with you."

That seemed to break the paralysis. "The two of us flew first to Irkutsk. A small plane, Jack was the only one light enough." He started to say more but then went back to where he'd been. "He only made it because I lost weight." Then wandered to his desk and started fiddling with improvised paperweights. A cracked cup, a piece of black glassy rock.

"Where are the others?"

He blinked as if he hadn't understood.

"Anna Louise, General Teng. Did he join you near the border?"

"Yes, Teng. Brave man. Too brave, perhaps."

What did that mean? "Mme. Sun is anxious to see him."

"I imagine she is. How is she adjusting? To our weather, among other things?"

She let her face show an appropriate measure of concern. "Not well. Everyone ignores her. Tells her they are busy. With Party congresses, plenums. I can't say as I understand all this."

"I can't say as I do either."

This was going nowhere. She searched for another topic. "The trip. It took a lot out of you."

He sighed but it came out more as a shudder. "I hadn't factored in the sand. The first week we had to drag the cars. After we got into the desert proper, the ground got harder, but by then there was no food. We lost two of our party, Karanova and a driver."

"Lost? You mean dead?"

He started in about hunting, how he'd brought along his Russian carbine to kill grouse. "After days of desert, suddenly we came upon grasslands. Hard as the journey had been, this felt like freedom. Cut off from China, Russia, even my former self. I woke each morning astonished to discover I was alive."

She wanted to remember him like this, free, astonished to be alive, wanted to turn away from the tentative man who was looking out the dirty window.

"The buffalo grass," he continued, "or whatever it was called, grew in ridges, shifting windblown lines anchored in black glassy sand. Above me was sky, a deep robin's egg blue, hard as enamel, glittering all the way to the far edges of the horizon. Clouds, puffs of them, hovering over the jagged peaks in all directions. I knew, any hour, we would encounter a scouting party."

He was describing some deep place of rest, Rayna knew, that was now lost.

"I took a fortifying breath and squinted. A bull elk stood in the tallest line of grass. He examined me, one shoulder twitching, his huge head overbalanced by his great rack of horns, knowing that a lone man, a Russian with an old carbine, was no match. I glanced at the sky, then at the elk, and that moment my happiness was immense." Borodin fixed on Rayna a long painful look. "Then came a horn blast; Percy Chen come to bring me back. The rescue team had been spotted." He took up the glassy rock and studied it. "Without turning my head, I waved him away, fixed my eyes on the elk, raised my gun. I was preparing to advance on this beast, go down on one knee, lift my rifle and slaughter it. Furiously, I waved, ordering Percy to leave."

Borodin moved over to the bureau to pour Rayna some water, then wandered back to the widow. "Perhaps Percy was taken in by this charade, the great white hunter poised a good hundred yards too far from the kill. Anyway, he left. The gears on his truck engaged. Sand whooshed from beneath the tires as he backed down the hill. I was alone. The sky enclosed me, the elk held me in his gaze. I looked at the gun, pointed down at the grass as it rested on my knee, and gave a moment's thanksgiving, to be left with only one obligation: to murder this magnificent creature who stared at me with no fear."

The story had become unsettling. "And did you?"

Borodin flipped the edge of the limp curtain and came back to his empty desk, fingering the black jagged rock that must have come from the grasslands. "In reality I felt no such obligation. No chance, even, to shoot him. But I felt the weight of the moment, the hard choice between action or inaction. Did history, eternity, require that I punctuate this glorious moment with an announcement that Borodin was here? Or was my obligation more complex, my responsibility one of silence? Silence, with its fearful possibility that Borodin was not here, that no one was here, that no one had ever been here to feel this warm earth, this still, enameled sky?" He pressed both sets of fingers down hard on the bare oak desk. "You can see what this trek has taken from me. My senses, apparently."

I love you, she wanted to say, but knew what he was telling her. That he was the magnificent elk that she must let go. So she said nothing and he responded in like manner.

Her plan had been to tell him that Chen had left Bill high and dry. That Mme. Sun was leaving her high and dry, that she was as good as homeless, her only recourse to enroll in the Lenin School so as to get a stipend and a place to live. But these claims against his energy seemed pointless. He was still in the Gobi, caught in the dilemma of action or inaction. She would have to give him time and space to recover.

Two days later Eugene Chen arrived with Mme. Sun. A day after that, General Teng, Anna Louise and the rest of the party from Irkutsk. Rayna had heard nothing further from the Lenin School and was on her third stint of temporary housing. The foreign press corps had taken a grudging collective responsibility, and every third or fourth day she was given a new address and a brisk farewell, sent off with her three overstuffed bags to sleep on someone else's couch or floor. It almost made her wish for the isolation of the Sugar Palace.

Her only news of Mme. Sun came from Chen's daughters. One afternoon she dropped by to hear Jack Chen give his account of the Gobi trip, the cold reception Bee had received in Mongolia. "Ulan Bator was like a third-rate fairy tale," Jack said. "A handful of modern cement buildings and then miles of dusty yurts. Wonderful shaggy goats everywhere. The women were all covered up so it was impossible to tell who was young or old." He paused. "The younger ones smelled different, though."

Yolanda interrupted. "Don't tell us about stinky women, tell us about—"

Rayna hushed her. "Tell us about Bee, what you meant by a cold reception."

"Well, on the second day, we were all herded into this giant yurt for a meeting of the Mongolian People's Party. It was a round cement enclosure topped by the usual felt roof and lined along the walls with tribal rugs to keep it warm."

"Did Bee make a speech? Were there questions?"

"Both. He was escorted on stage by a squad of Russian army officers. Not sure whether he was being protected or whether it was some kind of ceremonial escort. Anyway, he launched into a prepared speech, read it word for word. You know Bee never gave prepared speeches, but this one he read. It was in Russian, so I didn't catch any of it, but afterward someone, a Mongolian in a black suit, asked him a question in English and he answered in English. The gist of it was that Russia had done the best it could, that the Chinese revolution was not a communist one, that it was a revolution for independence and unification. Well, that seemed the wrong answer, because all hell broke loose. Some burly Russian in the back rose and barked out harsh words and Borodin backed away, raised up his hands—" Jack made the motion of surrender. "And apologized in both Russian and English, said he misspoke, that he had just come through the desert and his thinking was affected, and then the guards hauled him away."

Suddenly she was bone weary, realizing how far she had traveled from the comradeship of China. Now they were all dangling alone.

Sylvia switched the conversation, anxious to tell her brother about another uproar. That while Mme. Sun was in the Crimea, a scandal story, complete with a picture of Chen and the Lady squinting in the sun, had appeared in all the foreign newspapers claiming that Mme. Sun and Eugene Chen were engaged. The girls pealed with laughter, but then let Rayna know their father had told them Mme. Sun was furious with Rayna for not stopping the story. The same canard had circulated in Shanghai, of course, but now that it had leapt into the international press, Rayna supposed in Chen's mind she should be held accountable. The fact that *The New York Times* claimed the report had been verified by *Novasti*, the Soviet press agency, would do little to mollify Mme. Sun.

So the next day, Rayna made a point to visit the Sugar Palace and apologize to the Lady for what she had failed to do. After a long wait in the drafty hall, a housekeeper showed her into the gloomy living room with its two massive chairs flanking the unlit fireplace. Mme. Sun was sitting on one throne and General Teng on the other. Teng got up and took a side chair and motioned for Rayna to take the big empty one. She felt dwarfed inside its wooden arms and began a profuse apology.

Mme. Sun waved it away. "Rayna, my dear, I know you are not to blame. This is the way of our friend Chen, shifting responsibility for uncomfortable events. In a manner, it is a blessing. Now there can be no question of my being in his constant presence, adding fuel to the fire."

She glanced at Teng for confirmation of her little joke, looking happier than Rayna had ever seen her. The Crimean sun had done her good, but Rayna suspected it was the long-hoped-for arrival of General Teng. His journey did not seem to have taken any toll. He sat upright, ready to spring into action, the shock of black hair shiny against an unlined brow. Mme. Sun took up Rayna's hand. "General Teng has been filling me in on the China situation. My sister Mai-ling is preparing to marry General Chiang. Dreadful, of course. I wonder at the pressure our mother is under. Of course, Elder Sister is behind this." She took a deep breath and changed course. "But that is neither here nor there. The question I have been discussing with General Teng is where do we go from here. I mean our little band in Moscow. What course my late husband would have chosen: to align ourselves with the Russians or regroup and build support in the West."

Rayna was struck by the realization that Mme. Sun had not yet made that choice.

General Teng spoke in a burst of Chinese. Mme. Sun nodded and then resumed her explanation. "I fear we will soon have to decide. The coalition at home seems shattered. The Chinese Communists have been instructed to have nothing to do with our movement. It is the Comintern, of course, that gives these orders. General Teng plans to address their plenum tonight to explain why this policy is unwise."

Rayna thought of Mike Gold, his advice not to get involved in the China business. "You remember Jimmy Sheean? He's gone off to London to drum up work. He's got a New York agent who he says can put together an American tour for you. I said I'd speak to you about it."

General Teng was sitting at full attention. She wondered if he was following this conversation. Or thinking about microphones. "But that's just Jimmy talking," she backtracked. "I imagine it will come to nothing." At least she'd planted the idea. But she must be more careful about what she said. And then wondered if her upcoming Lenin School interview would require an explanation of the advice she seemed to have given to Mme. Sun.

At the end of the visit they agreed to meet the next day. Krupskaya had sent an invitation for a carriage ride and Mme. Sun was anxious to accept.

CHAPTER 16

Later that afternoon Rayna called the number she was given and was told to report for her second interview. Mushkin was waiting at the same small desk. This time he did not offer to take her coat.

"Mrs. Prohme," he began. "We shall continue to call you Mrs. Prohme since that is the name you are known by, although our information suggests that you have a common-law relationship, is that correct?"

She felt herself color. "Well, yes. But we intend to spend our lives together. He is in Shanghai, as you know, in straitened circumstances. I was hoping—"

"I'm afraid that is out of the question. You are aware, are you not, that admission to the Lenin School requires an extended period when all outside communications cease. Occasionally immediate family members are exempt, but in this case—"

"But he's my husband." She tried to phrase this in a way that sounded resolute. "I have a responsibility to him."

Mushkin shuffled papers as he suppressed a smile. "In that case, perhaps you should withdraw your request."

"I can't! What I mean is, I can't turn back—" And here she faltered. "—on all I have committed myself to."

The pause was deadly. "And what is that, exactly?"

She wasn't sure what to say. She had written an essay, required in the initial application, which detailed her growing clarity about what the Chinese revolution meant, the central place of social reform and her place in it, if only she were properly trained. He had the essay, she had spent hours on it. Let it stand. "I want to stay in Moscow until events in China become clear. In the meantime I will study Marxist theory so I can better understand the instructions we were given."

"You mean the instructions Comrade Borodin was given?"

"Yes."

"And Comrade Borodin shared with you the content of those instructions?"

"Of course not." She hurried to set things straight. "I just assumed my instructions were in line with his instructions." There was a pause while she studied her ragged fingernails. "Please. I want to help. In any way I can. I'll tell Bill that we can't communicate for a few weeks. Or months. As long as we know how long, we can manage. Provided he has some kind of job while he waits." She looked up hopefully to encounter a stone face. "You can understand that, can't you?"

A flicker of something. Then it was gone as he consulted his page of notes. "Mrs. Prohme, let me tell you what is expected. While your candidacy is being assessed."

Her heart rose. Maybe she would make it.

"You are to tell your common-law husband nothing. We have made arrangements for him to receive an offer of work in Manila. Here in Moscow, for the next several weeks, you will continue to do what you are doing."

What is that? She wanted to ask, but didn't.

He continued. "You are to maintain your connection to Mme. Sun. Find out her thinking with respect to China and the role that the Soviet Government is prepared to play in her future."

She did not like the smile that accompanied that last statement. "And Commander Borodin?" She asked this to lead him away from Mme. Sun and her supposed future.

"Do not contact him or discuss this assignment with him or anyone else."

"What if he contacts me?"

"He will not."

"What if Mme. Sun asks me to speak to him?"

He considered. "Tell me first."

"And how am I to contact you? Call *Tass* every day, ask for a message?"

"Yes." The interview seemed to be over, but there was one more thing. "General Teng." He said this as if it were an afterthought.

"Yes?"

"Do you know him?"

Rayna wondered if he knew about the morning meeting. She decided he did. "Not well. I saw him earlier today in the company of Mme. Sun."

"What did they discuss?"

"A lot of it was in Chinese. I believe it had to do with their confusion as to the intentions and wishes of the Soviet Government."

He nodded, "Good. I want a written account. Now you must report next door for a full medical exam. That is all."

She walked out realizing what she was being asked to do. Spy on Mme. Sun.

That evening, as she was sitting at a makeshift desk composed of suitcases piled high in the hallway beside the toilet used by four families, she was rereading Bill's telegram. It contained the heady news that he had been offered a job in Manila and wanted her to join him. She put aside the useless attempt to write a report on her meeting with Mme. Sun and instead pondered this new complexity. She was not supposed to tell Bill what she was doing and so could not respond to his wish, more like a command, that she join him. But she could pretend she hadn't gotten the telegram. Their letters had all gone astray so why not a telegram? She would wait for a second one and then decide.

In the meantime, she had to get out of this current squalid place. She tore up the hopeless draft and flushed it down the toilet, then examined her face in the pockmarked mirror. The smile was now fleeting, her face narrower, more strained. Good, she'd had enough of being called an elf. She went back to the room and got her oversized trench coat, pulled on her new felt boots, and went out for a night stroll even though the temperature was well below freezing.

Her destination was the lobby of the Metropole, where it was warm and there was enough light to take a second crack at the report if she could ever figure out what to say. By a stroke of good fortune she spied Mike Gold making his way across the threadbare carpet.

"Mike! What are you doing here?"

"I live here, remember? Well, not live exactly, it just seems like it. Meetings, what can I say?"

A thought struck her. "Was there a Comintern plenum earlier this evening? One on China?"

He looked at her with a thoughtful expression. "Why do you ask?"

"I met a man today, General Teng. He accompanied Bee across the Gobi and I heard Mme. Sun say he planned to address the plenum."

"He did. A disaster. Brave man, though. When the Boss gets word, he's going to go through the roof. If I were you, I'd stay away from General Teng. And his mistress."

"You mean Mme. Sun? She's not his mistress."

"I meant in the courtly sense. Although I wouldn't be surprised if that is the next bit of inspired gossip. Post-Chen. I gather she's put him out to pasture."

Rayna wasn't sure whether Mike was telling her things she should know or warning her with information he wasn't supposed to tell. Or maybe they were just chattering on. She decided they were just chattering. "What do you think the Boss is going to do?" It made her jittery to call him that. Joseph Stalin sounding like some Chicago hoodlum.

185

He caught some of her unease. "I'd say," he responded softly, so softly that she almost couldn't hear, "that General Teng and his mistress should be very careful. Accidents might befall. It's been known to happen." Then he spoke in a loud and very different voice. "The Chairman is always open to differing views. I'm sure General Teng will get his wish for a full discussion."

Then Mike checked his watch, put a finger to his lips, bent down and kissed her cheek. "Take care of yourself. You look awful."

The next morning she was told, yet again, that she needed to find another place to sleep. As she was packing up, word came that Mme. Sun wished her to join in the outing with Krupskaya. The address given was Sun Yat-sen University, just a mile down from the Kremlin near the Boulevard Ring. First she had to move her things, then spend a few minutes thanking her new hostess. Finally she was able to hail a cab with her last few kopeks to get to the university on time. It was a former high school set on a small square with two dormitories, a classroom building and what looked like a headmaster's residence. In the headmaster's house she was shown to a small alcove. Mme. Sun was sitting at a mother-of-pearl inlaid desk. "Sit down," the Lady said, holding out a welcoming hand. "Do you like my new office?"

Rayna looked around the room and wondered about microphones. If Mme. Sun thought she was free of that she was mistaken. "I do. It will be warmer here, not so many drafts." She was making a joke. The heating plant next door was billowing out voluminous clouds of wet steam.

Mme. Sun smiled as if this were just the right answer. "I thought so as well. Come, our transportation is waiting."

The car was driven by a Chinese cadet rather than the customary Russian. "You see?" Mme. Sun explained as they settled back into the upholstery. "Here I feel more like I am at home." In her fur-collared coat she looked almost comfortable in the gray October light.

"Jimmy Sheean said he'd be back soon," Rayna offered. "He gave me money to rent him two rooms. Do you think I can in good conscience use one before he arrives?"

"I don't see why not."

"I've got reports to write," Rayna explained. "I need someplace with peace and quiet."

"Yes, privacy. A hard thing to find in this vast city." They were pulling up at a riding stable at the edge of a hunting park on the far side of the river. "We are going for a sleigh ride, isn't that splendid?" She waved to Krupskaya who was wrapped in black sable and standing beside a gaily bedecked Russian sleigh. The two great furry horses were pawing at the slush, anxious to be off, while the groom held the reins. He helped the three women climb in.

"Welcome." Krupskaya grasped her guests' outstretched hands with bony fingers that were surprisingly strong. "Let me settle the robe over you both." She spoke in Russian to the driver and with a jerk they set off on the wide forest path. "Not a long journey, we are just going around in a great circle, but it will give you some sense of one of our better winter pastimes."

"Thank you," Mme. Sun murmured and waited.

"I thought it would be useful," Krupskaya continued, "to give you a survey of how we do things here in the Soviet Union. These days. Not how it was done in the old days when our husbands were alive." Still Mme. Sun waited. "I hear your General Teng made quite a splash with Comrade Stalin last night. I understand the argument over strategy and tactics for China went on for over an hour." Krupskaya turned to Rayna. "I don't know if you know, but Chairman Stalin does almost all of his work between midnight and dawn. There is a wicked jape on the streets that he can't sleep because of a guilty conscience but I wouldn't know about that."

They came to a fork in the path and Krupskaya commanded the driver to take the narrower way. "I thought it would be helpful if we had an honest talk. Not a disloyal talk, but a cautionary one. Don't worry. My driver doesn't speak English and is handpicked. I don't believe they have gotten around to bugging the forest yet, but who knows?"

What about the sleigh? Rayna wondered.

Krupskaya seemed to pick up on her thought. "Nevertheless, let us stop here and have a brief walk to inspect our Russian forest treasures." She called out for the sleigh to halt and the driver came around to help each of them down. With only a few inches of snow on the ground it was easy to identify the varieties of moss and creepers that still retained their waxy leaves. "This one is your English mistletoe," Krupskaya said, holding up a loose strand that had dropped from a branch on an otherwise strangled tree. "A parasite. We Soviets don't like parasites, so we frown on this even though in the West it is used to spark love." She dropped the creeper. "It is poisonous and we often use it as an ingredient in one of our famous Russian fatal concoctions."

She moved further into the woods and began prying a heavy pad of moss from the side of a birch tree. "Birch trees need air around them or they begin to rot. They are susceptible to insect infestation and our cold winters serve to kill much that threatens them. They don't transplant well to southern climates, as I am sure many of your lovely Chinese specimens don't transplant well here." She stopped to face Mme. Sun. "We are far enough into the woods for me to tell you that your General Teng is in grave danger. He spoke the truth last night, first to the Comintern and then to Comrade Stalin, about the understanding that my husband had with yours: that the Chinese revolution should be permitted to take its course, that your husband's Three Principles, while not Lenin's blueprint for Soviet Russia, were a sufficient basis for the two men and their countries to find common ground. Unfortunately, Comrade Stalin does not have such a subtle mind. He understands only the iron fist. General Teng should beware of that iron fist. As should you."

After a moment Mme. Sun spoke. "Thank you. You are most generous in your advice. I will reflect on it most seriously. May I ask the extent of my own peril, as you see it?"

Krupskaya considered. "I don't think they will use violence against you. It is too public. Although I would be concerned about poison, the slow kind that can't be traced. I understand you have a delicate constitution. It is well known."

"Yes."

Rayna now understood the need for a Chinese cook.

"However, if they wanted to poison you they would have done so by now. So I suggest you continue to be inscrutable and find a pretext for getting out of the country. Your sister's wedding?"

"No. An event too shameful."

"Europe then. Some kind of conference. Surely you can arrange that."

"Perhaps."

They were nearing the sleigh, Krupskaya still holding onto the tuft of moss. She gave it to the driver and he accepted with a big smile. "His wife likes these small gifts," Krupskaya explained. "And you," she turned to Rayna and spoke in a low voice. "No report of this, you understand?"

CHAPTER 17

After days of searching, she found two rooms, outrageously expensive, a large main room and a microscopic adjoining one. The closet, that's what she called it, would barely fit a bed, but had its own door to the hall and so could be rented as a separate room. She put down all of Jimmy's money on a two-month contract, figuring she would take the closet and pay Jimmy back when she got into the Lenin School. That was the excuse she would use to hold off Bill, that at present she had no money to travel.

At long last she got a bundle of piteous letters, and she assumed Bill got a similar windfall before departing for Manila. She was sure now that they had been held, for whatever reason, and that the wheels of Moscow bureaucracy were now making a small grudging turn. Her trip down the Yangtze a mere three months ago now seemed eons past. Then she had been so sure that the stars in her life would align. How trusting that girl had been. For that's what she thought now of her former self, a 33-year-old girl. Well, no more. She remembered Mme. Sun telling her about Pinyang, the warrior princess, how the emperor had ordered military music at her funeral. While Rayna was being fitted for the gold dress, she had imagined leading such an army, being a woman warrior, capable, courageous and sure.

Instead she found herself in bitter cold Moscow mired

not in one, but three impossible situations. Bill, how to keep him safe and not so lonely that he arrived in Moscow uninvited. Mme. Sun, how to protect her in this treacherous political sinkhole. Bee, how to keep open the door of a possible life with him, official or otherwise. On reflection, she realized that her efforts to enter the Lenin School were a way to braid together all these loyalties. She must stay useful to Bee, wait through his internal exile. Then they could embark together, if not to China, then India or Turkey, some place with a nascent revolutionary movement. She'd heard that his wife had arrived, that Anna Louise was writing an account of Fanya's miraculous escape. Rayna was jealous of her easy access to both Borodins, irritated that Mushkin had ordered her to have no contact with Bee.

The closest she could get was to the Chen girls. If she ran into their father she would use the occasion to crow about Bill's job in Manila, as well as find out what ailment, real or feigned, was keeping Mme. Sun from seeing visitors. As she doled out the last of Jimmy's money to the landlady and clambered down three flights to drag up her overstuffed bags, she wondered about General Teng, whether he was allowed to see the Lady, whether the storm caused by his remarks at the Comintern had abated.

The girls were out, but Jack Chen was typing a report on his father's brand new Remington. As she came in, he pulled out the page and put it face down on a pile.

"How's tricks?" he grinned, an old joke between them.

"Pretty tricky," she replied. That's another thing that had changed. She no longer felt like bantering.

"You look tired."

"Alas, it appears I am no longer young." When he didn't say anything, she asked about Bee, whether he ever came into Chen's office.

"Not much," Jack replied. "Anna Louise appears once

a day to borrow paper. For some reason we have an allotment and the great man doesn't."

"Don't call him that," she said in a sharp voice and when he gave her a puzzled look she added, "It seems so mocking, given the circumstances."

"Yeah," Jack agreed. "Even my old man feels the heat." That interested her. "In what way?"

Now he grew cautious. "Oh, you know, the Which-Side-Are-You-On thing. The cadets at Sun Yat-sen are having a knockdown tumble."

"Tumble?"

"KMT vs. Comintern. There's talk they're going to ship all the KMT students back."

She hadn't known that. Wished, for a moment, she didn't, because going back meant certain death at the hands of General Chiang. There was a report due to Mushkin later that day and she was having trouble keeping track of what she knew and what she cared not to know. The whole enterprise gave her a massive headache. Or maybe it was the wet cold. Or the smell of wood rot that seemed to hover in every rental room in Moscow. All said, she would have preferred to be in China, a woman warrior in a gold dress. "What's the matter with Mme. Sun?" she asked. "Illness or nerves?"

Jack looked surprised. "Didn't you know? She's gone back to the Crimea. Left two days ago."

"With your father?"

"No. Not sure who she went with."

"Oh." Abandoned without a word. Rayna turned to leave and ran into Anna Louise on her way to steal more paper.

"Rayna! I haven't seen you in weeks."

"I hear Fanya Borodin is back. That you are writing an account of her escape."

Anna Louise launched into a detailed account. The bribes, how they smuggled her out disguised as a nun. Rayna was only half listening. "How is Bee doing? Is he back at work?"

192

Anna Louise took umbrage. "Of course. He's very much at work, dictating reports to me."

Rayna absorbed this jab. "I thought you were writing about the Gobi. How many things can you write about at once?" What she meant was, why has Bee chosen you and not me?

Just then, she saw Bee himself at the far end of the hall. She waved and planted herself smack in front of Anna Louise so she would have the excuse to intercept him with a hug. He accepted the embrace with forbearance.

She had a reason for this. "Jack tells me the Lady has left town," she murmured into his soap-scented neck.

He stepped back and nodded with grave eyes, suggesting that this was something he did not wish to hear about.

Anna Louise, however, was anxious to share all her news. "General Teng, that poor soul, is speaking tonight at Sun Yat-sen. Do you want to go?"

Rayna thought about Krupskaya's warning, sure now that was the reason for Mme. Sun's sudden departure. She figured the Lenin School might consider it part of her assignment, to monitor the pronouncements of General Teng. If not, Mushkin would certainly wave her off if she asked him. Borodin got there first.

"I don't think that is wise."

Suddenly irritation broke through. "Why is everyone trying to quarantine me?"

He lifted his hands. "As you wish."

To change the subject she said, "I've rented two rooms for Jimmy. He's due back in ten days." She kept her position in front of Anna Louise and made a show of putting on her coat, opening it wide to shield her next whispered comment. "One room's an office. You could use it."

His face showed cautious interest. "My place is a madhouse," he agreed in a low voice.

"The address, I'll leave it with Jack. Do you want to see it?"

He nodded, thought. "Tomorrow? Ten?"

She turned and smiled at a less-than-pleased Anna Louise and announced that she'd forgotten to leave something with Jack.

Excited and proud, she went back to her new apartment and spent two hours cleaning. The main room had two beds and she thought she could push the smaller one into the closet room and move the two chipped dressers on either side of the door between them. But she didn't have the energy. Her head was pounding as she worked on hands and knees to scrub the filthy floor. The carbolic soap made her eyes sting and she found herself weeping, silently, in a way she persuaded herself was a reaction to the fumes.

At four she presented herself to Comrade Mushkin at his Comintern office. He was again sitting spider-still at his small desk, with her growing file in front of him. He looked up. "I see you've failed to be fully honest."

She decided to bluster it out. "I'm sorry?"

"Sorry?"

"That's just an American way of saying I don't understand."

He sniffed at that. "First, you mislead us as to your marital status, and then you fail to report on a meeting you arranged between Mme. Sun and Krupskaya."

"I didn't arrange it. A letter came through the regular mail. I didn't see the invitation so I didn't know if I was included or not."

"But you went."

"Yes. Mme. Sun invited me at the last minute and I thought that was what you expected me to do."

"I expected you to tell me."

"I believed I was to put such things in my weekly report. Here." She shoved five handwritten pages at him. "I don't have a typewriter. And no space to collect my thoughts. I'm homeless, as you know." In the report she had composed a brief paragraph about the sleigh ride, couching the advice Krupskaya gave as designed to help Mme. Sun understand the importance of seeing things through Soviet eyes. She wondered at the reliability of the coach driver. If he were a spy, her future was bleak.

Mushkin glanced at the report and put it in the folder. She made a mental note not to mention the rooms she'd rented until the next report, so that her meeting with Borodin might escape attention. For a while.

Mushkin was now taking out stapled pages from the middle of his pile. "Your overall health is something we are concerned about." They had prodded and poked her after the last visit and asked a million questions. "The man you had been living with, William Prohme, is an advanced consumptive."

"I know. That's why I am concerned about him."

"We may not let him into the Soviet Union on health grounds."

Her heart sank but she tried not to let it show. "It's contained."

"You could be a carrier."

"I could," she admitted. "But I'm here. Going to receptions with heads of state. Taking sleigh rides with the widow of Lenin. If I am, I'm already a menace." Why was she saying this? Was she trying to get herself kicked out for being sassy?

He raised his eyebrows and made another small note. "It says here you had typhoid as a child. Describe, please."

She took the moment to consider. She had worked mightily to downplay that during the medical interview, "I explained it all, it must be in there." He waited. "I was ten," she said in a sulky voice, "late to catch that disease. My father had a farm not far from Chicago, and he hired men, sometimes, from the city. I'm guessing that's how I got exposed." She realized she'd always held that theory, that her father had hired infected derelicts from Michigan Avenue to harvest his crops, but then realized that was silly. She had come to China to live among people with worse diseases.

Why blame her father? It was the intention, she decided. His was to save money. Hers, to save people.

"Tell me about your symptoms."

Again she glossed over it. The year she spent in bed. The blinding pain behind her eyes. The wraithlike hallucinations that visited her in the darkened room. "I was put to bed, that was the standard treatment. It wasn't rheumatic fever but that was the initial diagnosis and in those days doctors felt bed rest was the universal cure." She stopped there, hoping he was done.

"What symptoms, if any, persisted?"

"I was weak for a while. But I caught up in school and was only a year late attending university."

He consulted his papers. "Where you met your first husband."

"Yes."

"Any trouble concentrating, doing school work?"

"No. I've always been good at that. Getting work done. I'm sure at the Lenin School—"

He cut her off. "That is premature. You are being vetted. There is much in your record—" He motioned to the folder. "To disqualify you."

She shifted in her seat, both ashamed and oddly proud at the prospect of being disqualified. She desperately wanted to talk to Bee, to talk this through with someone she could trust. She needed to know about the people making the decisions for the Lenin School.

CHAPTER 18

Teng stood at the front of an auditorium crowded with Chinese cadets, some in KMT military uniform, some wearing the insignia of the newly formed Chinese Red Army. Scattered among them were teachers of one nationality or another and a crop of unidentified Russians. No press allowed, but Anna Louise had managed to get Rayna credentials that were left at the door. When she arrived, Anna Louise was down front, talking to a Russian, so Rayna squeezed in the standing crowd at the back. The introductions, going on in Russian and Chinese, were nearing an end. General Teng bowed his head to his hosts and then started speaking. There was simultaneous translation in Russian but no one to help her by whispering the essentials.

Teng began in a low voice, using disarmingly gentle gestures. Rayna guessed these were ritual thanks being given out. Then the tone shifted. She knew enough Chinese to determine that he was speaking of events in Hankow and Shanghai, of the split in the KMT that led to his being in Moscow. He bowed in the direction of students wearing the Chinese Communist insignia, and Rayna guessed he was speaking of the long and fruitful relationship between the CCP and the KMT. It was a recitation Rayna had heard many times. It was, in fact, the daily content of *The People's Tribune*, a declaration that she could see, from a distance, was more wish than reality.

All of a sudden her thoughts returned to Dan, how her beloved dog used to sit at her feet while she pounded out one story after another about the inseparable bond between the KMT and the CCP. She had failed Dan, persuading herself that she could keep them both safe. Now Bill was heading to Manila. He would never have been able to transport Dan there. He had never liked Dan in the first place. A flush of shame came over her, that she could so easily have forgotten in these past hectic weeks a creature she had once vowed to love and protect.

The tone of speech had shifted. Now there was a harsh, deliberate note. The audience was stirring, some twisting back in a way that bespoke anger, others leaning forward to catch every word. The men in suits, the Russians, were stone-faced. She could guess what General Teng was saying, repeating the assertions that had gotten him in such hot water with the Comintern and Chairman Stalin. That the KMT was the wellspring of the Chinese revolution, its goals embodied in Dr. Sun's Three Principles. And while the continuing support of the Chinese Communist Party and the Russian Government was much appreciated, the KMT's mission now was to lead the effort to reverse General Chiang's unlawful coup.

Unstated, of course, was the implication that what remained of Mme. Sun's wing of the KMT would not remold itself according to the dictates of Moscow or fold itself into the Chinese Communist Party. Now a cadet from the CCP stood and shouted something. Teng started to respond but other students, the ones who wore KMT insignia and were hanging on every word, rose and shouted down the heckler. Teachers tried to bring order, but by then half the audience was on its feet. General Teng seemed unsurprised by this tumult. But the Russians did not like it one bit. Three of them took to the stage and pulled General Teng aside. Suddenly the aisles were filled with rough looking Russians in uniforms. The shouting cadets took note and fell silent. One of the Russians on stage commandeered the microphone. The tone was unmistakable. He was in charge.

Teng was brought back to the podium to face a series of harsh questions. He seemed impervious. Ranya imagined that he had been subjected to worse at the Comintern plenum and in his late night session with Chairman Stalin. But this was different. He was speaking not to the Russians but to the Chinese cadets, presenting a version of China's recent history that was supposed to be discredited and sealed. His view was not the current Soviet view. Teng held to what Borodin was also trying to live down, what Krupskaya had alluded to on the sleigh ride. The old terms of the partnership that began in 1923 when Lenin first sent Borodin to help Dr. Sun. Help given with the hope that Russia's support would move Dr. Sun farther to the left. The Chinese Communist Party had flourished under that agreement without either side fully agreeing on underlying principles. Now things had changed. Now there was only one correct line for China and it originated in Moscow. That was what Rayna took from the way General Teng moved his hand in a chopping motion to delineate the Chinese and Russian positions.

Teng was being escorted from the stage. The way he held his wrists looked as if he were mocking his handlers, as if he were already in shackles. One last bit of theater for the crowd. Some were leaving, but only a few. Most were standing in groups whispering among themselves while the Russians manning the aisles moved in to break up their huddles. Anna Louse was coming toward her.

"Well!" Anna Louise said in a triumphant voice. "What did you make of that?"

"Not much." For once Rayna was glad she spoke neither Russian nor Chinese." What was the ruckus about?"

"Teng being stubborn. It will get him in hot water."

"What do you think will happen?"

"Don't know," Anna Louise's voice took on a studied unconcern. "A good talking to, I should think. How long it will go on…" She shrugged, suggesting neither a pleasant nor short interlude.

If only it were that, a slap on the wrist. Mme. Sun must have agreed to the speech. It must be part of some bigger plan. But Rayna didn't know that, and that was just as well. Because she had to report all this to Mushkin, and ignorance, she was discovering, was a precious commodity.

The next day at the appointed hour she was sitting on the bed in Jimmy's room waiting for Borodin. Dan kept coming to mind, in spite of her effort not to reproach herself for failed intentions. She wondered about Bee's intentions. She was not so ignorant as to think he would leave his wife. Still, she thought that in some way her faith in him was essential. She was his link to China, she saw him as he wanted to see himself and that mattered.

The thought made her shiver, and she realized that there was no heat in this overpriced room. She noticed once more the cracked ceiling, the flaking paint, the black accumulation along the baseboards. She would have to go over it all again with carbolic soap. She checked her watch. Where was Bee?

The many things that could have kept him assailed her: illness, incarceration, an irate wife. She refused to think that he didn't love her enough to risk coming. Footsteps on the stair, light ones that skipped a beat. A knock, and when she opened the door, a small boy, nose running, which he swiped with the same hand he used to shove a piece of paper at her. *Gospodin*, he said, meaning an old fashioned fellow. Not a comrade. The note was from Bee, in a scrawled hand, saying he'd been detained, that she should meet him at three, at the Novodevichy Cemetery, at the big iron gate beside the convent.

It wasn't a complete brush-off, she was thankful for that. She gave up on the carbolic soap and spent the next four hours writing letters, long delayed ones to her father, sister, Helen, whose husband Dan had been the source of her dog-naming impulse. Jimmy Sheean had dropped Rayna's note to Helen in the mail when he went through Berlin and it had rekindled a correspondence. Helen and Dan had an understanding. When their house burned down in the Berkeley fire just before Rayna had left for China the first time, they'd rebuilt it as two small houses side-by-side. That seemed like a perfect way to live together. Now Helen had taken up residence in Switzerland seemingly without any impact on her marriage. Rayna longed to pour out to Helen all her frustrations about Bill, the weakness that led her to take up with him, how his dauntless self-confidence had so completely collapsed.

Of course she'd long since learned that it was a false front. Even before she'd allowed herself to take on Bill's last name, she knew how desperate he was for recognition. At one low moment she'd written to Raph, hinting that all was not well. But he'd written back, in a tone tinged with triumph, that he'd recently remarried. Soon after, she and Bill went to China. And Bill got sicker, more unsure of himself. Determined to fashion some kind of victory out of her string of rash decisions, she'd pushed them both deep into the world of Mikhail Borodin.

And against all odds, it had worked. Bill had gained enough status to keep him afloat, and she'd became editor of *The People's Tribune*, she without any journalism credentials to speak of. She was, as well, personal aide to Borodin. And lover, but that came later. In Hankow she had become what she had always wanted. To be filled with purpose. One of a kind.

Now she was in Moscow, at the gate of the Novodevichy Cemetery, trying to hold on, trying to find the magic thread that would keep it all cinched together. She looked at her watch. Fifteen past. The sun was setting and the slush beginning to freeze. Then she saw him, hatless, coat open to the wind. He carried an umbrella and a newspaper, English, pink paper, *The Financial Times*. No wonder the boy had called him *Gospodin*.

With a flick of the head he indicated not to recognize him. He walked left on the path, while she stood with her back to him surveying the gold domes of the monastery, then turned the other way and cut back behind the ponderous gravestones. He was waiting for her in front of the Orthodox tombs. "I come here often," he said. "The quiet of the dead."

She didn't like the sound of that.

He continued. "I agreed to see you in a moment of weakness. You looked lovely there with Anna Louise in the hall. I forgot myself."

He was like a kid trying to play school principal. She didn't believe his gruffness for a minute.

"It has come to my attention that, against my advice, you have gone ahead and applied for admission to the Lenin School."

She nodded. "I have."

"It is a bad idea. Things are too unsettled. If you think that somehow it is a way we can continue..." He left that thought unfinished. Rayna was not sure what kind of continuance he meant.

She took it the way she wanted to, what she believed he wanted as well. "I'll wait. For as long as it takes. I don't mean your wife. I have no claims on that. I mean what we had in China. All of it. The malaria, the broken arm." She smiled at what she didn't say, Kuling. It was the first happy moment in weeks.

The frozen look on his face thawed a little. "I reproach myself for letting you come to Moscow. It was selfish."

She took that as an opening. "I know something you don't know. That you're American as much as Russian, and that American part is what 'selfishly', as you put it, wants me near you. Besides, you didn't make me come. What a loss if I had not come to belong to that great movement you conjured into being."

Now an almost joyful sound leaked out from a face that

struggled not to smile. "Yes, conjured, that is a good word for it. I was a magician pulling rabbits from a hat."

"With a long red scarf up your sleeve."

The frozen look returned. "That, too." Then, "Tell me, how is Mme. Sun?"

"I haven't heard. I don't know if I am part of her circle any longer or not. She pulls me to her and then the next day disappears without a word."

"Like me, she is enchanted with you, afraid for your safety."

"No one should fear for my safety. Without you, without her, I am a trifle, a distraction at best."

He put both hands on her shoulders. "You must not speak that way. Look at you, no more than skin and bones."

"I thought you said I was enchanting."

"That too. But you are under too much pressure." A pause while he considered something. "What do they say to you at the Lenin School?"

"That they have not accepted me. I am suspect on a number of levels. Still, Mr. Browder recommended me, so they can't reject me out of hand. I think they are trying to make a test of my loyalty, then reject me on spurious grounds."

"Being associated with me and Mme. Sun are not spurious grounds. Still, that would not be such a bad outcome."

"Then what would I do? Go home? I'll never go home. And don't tell me to go back to Bill. That, too, I fear, is *kaput*." She had another thought, one that made her laugh. "There's always Jimmy Sheean. He wants to take me away."

She could see Bee was uncomfortable with that prospect. With care he assented to this idea. "You could do worse."

"Be the companion of a world-class reporter? Or

someone who thinks he is? I've done that, thank you, been someone's muse. I'll be yours but no one else's."

They both were silent. Shadows were creeping up the tombstones. The convent bell rang to signal the gates would soon close. "I love you," she said.

His lips moved. "And I you." The words inaudible but that's what she wanted him to have said. Then, "You must go." This in a louder voice as he reached out to set her in motion, letting his hand touch her cheek for the barest moment. "As must I. Each to our destiny."

And with that he slipped behind the mausoleum with its ancient Cyrillic markings and left her with a sliver of dread working its way inside.

Part III
Time to Choose

CHAPTER 19

She could see Jimmy leaning out the window as the train pulled into the October Station, a great pink pile that used to be called the Byelorussian Station, but had been renamed in honor of the revolution. But then they changed the calendar so now Revolution Day was on November 7th, the day Jimmy was returning, a full month after he had promised.

She fingered his several letters stashed in her pocket, ones that recounted his mighty efforts at money grubbing and the whirl of social activities with old chums in London and Paris and Berlin. She had written him twice, once to tell him about the rooms, the second to announce she'd be paying half as soon as her stipend came through. She didn't mention the Lenin School, hoping he had forgotten about that. If he asked, she'd be vague, say nothing was set. Which was true. After the last interview they'd turned her over to a sallow female psychiatrist who mainly seemed interested in her childhood. Then came the usual battery of doctors who thumped her chest and pounded her back and questioned her at length about her illnesses.

The train was screeching to a halt, the brakes gushing out great billows of steam. Jimmy, red-eyed and rumpled, appeared on the platform between the cars. It was snowing, just starting. He stepped down, still not catching sight of her. People pushed past him as his eyes scanned the concourse. Then he shouted, his voice sounding hoarse and cross. She waved, let him come to her, gave him the bouquet of deep red roses she'd bought the night before and tried to freshen up by brushing through the snow.

He hugged her until the roses were smashed to a pulp, said he was glad to be here. She let him hang on for a few seconds, then pulled back and took his arm to hurry him to claim his luggage. At seven in the morning the sky was dark and the streets deserted except for small armies of *babushkas* manning their short-handled brooms. Moscow was getting its final lick and dab for Revolution Day, the parade in Red Square. She talked all the way to the apartment, pointing out scaffolding on the new radio building, restoration work on the Manezh, how traffic routing had blocked the Krymskiy Bridge. He wasn't paying attention, seemed restless and distracted. She guessed she was talking too much. When she led him up three flights of stairs, all she could see was the grime on the walls, the broken light fixtures.

The rooms were fine, he said, he'd put up with worse, though not in a Russian winter. The *matrushka*, who managed the house and had insisted on showing them up, was another matter. "A temple dog," he observed after he'd tipped her to leave. "Short, fierce and carved of stone." Then he insisted Rayna show him the second room, the tiny one that both connected and had a separate entrance to the hall. He objected to her allocation of quarters, saying the large room should be hers, that he would take the tiny cell with the cot.

No, she said, she was only staying a week, or maybe two, just until things worked out, then apologized for the barricade of bureaus on either side of the connecting door. "The matrushka is concerned about propriety."

"More like property," he countered. "The capitalist kind. To prove to the inspectors that the rooms have been rented separately. I imagine she gets some kind of subsidy for each."

Rayna was irritated at the negative tone. "Why are you being so ungenerous?" Somewhere along the way the roses had disappeared.

He put his suitcase on the bed, opened it, let his eyes settle on the barricaded door. "Because I see things as they are."

Her hand crept to her throat. She coughed. She had developed a persistent cough.

He pulled out his shaving kit, walked six steps, put it down on the bureau. The jerky movements reminded her of Bill.

"Jimmy, what's happened?"

"Nothing," he said. "A late night."

"It's more than that." He was pulling out his pinstripe pajamas, a blue silk robe, looking around for a place to hang them. "It's as if you're seeing through things."

He didn't deny the claim. "It's my job to see things as they are, look through the surface ugliness to the real underlying ugliness." Then he added, "I don't think we should talk about it."

She could see him wondering how on earth this was ever going to work.

"It's just a shock, coming back." He took out his spare pair of oxfords, slid them under the bed, then his calfskin slippers. He held them, one in each hand, looking at her as if he wanted to sweep away the suitcase, to take her down on the bed and ravish her. She looked at the barricaded door, saw him following her look.

"I think we should talk about it," she said.

"All right." He unpacked his winter suit from a garment bag that proclaimed it was made on Saville Row, hung it on its polished wooden hanger beneath the bathrobe on the room's one hook. "As promised, I have a signed offer of a lecture tour for Mme. Sun. Eight weeks in the United States. But I'll only give it to her on the condition you come too."

She drew in her breath. "That's very selfish."

"I am that, selfish." He seemed pleased at the sound of

that, took his six shirts folded over cardboard, walked over and shoved them into a drawer. "We capitalists are."

"Jimmy." She was breathing hard, trying to make sense of the changes that had come over him. "Why are you trying to hurt me?"

"I'm not," he protested, waving his three regimental striped neckties. "I'm trying to make you see that this is nothing but a grim fantasy. All of it, the gray morning, the disheveled streets, the claustrophobic sense of a revolution gone bad. Do you know what they are going to do to Trotsky?" He ran a finger across his throat. "*Kaput*. The revolution is spent, just like China." He was watching her, how her fingers began to pluck lint from her skirt. "It's just—" His voice went soft as he moved closer. "I've seen it all before. When they don't know what to do, they turn and eat each other."

She tried to laugh but came up coughing instead. But she let it go on awhile, because it derailed his diatribe, brought out his tender feelings. She surprised herself by grabbing his arm and holding it with unexpected feeling. "Jimmy, please don't do this. I need you to believe." Then she coughed some more and let him take hold of her while she shuddered through it.

He spread his fingers across her back and pressed her to him until she felt herself relax. He said he was sorry, that she didn't look well. "Lie down for a while in my big, big bed," he said, making a joke of it. "Go on, I'll finish unpacking and you have a nap before the parade."

She protested she should be in the other room, but he refused to let her move, arranging blankets around her and instructing her to sleep for a blessed hour.

She woke with a start, having had the usual dream of wild dogs chasing her. Her body jerked as he sat down beside her, stroking her forehead like he owned it. That made her sit up and insist on getting ready for the parade.

They decided to walk the two miles, and on the way the arguments started up again.

She was wearing her one decent winter dress and a wool hat she'd bought with the last of her money. She'd been hoping for what from Jimmy's arrival? A return to the alignment of world view? When he told her he was wintering in Moscow, she thought he was committed to the cause, the belief that Mikhail Borodin could find a way for Mme. Sun to begin anew.

Of course much had happened since then. Her interviews at the Lenin School for one. Mme. Sun's decision to keep her own counsel. Rayna hadn't had a moment with the Lady since she'd returned from the Crimea. And the last conversation with Bee had been disheartening. But she didn't say any of that to Jimmy. Instead she switched on her best smile and concentrated on telling funny stories about their shrewish landlady. "I can't tell you all the shouting matches we've had. I don't know enough Russian to make hide nor hair of what she says. I think she's accusing me of running a bawdy house. I brought a couple of Russians friends over and she insisted it was only for 'the American', and I can assure you she didn't mean me. Let her kick me out if she doesn't think having the door blocked on both sides is enough propriety."

"I could marry you," Jimmy offered with a half-serious expression.

Her reaction was to laugh. "Bigamy's not legal even here." She didn't tell him bigamy wasn't the problem, didn't go into the matter of her exact marital status. Instead she began to explain her belief that the dark clouds would soon wash away and Bee would be able to get back to promoting the fortunes of Mme. Sun.

"Not going to happen," Jimmy said, "I've been talking to colleagues in Berlin. Getting a line on our friend, Comrade Stalin. Do you know this whole cock-up in China

211

was his doing? Wanted to make sure Trotsky didn't prove to be right — that supporting the Chinese merchant class was a losing strategy, that some new warlord like General Chiang was bound to emerge, seize power and turn on the Chinese Communists."

She remembered what she had witnessed at Sun Yat-sen University, the various factions shouting at each other. "I don't know about that," she conceded, trying not to acknowledge the truth of what he was saying. "All I can do is try to help."

"Help who? Borodin? I don't know as he wants your help. Has he asked for it?"

She wasn't going to tell Jimmy about Bee's suggestion that she go home to Chicago or back to Bill in Manila or off to Europe with none other than Jimmy Sheean.

Jimmy took her silence as a no. "Mme. Sun? Look, I'd love to help with Mme. Sun, but understand that she's the head of the bourgeois faction Stalin first supported and now has no use for. He's casting a wide net for scapegoats. The sooner she realizes that the better."

Rayna squeezed her eyes shut. Already her head was pounding and it had only been four hours since she'd met him at the train. How was she going to endure being his roommate for weeks even if she was separated by a door and two dressers?

She suggested they sing, tried a few bars of "The Yanks are Coming," but he would have none of it.

"What does Borodin hope to accomplish?" he persisted. "How can Mme. Sun's staying on possibly further her cause?"

She could tell by the way he put it that Jimmy thought his American lecture tour was a God send. She couldn't explain that Mme. Sun was no longer consulting her, that Eugene Chen had turned on them both, that General Teng had arrived out of the mist and Mme. Sun now seemed to be taking her direction from him.

212

Nevertheless, he seemed to be reading her thoughts. "This General Teng, tell me about him. There was a picture of him with Mme. Sun, very cozy. Taken in Tiblisi, I think."

Rayna was amazed. "What paper? Did it say when the picture was taken?"

Now Jimmy got vague. "Berlin, I think. Someone showed it to me over cocktails. Knew I was interested in China."

She told him about Teng's reception at Sun Yat-sen University, not bothering about the disastrous meeting with Stalin. "He's disappeared. No one knows where. If he's in Tiblisi with Mme. Sun—"

"Not any more, I'll bet."

She asked what he meant.

"He's either dead or escaped. Mark my words. Stalin has no use for opposition, least of all Chinese."

A prickle of alarm. She considered the implication of that.

But by the time they got to Red Square, she felt better. Maybe things would be all right after all. She had standing-only tickets across from the reviewing stands, so they were locked eight deep in rows of excited Soviet citizenry. She'd insisted they get there early, but four hours later, when the sun was casting long shadows, her energy began to leak out at an alarming rate. Still, along with her neighbors, she applauded each new battalion and tank.

She was chilled to the bone but would not admit it. Jimmy, however, was sighing out great plumes of impatience, petulant that she had dragged him here an hour early.

"We wouldn't have gotten a good place if I hadn't."

"At least you're warm." He pointed at the gray woolen leggings he'd brought from London.

"I offered you the money for them. You promised to mail them and then forgot."

"But they arrived. Wrapped in silver paper. The guards at the border were most suspicious."

"You should have bought some for yourself."

"In the ladies' underwear department?"

"You know what I mean."

Then he complained that military parades were boring, that you could only take in so many tanks and bands and regiments.

"Shhh!" She was irritated she'd brought him. If she craned her neck she could see Mme. Sun on the dignitaries' stand, not warmly dressed, she was sure, and Eugene Chen in a big Russian hat smiling and shaking hands with whatever dignitaries he could corner.

"Let's get a drink," Jimmy suggested.

"Shhh!" And then, "Can't you let the occasion, the whole solemn meaning of it, register?"

"I don't register solemn occasions. And nobody I see is solemn — look over there." He pointed to a screeching band of school kids waving little flags, red kerchiefs prominent around their bundled necks.

"You know what I mean." She was torn between anger at how he was countering her argument and a desire to be transported by this mighty show of Soviet accomplishment.

"I don't, actually." Jimmy wanted to leave and get his drink. The cadets from Sun Yat-sen University were marching past. Rayna was looking through the accompanying row of tanks to see if General Teng was, perhaps, on the dignitary stand with Mme. Sun. Then came a flutter, a momentary halt to the parade, a murmur in the crowd. To the far right she saw a dozen policemen making their way from the viewing stand, pulling off cadets from the front row, a banner snatched up from where it had fallen.

Now Jimmy had his excuse to find out what the commotion was. She doubted he'd come back. It was nearly four. She hadn't eaten since dawn and there would be another good hour of marching. Fatigue roared back and she admitted to herself that this parade had not turned out to be the momentous event she had hoped.

She decided to find Bee. She'd caught a glimpse of him

with Fanya in her brown fur coat on the second-tier dignitary stand. She made her way through the marchers at a designated crossing point and went up to where she'd last seen him.

People were beginning to trickle down from the risers, to go to the toilets or buy a fortifying drink from the vendors. She attached herself to a returning cluster and managed to slip past the guard who had given up checking every last credential. Borodin and Fanya were on the top row, at the mercy of the wind, and Fanya had cheeks the color of beets.

"Mme. Borodin," Rayna began, "how nice to see you."

Fanya ignored her and began talking to someone on her left. Rayna turned to Bee. "Jimmy Sheean's back. He's gone off to find out what the commotion was."

No reply. Borodin scanned the horizon. She tried again. "He says General Teng has gone to Tiblisi. Do you know anything about that?"

Now he reacted. A steel grip on her arm as he steered her away from the crowd. With his back to the people moving up and down the risers, he positioned her so that his words were not overheard. "That is not a helpful line of inquiry. Tell Mr. Sheean that."

She wasn't going to let that stand. "Mr. Sheean also says you are inviting press to your rooms for a post-parade reception. He wants to know if he can come. And bring a guest." She blinked.

He nodded, too agitated it seemed by being in an extended conversation with her to protest. She smiled and followed him as he returned to his seat, stuck out her hand in a failed attempt to engage Mme. Bee's gloved one, then made her way down the rickety reviewing stand. Mme. Sun would be at the reception, she was sure of that.

She skipped out on the last hour and arrived back at the rooms to find Jimmy reeking of vodka and in an expansive mood. "You know what I found out?" he crowed.

She didn't want to hear about it. She wanted to lie down

so as to be rested for the reception. "Later," she said, heading into the hall so as not to have to move the two dressers.

He stopped her with a hand on her arm. "You have to hear this."

She gave up. Jimmy was in full-speed mode. She sat on his unmade bed, resting her cheek against the wall and closed her eyes.

"It was Chinese cadets. Apparently part of a Trotsky faction. Ones who feel as Trotsky does, that Stalin is trying to pretend he has always opposed any truck with General Chiang." He paused and searched for a glass to pour himself a short refresher. "Want some?" She shook her head. He continued. "Apparently they unfurled a handmade banner, probably some saying of Trotsky's. Anyway it was taken, as intended, as a direct shot at Comrade Stalin's moves to sideline his archenemy."

She must have drifted off because the next thing she knew he was bending over her and shouting. "Don't you understand? You've got to get out of here. Anyone connected with the old China policy is doomed."

She blinked and tried to remember what she had been dreaming. It had been a lovely dream, something about clouds. She was on her back in a warm field and the sky was blue and she felt herself sinking into the earth. Now here was Jimmy with his vodka breath yelling at her. "We've got to go," she said, sitting up. "We're late."

So they dressed and went out again into the dark and cold. She was glad she'd fallen asleep and missed half of Jimmy's oration, because she was sick of hearing him tell her she was doomed unless she went off with him to Europe.

CHAPTER 20

There were guards checking invitations at the entrance to the Metropole, and Rayna found out she and Jimmy were not on any list. She was embarrassed because having access to Borodin was about the only credential she had, but then remembered Fanya's glowering expression and decided that the wife had been the source of the snub. Just then Anna Louse bustled past, and Jimmy waylaid her with his artful smile. Always ready to help an attractive male journalist, Anna Louise spoke to someone who sorted it out. So Jimmy got his credential, which allowed a ticket for one companion and Rayna was finally allowed into the place where she had lived just a short time before.

The lobby was full, hotel staff directing guests to receptions on various floors. They had a pass for the China office, so they went there first, thinking that the most likely place to intercept Mme. Sun. No one was there except Jack Chen and a table full of soft crackers and warm Georgian wine.

"Nobody came," Jack said with studied resignation. "I guess the Chinese delegation is not the place to visit."

Jimmy wanted to know if Jack knew anything about the cadets and their banner.

"Nope," Jack insisted, but Rayna thought he probably did. She asked if Mme. Sun were around. "Up at Borodin's," he said, pointing to the floor above. "My dad escorted her there in a brave show of face."

Jimmy insisted on staying to sample the wine, but after a few minutes they made their way down the hall to the elevators. The Borodin reception was also thin, maybe twenty people in all. Jimmy did a quick survey and whispered, "No one important that I can see." Fanya was bustling about, urging food on everyone, exclaiming how wonderful the parade was. "The best ever," she said, glaring at Jimmy when he declined the smoked eel. A waitress came and took Rayna's coat to the other room. Rayna surveyed the guests, mostly foreign journalists clumped around the oddly-placed furniture, and tried to put a finger on why everything seemed so strained.

Borodin was by his desk pouring drinks, expounding his theory of the British working class. His two listeners were checking their watches. Jimmy, who had not yet surrendered his coat, whispered that Mme. Sun was in the adjoining room and that he was going to check out other receptions. Rayna watched him go, deciding she was glad to see him off. Once again, she was sorry that she'd welcomed him back. She was alone. More alone than she had ever been in her life. The question was what to make of it. Mme. Sun floated in and began talking to Bee who was now stationed by the windows. Rayna put down her glass and straightened. Too quickly. The view in front of her buckled. She had the unpleasant sensation that her head was rolling across the floor. She shut her eyes, smoothed down her dress, then made her way over to join them.

Mme. Sun was speaking in a low urgent voice of her need for an exit visa. As Rayna came in earshot she heard Borodin's reply, that now was not the time to make such a request. "It might seem your Soviet hosts are neglectful, but that is not the case. Not an intentional slight."

Mme. Sun's voice was firm. "No slight, I am sure of that." She paused to let her meaning sink in. "Perhaps you could convey to the appropriate parties that it is a matter of health."

"Your health?" Borodin switched to his solicitous voice. "In that case, perhaps an extended return—"

His suggestion, not fully voiced, that Mme. Sun go back to the warm sun of the Crimea, prompted Rayna to intervene. "Jimmy Sheean brought back a contract for Mme. Sun to do an American lecture tour. Surely that is a good reason for a visa." Fanya Borodin, passing with a tray, stopped to register this brazen suggestion. "I haven't yet—" Irritated by her impulse to backpedal, Rayna stiffened her voice. "I haven't yet mentioned it to Mme. Sun. Jimmy just told me this morning."

Mme. Sun took a moment to scan Rayna's face, then Borodin's. "Now is not the time," she agreed, putting a hand on Rayna's arm. "Though the idea, from a purely personal standpoint, has much attraction." She bowed to her host, her hostess, all the while tightening her clutch on Rayna's arm. "Perhaps you could find me my wrap," she murmured and led Rayna off to the dwindling pile of coats on Fanya's bed. "We must talk," Mme. Sun continued in a low voice. "I have missed you."

Rayna waited, wanting to point out that it was Mme. Sun who had abandoned her. "You never mentioned you were leaving," she finally said.

"That is true. I will explain it in time. Perhaps you could come by this evening?"

Rayna's heart sank. She had barely slept the night before. "Yes, when?"

"In two hours, shall we say? At my new quarters at my husband's university."

Odd but charming, the way she put it, her husband's university, as if the university were still loyal to her husband's principles.

She found Jimmy a few minutes later in the hard currency bar with a half dozen cronies. She begged a headache and borrowed some money for a *droshky*. Because of traffic cordons, the ride took a half hour, and by the time she climbed the steps to her closet room she was frozen. Afraid to sleep for fear she'd never wake on time, she spent the next hour writing a letter to Bill, explaining the wonders of the Revolution Day parade and the glorious receptions after.

She had an interview at the Lenin School the next day and so, when the letter was finished, she tried to pull together some kind of report for them. She wished she'd had the interview the day before, so she could say in all honesty she hadn't seen Mme. Sun. Now she was going to have to report whatever she found out about the Lady's sudden departure for the Crimea, the whereabouts of General Teng, as well as what she knew from Jimmy about the Chinese cadets. Not on paper, that would be a mistake, but in the verbal report that was the last item required at each interview. She had to get away from Jimmy Sheean, that much was clear. And find a way to earn some money.

There were no *droshkies* so she walked the long blocks to Sun Yat-sen, wondering what she would tell Mme. Sun about the Lenin School, that she'd been asked to be a spy as her price of admission. When she was directed to Mme. Sun's office, she was grateful for the glowing fire and steaming samovar. Mme. Sun was solicitous. "I am sorry you had to walk and that you are so cold. Perhaps you should stay the night. I am sure I can find a room."

Rayna's heart swelled with the sense she was once again being taken in, made part of the team. Mme. Sun motioned to her to keep on her coat. "It would be best if we step outside,"

Rayna understood. "Yes, it would be nice to get some fresh air," she agreed as she pulled herself away from the warm grate while the Lady took up her padded silk overcoat.

Mme. Sun guided them to a copse of trees that provided some shelter from the wind. "You look tired."

"I am," Rayna conceded. "It's been hard. I don't feel as if I belong any place."

"For me as well. That is why I have decided to go to Berlin.

220

There is a conference I've been invited to. Why I made my visa request."

"I don't think Bee can do anything. If he could, he would." Mme. Sun seemed to question that. "I am sure he has been advised not to concern himself with our affairs."

Rayna hesitated before asking the next question. "Do you think he will ever get back to concerning himself with our best interests?"

A smile. "You still think of yourself as one with our best interests. That is a difficult position to be in here in Moscow."

"I know." Then, "Jimmy Sheean wants me to go with him to Berlin, or London, he doesn't care which."

"Do you want to?"

Now it was her turn to smile. "Go with him? No, but Bee keeps urging me to get out and I don't seem to have much enthusiasm for Manila."

After a bit, Mme. Sun probed further. "You must decide what is important and then devote yourself to it. You are stretched too thin by too many different loyalties."

Another long silence, Rayna agreeing that too many loyalties was indeed the problem. She wanted to tell Mme. Sun about the Lenin School but the conversation veered in another direction.

"General Teng is in Berlin. In hiding of course. I intend to join him."

Now Rayna would be faced with whether to report that news.

"Between General Chiang courting my sister and the Chinese Communists taking orders from Moscow, it is difficult indeed. If I stay any longer I will be forced to align myself with the Moscow position."

Another statement she would have to decide whether to report.

"I cannot tell you if you should go off with Jimmy Sheean, but if you should decide to visit Berlin it would be soothing to have your companionship."

That was a statement Rayna was sure she would not report.

Mme. Sun continued. "However, if you decide you must stay, that can be helpful too. I know you are hopeful that Commander Borodin will again be allowed to take up his special mission in China. I hope that too. And if you were to assist him, that would be an excellent application of your devotion and talents." She paused and then added, "I cannot but believe that someday we will all three come into harmonious alignment. China and Russia need each other. This current impasse — let us say it is not important. And the three of us will surely meet again."

Rayna bit her lower lip, mostly to see if she could feel anything. "But first you must get that exit visa."

"Yes." Mme. Sun took her arm and guided her back to the warmth and light. Rayna declined the couch but accepted the offer of a ride back to Jimmy's.

The next morning, at breakfast by Jimmy's window, Rayna told him a truncated version of her late night meeting with Mme. Sun. He was gleeful, jumping to the conclusion that she would come with him to Berlin and that, from there, they could together convince Mme. Sun to take up the tour.

She explained that because Mme. Sun was reluctant to cause any estrangement between herself and Moscow, she doubted the tour would be agreed to. He turned morose when she announced she would not be accompanying him to Berlin, that her plan was to stay on in Moscow. Another long jumpy conversation ensued, which centered on how she would manage with no money and no place to stay. Jimmy declared that the Soviet Union was, for him, of no further interest, that he was going to write his piece and get out. He tried to persuade her to eat something, some tea biscuits he had brought from the hotel the night before. She refused, saying she wasn't hungry. She watched him drum his fingers on the battered table and look out the cloudy window, then mentioned a conference she planned to attend later that week.

"The Friends of the Soviet Union?" He could barely conceal his disdain. "What kind of organization is that?"

She said nothing, resolving not to bring up the Lenin School, hoping he would forget that she had ever mentioned it. Then they got onto the subject of Trotsky, the story that was being run in the morning *New York Times*. Jimmy repeated that the banner was a direct affront, that those cadets who had carried it were sure to be locked away or worse. She said he was exaggerating. He said she should go back to a free country, any free country, that from there things would look different.

"What it really comes down to," she said, "is that you don't believe. In anything, from what I can tell. How sad."

"What it comes down to," he countered, "is that I love you. That thunderbolt hit me while I was away. Hard on the heels of the realization that I had no use for the Soviet Union."

It was an awkward moment, one she didn't want to deal with. So she laughed, and that felt good, a glee that came up from nowhere and almost smoothed things over. She told him she didn't mind that he loved her, and left it at that.

Then she reminded him she had an urgent appointment and he extracted a promise that she would meet him at the hard currency bar at the Savoy at seven. "If you buy me dinner," she said, and he agreed.

Then she went out into the hall and back through the front door of her closet room and picked up her report that she'd squirreled away and walked the mile and a half to the interview. Mushkin greeted her with a hard expression. "You met with Mme. Sun," he said, lighting a cigarette from the tag end of the last.

"Yes," she said, and handed him the report. "I didn't think it wise to put it in writing."

"You went to Comrade Borodin's rooms. You were told not to."

"Yes. My journalist friend Jimmy Sheean wanted to go. He's trying to interview him."

"Did he succeed?"

"Not really. There weren't many people there. He went off with some journalists to seek bigger fish to fry."

"Bigger fish?"

"More important people."

He liked that. "So then you took up a conversation with Mme. Sun?"

"She came in just as Jimmy left. She was gathering her coat at the same time as I was, and she asked me to come by her office at the university." She assumed he knew Mme. Sun had taken space there.

"And so, tell me please, in precise detail, everything that was said."

She told him about half of it. That Mme. Sun was the one who wanted to talk by the copse of trees. Skipped the part about General Teng, the Lady's plan to join him in Berlin. She glossed over the advice to narrow her loyalties and instead recounted what she understood to be Mme. Sun's thinking about how to foster her husband's Three Principles. "She is very clear that the Soviet Union and China need to continue their special relationship. That China cannot become free without Russia's support. But she is also aware that her husband's path is not exactly the path of the Chinese Communists, and she sees her role as maintaining a 'third way' for those opposed to General Chiang but not yet ready to embrace all the tenants of Marxism."

He listened to this speech, the one she had rehearsed over and over on the long walk. "And you, what do you make of Mme. Sun's analysis?"

"I think it is wishful thinking. But then, Dr. Sun was not my husband."

He nodded. "The irrational thinking of a grieving widow."

"Something like that." She made a silent apology to Mme. Sun.

That must have been what prompted her to think about the remarkable conversation initiated by Krupskaya. What Krupskaya was trying to say, she now realized, was that widows had a special power, that they could speak the truth, and that while their enemies would dismiss them as silly women, they dared not silence them. Rayna thought of Mei-hui, her beloved Dan. She must do whatever she could to make sure Mme. Sun was not silenced.

After another medical exam and a long list of questions about the year she spent recovering from typhus, she was finally able to escape. She dared not ask when this would be over, but each week she became more hopeful they might accept her, in spite of her age, apparent ill health and shaky knowledge of Marxist dogma. She had a special relationship with Mme. Sun, a person of interest to the Soviet hierarchy, and maybe that would be enough to get her in.

She was only a quarter of an hour late meeting Jimmy in the Savoy bar. After a round of drinks, she pressed him to order dinner. She had not eaten all day. Service was slow and by the time it arrived she was too tired to eat much, a few bites of potato and a spoonful of stewed greens.

When they got back to their rooms he wouldn't let her go, insisting that she come into his parlor for a nightcap.

"Shhh! You'll wake the gorgon," she said, finally agreeing, but first going through the front door into her closet room and then going through the whole routine of moving her dresser, unbolting the connecting door and then moving aside his dresser. When she came into his room she sat on his bed, studied her hands while he took up where he'd left off.

"You've got to come down on one side or the other. West or East. The One or the Many." He was angry at her stubbornness, and pressed on, claiming that freedom was innately superior to equality, that equality was mere leveling. "Liberty or equality, one or the other. And you, my dear lady, have to choose." He tipped back his glass, satisfied at his accounting.

Her voice, when she spoke, was spent of all emotion. "What about fraternity, Jimmy? Where does that fit in?" It was if she were speaking from a great distance. "Doesn't that count for anything?"

He examined her face through the bottom of his glass, spun it around to take in the door where his heavy silk robe hung. It was deep blue, the long sash with two tassels arranged in majestic counterweight. That moment she hated him. "What do you want me to say?" There was a blur in his words. "Boola, boola?"

She stood, putting up a hand to ward off any further attack. "Good night, Jimmy," She could feel his watery eyes on her as she marched over to squeeze past the dresser, unbolt the door, slip through, then bolt it from the other side. She half hoped he could hear as she shoved her bureau back, shoving instead of lifting, putting too much strain on the weak back leg. She supposed the landlady would evict her for that, damaging the people's furniture. She had to get out of here, find a way to make the Lenin School accept her. Without caring if he heard, she flung herself over the noisy bedsprings and made no effort to stifle her long overdue sobs.

CHAPTER 21

The next morning she got up early and snuck out so as not to talk to Jimmy. She walked the streets, making a mental list of all the people in Moscow she knew, the few with pull. There was Mike Gold, if she could find him. The man at the *Tass* office who had helped her. The reporters who had let her stay for a night or two. Since she was near the *Tass* office she decided to start there.

"Is Comrade Rykoff in?"

The woman at reception looked blank.

"I've spoken with him before, he's helped me with—" Then she stopped. Rykoff could do nothing, she was sure of that. All she would do was get him in trouble. "I'm sorry. I just realized I've come to the wrong place." She fled, resolving to think this through more clearly, deciding to start with the *New York Times* reporter who had written the story about the Chinese cadets.

Walter Duranty was still asleep but his Russian housekeeper, or maybe it was his female companion, offered coffee while she waited for him wake up and finish shaving. When he came out of the laundry closet that doubled as a bathroom sink, he yawned while waiting to learn the reason for her visit.

"I think I have a story," she began, still finding her way. "Jimmy Sheean showed me the piece you did on the Chinese cadets."

She could see interest and something else register in his eyes. "What would you know about that?"

"Nothing really. I know there are factions at Sun Yat-sen, I saw them shouting at each other after General Teng spoke." She had not planned to bring up General Teng. "I wanted to talk to you about Mme. Sun," she hurried on. "She plans to attend a world peace conference in Berlin. They are holding up her exit visa. Maybe because of the cadets."

His face was skeptical.

"According to your article, the banner was expressing support for Trotsky. Mme. Sun couldn't have had anything to do with that."

Duranty sighed, reached for his first cigarette of the day. "My dear, you haven't the faintest idea of how convoluted thinking is in this city. How a perfectly convincing case could be made that your Chinese widow had urged those cadets to unfurl that flag."

"I don't understand."

"To embarrass the newly elected Chairman."

That was a far stretch. But he said newly elected. Did that mean that Stalin's tenure might not last? She supposed that was Bee's only hope. "But whatever the logic, it's not true." She fixed her most earnest expression on him. "You know that. And your paper could do something to make that point. Randall Gould put pressure on in Peking to let Mme. Borodin go."

Duranty drew in a lungful of smoke and examined her. "You want me to piss-off my contacts by raising this? It's probably just bureaucracy at its worst. And believe me, Soviet bureaucracy is the worst."

She returned his cold appraising look. "If it's just bureaucracy, a little pressure won't hurt. And I imagine you've already pissed-off those at the top with your cadet story."

He shrugged and crushed out his cigarette. Took the cup of coffee offered by his Russian bedmate and reached for a pad of paper. "All right, tell me the details. I'll see what I can do."

She did the same with Chamberlain of the *Christian Science Monitor*, Knapf of *UPI*, and Harrison George, Earl Browder's deputy. With George, who was an old friend of Bill's, she reminded him that Browder had written a letter for the Lenin School on her behalf. Unlike the journalists, he was guarded, offering no encouragement, and she wondered if talking to him had been a smart idea. To put on a good face, she told him about Bill's job in Manila, and they chatted a bit about how things had been in the old days.

When she left his office about three, she was boiling hot. She hadn't eaten any breakfast and didn't want to use her last kopeks on food. So she went to Chen's office in the Metropole hoping to catch Jack and maybe find a few crumbs of both food and information. The room was locked. On an impulse she went up a floor and knocked on Borodin's door.

A rumble of irritation. "Who is it?"

She said nothing, hoping he'd think it was a messenger and open the door himself.

He did, eyes widening at her appearance. He shouted something over his shoulder and guided her into the hall. "You should not be here."

"I know. I must speak to you."

He said to meet him in twenty minutes at the back entrance of the Menazh, the old imperial riding stables that now housed art exhibits. So she went there and spent a half hour shivering in the cold while she waited for him to show up.

He finally did, apologizing for being late and taking her arm and steering her across the street and toward the river. It was dark by the time they reached the crest of the bridge. Traffic was thundering past and that made it a good place to talk. He stared down at the sluggish black water. "It is very foolish of you to keep knocking at my door."

"I know. I don't care for myself, but for you I apologize."

He didn't say anything to that.

"It's about Mme. Sun. Her exit visa. I've been talking to

229

everyone I can think of, trying to put pressure on to get it approved."

He looked at her with grave wonder. "That is a very bad idea. You have done this already?"

She nodded, and he turned once more to look in the water.

To redirect his attention she continued. "Mme. Sun invited me to join her in Berlin. The implication being that she does not plan to return." She did not mention General Teng. "But I've decided to stay here. Enroll in the Lenin School if they will have me. The vetting has been quite rigorous." She could see him preparing to say something, or maybe to restrain himself from saying what he thought.

"I've told you that is a dangerous course to take," he finally announced in a low voice. "You see this river? How the ice forms at the edges and then breaks off in sheets, collecting along the banks with other broken ice?" He reached out and took her frozen hand and sandwiched it between his. "Each night the temperature plunges lower and new ice forms. The morning sun loosens winter's grip, but it can never complete the job. Each day gets shorter and every night longer. Soon the ice will win. That is how it is in this city."

She knew what he meant. "I'm staying with you," she said, and felt herself relax because her decision was now made.

When she got back to her closet room there was an envelope slipped under her door. The letter, with no identifying letterhead, commanded her to report at six that evening for intake. When she arrived, she was shown into the same interview room. Mushkin was finishing dinner. He waved her to sit down and asked if she'd had anything to eat.

"No," she said. "My funds are in short supply."

"We shall have to address that." He pushed a button, a woman came in and he indicated to bring in a second tray. "Now," he continued, "my reports are that you visited *Tass*. On behalf of Mme. Sun. What made you do that?"

230

The tone was friendly but the implication wasn't.

"I feel responsible. I was the one who proposed she should come to Moscow."

He raised his eyebrows. "Not Commander Borodin?"

"He may have said something. I know he didn't think she would agree to it."

"And why did you think she would agree?"

Rayna tried to remember how it had been in Hankow, why she thought anything in that far away time. She felt herself flush, realizing for the first time that she had used Mme. Sun's friendship as a way to make herself useful to Bee. "She was my friend," she heard herself say, "I thought she would be welcomed here."

"And now you think she is not welcomed?"

It was a direct challenge. She would have to answer it. "No," she said, "I don't think she is."

He scribbled something in the notebook in front of him and motioned for her to eat. Then he stood and went outside and left her alone for several minutes. She toyed with the food, rearranged the beets and mutton, hungry but not really able to go through the motions of eating.

When he reentered his face had changed. "You are being moved to the next level. Report here for the next three days. You will get intensive political preparation. After that, a decision will be made." He removed the half-eaten food, handed her her coat and ushered her all the way down the slushy steps into the night.

For the next three days she fought to make sense of her situation. From dawn until after dark she sat in the same cramped room, bombarded with questions, requests for clarifications, given instructions to read and summarize various speeches, plenum reports and statistical charts. None of it made any sense; she felt as if she were on a conveyer belt with people throwing things at her. She simply could not untangle the dense prose and convoluted thought process that seemed to her so much gibberish.

But she didn't say so. She tried to remember things Bee had said, catch phrases he had used to instruct her.

They gave her food, indeed urged food on her, a tray of tea and bread when she arrived. Lunch was the same meat, now with potatoes and cabbage. She wasn't able to down much of that. At five they brought in another tray, more bread with stewed fruit, either crabapple or plum, and a thimble full of brandy. She felt like she was in a hospital and indeed, the way her head swam, she thought maybe she should be. She had no idea if her answers made sense or not, but they seemed to satisfy her instructors, who rotated every two hours and took furious notes, then left her with a curt nod. The last instructor of the day, just after she got her stewed fruit, directed her attention to her past life.

"Tell me when you first became politically aware."

She said China, that moment when she had encountered the dead baby depository. That didn't seem to reach the mark.

"Earlier than that."

She dredged up something about the dissolution of her first marriage, how she had made friends with politically-active people in New York.

"Yes, we know that. Earlier, please."

She was stumped. What did they want? "I'm sorry. I'm trying to tell you, but I don't know what to tell."

"Tell us about your childhood. What is was about your upbringing that led to this decision."

"You mean this decision here. To enter the Lenin School."

"Yes."

So she told them about the year she spent in bed, how half the time she felt she was living in another world. "Hallucinations, I guess."

He wrote something down. "You had a high fever?"

"Yes, I told them that. The doctors who examined me."

"Tell me how it was subjectively, your feelings of isolation, detachment from the bourgeois world."

She took a deep breath. She had never told anyone about this. "I felt unmoored. But also in possession of a deep secret."

"Go on."

She didn't want to, but offered a teaspoon more. "I was very sick, hovering on, well, you know. I knew that, there were whispers and my ears were fine. Anyway, sick as I was, because I was so sick, I felt destined. That I was holding on for some reason. That life was being given to me for a second time and that once I became well I would be granted a special mission."

"And now you have."

"Yes."

"And what is that?"

"Being here." She didn't tell him the whole truth. She didn't tell him about Bee or Mme. Sun.

"To what purpose?"

"China. What we started. With the girls in the villages. I want to continue." On that note he let her go.

Each night when she was released, wrung out like a wet rag, she made her way to the Metropole, hoping, she supposed, to meet Bee or someone else who could lend her some strength. She didn't want to go back to her closet room and take up arguments with Jimmy. The first night she ran into Anna Louise, who invited her to a political event, but she declined. The second night it was the Chen girls waltzing through on their way to a dance recital. She joined them and drifted along in their endless chatter. The third night it was the Chamberlains, who had been so kind as to take her in before Jimmy arrived. They saw her sitting in the lobby and came over.

"Are you all right?" Mrs. Chamberlain asked.

"Fine," she said, although she really wasn't.

"That tip you gave me panned out," her husband reported.

"I contacted Berlin and Mme. Sun has been invited to speak. I can't get any information from the Soviets, of course, and Mme. Sun has once again retreated into seclusion, but I'm working on getting a confirmation or denial as to her exit visa. If I don't get something in a day or two we'll run the story as is."

She looked up, grateful. "Thank you. I've got to be going now."

Jimmy, of course, was waiting when she got back. She pleaded exhaustion but he would have none of it. "You have to tell me where you've been. I've been frightened out of my wits. Afraid they've snatched you for all the ruckus you've kicked up."

She smiled. "I've been kicking up ruckus? Good."

He wasn't being put off. "Where have you been these last three days?"

"I can't tell you. It's secret."

"You have to tell me. I'm going to marry you."

"Oh." The words seemed fuzzy, he must have been drinking. She tried to absorb what he had said, make sense of it. Then, "Bill won't like that."

"Damn Bill." With that he tried to pull her into his arms, but in defense she simply slipped into oblivion. Turned out like a light. The next time she became aware it was morning. He had put her in his bed with all her clothes on minus her shoes.

"Where did you sleep?" she asked, seeing wan daylight and realizing she was supposed to report for the final interview.

"In your bed. I left the door open."

She lifted her head and was assaulted by a sloshing sensation, as if her brain was an urn of jostled water. "You've made gouges on the floor," she said, pointing out where he had dragged the dresser. "Landlady won't like that."

He sat beside her on the bed and took up her hand. "That's the other thing I need to fill you in on. I told the landlady to go to hell. Reserved two rooms at the Savoy. We're moving there this evening. Then I'll start booking us tickets to Berlin."

How did she begin to untangle this? When she spoke her voice came out as a low croak. "My interviews are over," she told him. "I should find out today."

"Find out what?"

"What I'm doing next."

CHAPTER 22

She made it clear to Jimmy she was not going to the Savoy. But next week's rent was due and she had no money to keep the place if Jimmy moved out. He followed her into her closet room and pleaded with her to come with him, to tell him what interviews, what she thought she was doing. Furious, she whipped her head back and forth, setting off a series of dull thuds behind her eyes, and told him instead that she had to wire Bill. That seemed to give him hope, although his hopes were not what she intended to wire. She wanted to see Mme. Sun, to find out if she knew more about the visa, but decided not. "I'm going out, that's all you need to know," she said as she wrapped a scarf around her neck and put on the thick gloves she'd picked up from a side table in the Metropole. Gad, she was becoming a thief in addition to a grifter and a vagrant. On the street she considered her next move.

With an hour to kill she went to the main telegraph office, to see if Bill had wired, but the answer was no. For some reason she began thinking of Dan, how her beloved dog had also been a vagrant. That stiffened her resolve to be more considerate of Bill, to compose a gentle ten-word wire and be done with it. But she couldn't think of ten words to explain what was swimming in her brain, and besides, she wouldn't have any news until she found out if the Lenin School was going to take her. So she left without sending anything and walked the long blocks back across town and stood outside the door until the appointed time. When the doorkeeper let her in she looked like a snow castle.

"This way," the woman said as she escorted her to the same dreary room. Mushkin was in his normal pose, studying files, presumably hers. He stood. "Congratulations. You've been admitted to the Lenin School. Short program to start. You're behind, so you'll need some tutoring but that can be arranged."

"When?"

"When begins the tutoring?"

"No, when can I start. I need to find someplace to live."

She watched him go through some more papers, his lips disapproving.

"Also, the monthly stipend," she reminded him. "I have no money."

He looked up. "We'll see what we can do."

This time he offered no food, but did come up with a half-month's stipend, and made some calls and finally was able to offer her temporary quarters beginning November 15th. Three days, somehow she could hold out for three days.

"One other question," she said as she was leaving, trying to suppress her great excitement. "When can I tell my husband?"

"You may tell him you are enrolling in a short academic course, that is all."

"And my friends?"

"What friends?"

"Journalists, for the most part."

"Tell them as little as possible."

With her new stash of rubles she took a droshky to the telegraph office and wired Bill that she would remain in Moscow for several weeks on a paying assignment. Then went back to Jimmy's rooms and intercepted the landlady and told her she would be staying only two more days and to collect the additional rent from Jimmy. Next door, he was well along in his packing. She watched his back as he folded his shirts into his expensive luggage. "Let's be friends," she suggested. "I can't stand it when you're mad at me."

He stopped, looked at her with red-rimmed eyes.

He's been crying, she realized, and her resolve softened. "Let me try to explain. I've been sworn to secrecy but that's not why I didn't say anything. It's because I wasn't sure it would happen."

She waited for him to ask what her momentous news was. But it seemed he already knew. "The Lenin School. That's what you've been angling for."

She was surprised and he saw that in her face.

"I've known all along. Guessed it anyway. You talked about it nonstop in China, and here at the beginning, then shut up about it when I came back."

"It's true," she said, "But they told me not to say anything."

His face hardened. "You know what this operation is. It's a bloody spy school. They break you down and fill your mind with their brutal version of reality and then make you a puppet. It's worse than the Catholic Church. You'll become a bloody Soviet nun."

She turned to go back to her closet room. "Don't do this, Jimmy. It's hard enough as it is."

He followed her into the hall. "Why? Why are you doing this? Did they give you a number? 024867? It's the end, you know." As she closed the door he was shouting, "The end of Rayna Prohme!"

An hour later he knocked, and after he promised not to make a scene, she opened the door. He said the least she could do before entering her nunnery was to have a last capitalist meal. "I'm too tired," she said, trying to beg off.

"Tomorrow night then. Wear your gold dress. I want to remember you in that." His face started to crumple, so she agreed, if only to put an end to this painful passage.

The next day it snowed so she spent the day in her room writing letters and drifting in and out of sleep. She was so tired, she couldn't think why, and puzzled. Why had they taken her on? She'd done badly, worse than badly, on the political instruction. Her explanation of why she wanted to be a communist was ridiculous. She wished she could be with Bee, in his warm arms, letting him tutor her, caressing her forehead and stomach and back. She had no one to talk to any more and that was the truth. She was on her own with a mission not yet accomplished. To protect Mme. Sun. After that she could rest.

At seven, a loud pounding on her door. She opened it to find Jimmy, bathed in snow and angry at her for not meeting him as planned. "Come on. Get up!"

It sounded like the voice of her father, so without protesting she obeyed, stumbling over and pulling out her gold dress from the bottom drawer. It was mussed, but not much, and the wrinkles would fall out, that was the nice thing about silk. Jimmy stood outside the door while she put it on. "OK. I'm ready."

"You didn't brush your hair."

She did that, more or less, then put on her trench coat and the flimsy straw slippers Bill had bought her at the Shanghai market.

The Hotel Savoy was busy, warm and noisy. A brass band was playing some Russian martial music. She wished she were back in Hankow, in the living room at the Lutheran mission, listening to smoky jazz and drinking warm beer with visiting journalists. That's what she missed in Moscow, the stolen moments of relaxation that nearby danger engendered. She missed the sense that Bee was protecting them. Now she felt she had to protect him. Jimmy was pulling off her coat to give to the hat check girl. "Come on. We're late."

She wondered how much he'd been drinking.

Enough, as it turned out. She couldn't eat, her throat had closed down. She looked around at the vaulted ceilings, the big windows looking out on Red Square, the onion turrets of St. Basil's. It felt festive, all these foreigners and important dignitaries, the band replaced by a string trio, a soothing rush of water plashing in the central tiled fountain. "I want to make a wish," she announced. "I need a kopek." She used to do this with her father, beg for a penny to throw in the big fountain at Chicago's Grant Park

Jimmy fished out a handful. "Be my guest."

She went over to the fountain to look at the orange carp that were lazing around in the shadows. She felt nauseous at the thought they would soon be someone's dinner but looked past their tail flicking to the glinting coins resting on the greenish bottom. Jimmy came up and put a hand on her waist. "Come with me," he said. "Up to my room."

She turned around and laughed. A giggle of relief and surprise that it was all out in the open, what he really wanted. "I'm going to become a nun," she reminded him. "Just like you said. A Soviet nun, number 347982. Monday I go into a chrysalis, change my name and don't emerge for six months. You'll have forgotten about me by then. They all will."

The thought made her shudder, the part about being forgotten, but she lit up her bright smile and steered Jimmy back to the table. He waved for more vodka. She made a concerted effort to eat a bite of the scalloped potatoes.

"I won't forget about you, ever," he said. "If I could figure out a way to kidnap you I would."

"How Caucasian," she said, thinking of bridal kidnappings, but realized that didn't sound right. Nothing about this evening was sounding right. "I need to go." She stood and pushed back her chair. The legs were wobbly or maybe she was. Just then she spotted Anna Louise near the window eating with a Russian woman she recognized but couldn't place. As she walked over, it felt like she was wading through gelatin. "Anna Louise, can I join you?" Then sat down in the empty chair and smiled brightly at the two of them.

"We were just leaving."

"Splendid. So am I. Where are you going?"

"To the awards ceremony, to see Clara Zetkin get her red star."

By this time Jimmy was standing over them. She turned to inform him of her plans. "I'm joining Anna Louise and—" She searched for the Russian woman's name.

"Kollentai," the woman put in.

Of course, the famous Kollentai, the Ambassador to somewhere, she'd met her at the Sugar Palace giving advice to Mme. Sun. "Do you know if Mme. Sun has been given her exit visa?"

Kollentai blinked and exchanged glances with Anna Louise. "Excuse me," she murmured. "You two go along. I have some business to attend." She slid away, all swishy crepe, every eye in the room following the well-shaped hips of the departing Ambassador.

"That was unwise," Anna Louise said. "Asking such a question."

"I don't care," Rayna said, and she didn't.

They made a show of inviting Jimmy to join them, but he was clearly beaten. She waited until he'd paid the check and then kissed him on the cheek and left with Anna Louise, feeling strangely invigorated by her rude and ill-advised question to Kollentai.

There was no droshky so they walked the half mile to the Kremlin gate. Her straw slippers were gummy ropes by then, but her feet, when she could feel them, were hot. Finally they made their way to the back of the great hall filled with Party faithful and squeezed into two seats in the middle of the third-to-last row. She felt happy to be among this throng, content that in just two days she would be safe in her Soviet chrysalis with a new name and no contact with the outside world. What name would she choose? Dan, she thought, maybe she would name herself after her dog. Or Planter, her beloved cat. Or De Costa, her Sephardic mother's name that Rayna had misunderstood as seraphic. She was an angel. A girl from Chicago. A Bolshevik.

The stage was a long way down. Rayna could see a speck of the ribbon being held up as Clara Zetkin, the German leader for women's rights, hobbled forward to accept her Order of the Red Flag. Everyone on stage rose to join the applause. Rayna clapped until her arms ached.

Clara Zetkin gave a stiff bow. Rayna watched as she fumbled for her handkerchief and gave a good long blow that set her orchid to trembling. Then Zetkin, done with sentiment, spread her thick legs, anchored herself at the podium, and let loose a torrent of German. Defiant words as she raised a mighty fist. The corsage shook. The audience roared. Rayna slipped into a joyous state, seeing summer at the Illinois State fair, farmers' wives in printed calico, thick forearms holding struggling piglets while their white underarms danced.

Another wave of applause as Clara Zetkin ended her exhortation; then the handkerchief, tears, Rayna's tears, everyone's tears as Zetkin made her way back to her seat. The master of ceremonies had already taken up the medal for the next presentation, the Hungarian leader, Bela Kun. Rayna bit her lip, thinking about what Anna Louise had said on the train in China, about how revolutions used up women. Then about Mme. Sun and what lay in store.

She was about to be sick. Rayna lifted her hands from where they'd been clenching her knees and saw two palm prints on the gold metallic dress. Green and brown highlights slid up and down the gleaming silk. Her stomach revolted. "Excuse me." She bolted, pressing her way past neighboring knees.

Anna Louise looked up. "Something wrong?" But Rayna shook her head. The urgency of her unwanted dinner rose as she fled up the aisle.

In the washroom, when she finished, she felt mostly guilt. About wasting Jimmy's expensive meal, missing the rest of the program, making a spectacle. She used some cardboard to clean up the sink, then realized she'd left her purse and didn't have a kopek to pay the woman at the door. She tried to escape on good terms, bowing and apologizing to the attendant as she backed out the door. She was still trying to explain about the purse when, moving backwards, she bumped into M.N. Roy.

He had been standing in her path and positioned himself so she parked her backside smack into his trousers, then placed ten bony fingers on her stomach settling her firmly against him. One arm slid up under her shoulder, turning her around so they stood face-to-face. A chuckle at her astonishment. While she was being caught and twirled, she'd been frightened, but when she saw the expression on his face she got angry.

"Who do you think you are?" She wished she'd hatched a more original line. Once, at the state fair, her brother Reddy had done something similar, grabbed her and pushed her down in a headlock to entertain a crowd of boys. "Prick!" she'd yelled, but she didn't think that was appropriate now. M.N. Roy was looking down her dress, probably wondering about the hand prints. She tried again. "Why are you following me?" She stepped back as she challenged him, not caring if he saw the wet splotches or not.

He took a step back as well, his eyes measuring the distance between her shoulders and knees. She hated this dress. "What do you want?" This time she didn't bother to hide her scorn.

"I have information about Mme. Sun," he responded, still smiling, letting the implication hang there, waiting for her to ask the rest. She didn't. "The exit visa," he prompted.

She considered whether she should. Ask. Or whether she should tell him to stick his head in a bucket, or someplace really crude. She was recalling the wild joy when she'd flown at Reddy, torn his shirt, scratched all down his face, the crowd of boys gone silent as she banged his head in the dirt. But then things had turned. The men from the beer tent came out to take up Reddy's defense. "Now little lady," they'd cautioned, laughing and elbowing each other. One of them picked her up, lifted her high on his shoulder. "The new champ!" Then he turned her upside down, held her screaming and kicking by both ankles, showing off her underpants and skinny stomach to the crowd. Then her father had come, stopped the men all right, gave them a good tongue lashing, got her right side up and straightened down her dress. But he'd blamed her afterwards.

She eyed Comrade Roy and tried to think what to do. Flying at him, scratching his face would do no good. She closed her eyes and balled her fists and stood still for a moment. Then her eyes opened. "Yes, I would like to know."

"Ah." His teeth flashed. "I'm so sorry, my dear, I really am. The Soviet Union does not feel it is in its best interest to accommodate the Lady's travel plans to Berlin." His eyes glistened. "You see, I took it up with the Boss himself." The womanish mouth became a smirk, the head moving from side-to-side. "I drafted the directive myself. It's sitting on his desk right now, waiting to be signed."

"He hasn't signed it yet." A question disguised as a statement.

He shrugged. What did she think she was going to do? "He works nights, I suppose you could go see him." His expression told her that was impossible.

"Maybe I will."

His eyes widened. "You can't. And neither can your Chinese widow." With a droll expression, he lifted his palms. "It's too late."

"We'll see." She looked him up and down the way he'd looked at her, her anger beginning to make her shake. The timid part of her was trying to figure out how to get away from him without causing a scene. But a different part of

244

her shoved past him, searching for the right exit word. "Prick!" she hissed, and left it at that.

The ceremony was over. People were starting to stream past, pulling her away from the hated M.N. Roy but blocking access to her purse. She let the crowd pull her toward the wide entrance doors, take her outside, where she realized she was also missing her coat. She considered trying to push back in but was afraid of running into Roy. "Prick," she repeated, then struck out for the guardhouse in the direction she had come. But she made a wrong turn and found herself in front of a row of brick houses, each with identical granite steps, iron railings and red doors. It reminded her of a stage set, a block in Greenwich Village. Just then an old lady with a small dog came shuffling toward her.

Rayna watched the woman approach. She closed her eyes, felt a deep shiver of exhaustion. The woman stopped. It was Krupskaya. "My dear, what are you doing out in this cold?"

"I came to see you," Rayna heard herself saying. "I'm Rayna Prohme, we took a sleigh ride together."

"I know who you are." She peered at Rayna and pulled at the urinating dog. "You're freezing. Come along."

Chapter 23

When Rayna's thoughts next came into focus she found herself wrapped in a quilt of crimson and gold, propped in a high-backed wooden couch, her feet encased in thick felt boots. She was holding a glass of tea, stirred with a dollop of jam, her body drifting and warm, wanting to stay there forever.

"Well," Krupskaya said from her matching chair nearby on the faded Persian carpet, "tell me why you have come to such a state."

Rayna let out a puff of dragon smoke and realized the air in the apartment was frigid. "You mean having no coat, my shredded shoes. That's not important. I've just learned that Comrade Roy has drafted a letter that blocks Mme. Sun from leaving the Soviet Union. She is to become an indefinite guest of the State."

Krupskaya held up a hand. "More slowly. Tell me why you feel you must get involved in this."

So Rayna told her how Mme. Sun's older sister planned to kill her, how the younger one was engaged to General Chiang. "You see, she has nowhere to go. I know Chairman Stalin made a hash of his China policy. Borodin says everyone must lie low until this resolves itself. But Mme. Sun is caught in the middle. She's become a trophy to be taunted and played with. I brought her to Moscow. I'm responsible." Her intentions suddenly clarified. "Take me to Comrade Stalin. I know General Teng had a private meeting." Before he fled for his life, she wanted to add, but didn't. "I must stop him from signing that directive."

Krupskaya thought it over. Turned her face to one side, maybe to hide a smile. "I see."

"What's the best way to get the Chairman to do what I want?" Even to Rayna's ears, this sounded ludicrous.

"That is a secret we should all like to know." Krupskaya's smile came full out before being tucked away. "What about this directive is so important?"

Rayna leaned forward, the slippery quilt falling off her shoulders. "She's a widow like you, inconvenient to the authorities. If they succeed in keeping her here, they will turn her upside down, shake her for their private enjoyment. And if that doesn't work, they will string her up, open her body—" Her throat seized and she couldn't go on.

Krupskaya was careful when she spoke. "You saw something like this in China?"

"Yes, a young girl."

"I, too, have seen such things." Krupskaya was looking around, taking stock. "And you think Mme. Sun is in danger of some such thing. Here, I mean."

"Yes."

"Then, we shall have to go to see the Chairman, hear what he has to say." Krupskaya put down her glass and patted Rayna's exposed foot. She went to the telephone, spoke quietly in Russian, then in a harsher tone. Finally she hung up. "They will call me," she said and took Rayna's glass to draw her more tea. "You are sure you want to do this?" She was folding Rayna's hands around the glass. "Are you well?"

"Will you come with me?" Rayna looked down as she asked this, concentrating on the heat in her hands.

"Nothing will come of this. Except punishment for you."

"I know."

Krupskaya considered. "What will you say?"

"I have no idea."

She shrugged. "Sometimes that is best." Then added, "He

loathes women. With a revulsion that is rooted in fear. Use that. And here is a wrap. You can't go out without that."

An hour later, at three in the morning, Rayna found herself sitting opposite Chairman Stalin, in a chair too big for her, in front of a giant mahogany desk with a green leather top. Krupskaya sat off to the side, so still she was almost invisible.

Joseph Stalin was dressed in military regalia, hands folded on his desk. Then he plucked at his jacket cuff, on a sleeve, Rayna remembered, that was tailored to hide a shorter left arm. He stared at her with yellow wolflike eyes.

Rayna tried to pull together what she should say. She looked around at the deep green walls, the wine-colored drapes. A pool of light from the desk lamp and a second standing lamp by the curtains threw the room in shadows. Panic rose in her chest, she felt a sharp need to urinate. What would happen if she wet herself on his leather chair?

Krupskaya cleared her throat, a sound Stalin copied. That settled her, the realization that he too was as off balance. She squinted at the bristling moustache, tracing the upper lip against the clipped hairs, noting the one stray that had not been trimmed, how it curled toward the soft flesh of his mouth.

Concentrate, she told herself, tell the truth, make it glow and fuse itself into a tight mass. Throw that truth out to engulf this man of power.

She studied her hands. Stalin cleared his throat, this time the sound dismissive. She returned her eyes to his face. "Have you heard the story of the three sisters?"

Stalin's interpreter, who stood in shadows, intoned the question in Russian. She waited until he was finished. "The fairy tale about One eye, Two Eye and Three Eye." This time, hesitation before the translation. She saw Stalin's eyes widen and so picked up the pace. "Mme. Sun is like Two Eye, wedged between two gorgon sisters. The older one looks with a single eye to the past, to the corruption and greed of old China. The younger one, who will marry General Chiang, has her three eyes set on the corruption and greed of the future."

She saw Stalin's hand slide under his desk, she supposed to a hidden alarm. He thinks I'm dangerous, or better yet, mad. Examining him with even greater intensity, willing him to submit to her logic, she continued. "Mme. Sun has two eyes, and with them can see China's dreadful present. She seems powerless." As she laid out this new evidence, Rayna leaned forward. "But that is not true. Because her vision contains China's truth, she is dangerous." She sat back, liking the sound of that, watching his hand halt on its way to the hidden alarm. Prick, she thought. She'd hurled that word at her father once and been strapped blue for her trouble.

Stalin's back stiffened, his hand undecided. Who is this woman, Rayna imagined him thinking, is she mad? Have I let in a mad woman? Again his fingers started to move, then he stopped, looked at Krupskaya, sitting there, impassive. Why had she brought this girl? Does this mean Krupskaya is aligning herself with Trotsky?

He grunted, to give the impression he was absorbing Rayna's words. She stared back at him. "Go on," he muttered as the interpreter translated. "Finish what you have to say. What is it you want?"

Rayna took a deep breath and raised her neck to full length, glad for once her unruly hair gave her an extra three inches. Then she exhaled, drawing herself back into her shoulders, and spoke with quiet reproach. "I would have wanted you to understand, to have welcomed Mme. Sun for what she represents, for the hope that is China. Not just China, the whole world." She stopped to let her disappointment show.

With an impassive face he examined her, but underneath she could detect the ghost of something unsettled. Her eerie voice continued. "But that is not possible, I see that now. You are fallible, I'm not making

249

any criticism of you personally." Rayna added this last when she saw his body start to twist, the left shoulder rise, the right arm pulling itself into a protective hug. The motion of a man exposed. She changed her tone, making it low, soothing, but continued to look at him, at the space between his eyes. "I understand now how the power of one nation's belief can poison another's, even if that is not intended. It comes from having only one eye. Or three." She stopped again, looked down to give him space to absorb this. Her voice took on a sense of resignation. "It is the same with people, they fail you, and sometimes not from hate or anger. Sometimes from love."

Stalin, she hoped by now, was thoroughly bewildered. Why was this American woman in his office? In the middle of the night, talking of past loves? She stared, imagining him wrapped in silken threads, imprisoned by Fates. Suddenly, both his hands splayed rigid on his desk. He began to rise, then stopped. Looked at Krupskaya, at the way she sat, then closed his eyes.

"I'm talking to you," Rayna continued in that ghostly voice that came from she knew not where. "Because you are the only one who can put it right. You have a directive on your desk, in that pile, about half way down." She pointed. With an involuntary movement he clutched at the papers, spilling pages across the floor. He barked at the interpreter to gather them up.

"One of them," Rayna continued, "is a letter to Mme. Sun." She pointed again, to a single page resting face down on the edge of the carpet and he motioned to his aide to fetch that very one to prove her wrong.

"It says," Rayna continued, hoping it was true, "that Mme. Sun is not free to leave, that she is a permanent guest of your government. A captive, in other words, until you decide to let her go." He looked at the page, flung it away.

Teeth clenched, he rose behind his massive desk, spoke in a growl to the man behind him. "What you ask is impossible," the aide intoned. "You cannot hope to barge in here and ask that the considered policy of the Supreme Soviet be reversed."

Krupskaya took this moment to speak. "Why not?" She spoke in English for Rayna's benefit, making the interpreter do his work. The audacity of the question hovered in the close air.

Stalin turned to her, his rage erupting. "What did you say?"

She didn't react, instead continued in English. "I said, 'Why not?'" A small shrug. "It seems to me we do a lot of things these days without much good reason."

That made him go pale. Rayna could see sweat beginning to form at his hairline. "What do you mean?" he said, or something like that, growled in Russian, his eyes narrowing, spitting out this challenge to his supreme authority. Only it isn't supreme, Rayna remembered, he hadn't yet stamped out all the opposition aligned with Trotsky.

Krupskaya shrugged again. "Busy times," she said, as if that explained it. Then held up her palms. "Why don't you give the girl what she wants? What does it matter to you?" She was speaking in a relaxed tone, that of an equal, without fear.

He turned and walked to the window, pulling aside the drape to stare into the Kremlin night. Then he decided something, flexed his fingers, returned to his desk. He spoke in a low voice to his interpreter, who went into an alcove and emerged with a tray carrying three small cups. He handed the Turkish coffee first to his employer, who drank it straight down, then one to Rayna and a third to Krupskaya. Rayna raised the cup, then caught a slight motion of Krupskaya's head. She put it down, wishing she could wipe off the bitter trace of the just-tasted coffee.

Then the Chairman's mood shifted. He granted them both a tight smile, spoke again in Russian with an indication that it be translated. "Krupskaya, I'll make an accommodation with you. This girl, her fantasy about Mme. Sun, I will not deal with. But with you, our esteemed Leader's widow, a member of the Central Committee, with you I will have a candid discussion." He motioned for her to move closer to his desk. The interpreter helped resettle the chair. "Tell me," he continued with a broad yellow-toothed smile, "tell me what you want. It shall be yours."

They spoke in Russian for a minute or two and then, with great show, the Chairman took out a sheet of paper and wrote a short note and signed it. He handed it over to Krupskaya.

"What does it say?" Rayna asked.

"An instruction to give her the visa," Krupskaya murmured, then stood and motioned for Rayna to do the same.

"I want it in English, too."

A severe look from Krupskaya. Rayna shook her head. "Mme. Sun does not speak Russian." Reluctantly Krupskaya handed the sheet back and spoke to Stalin in an apologetic tone.

He looked exasperated but then, with an effort at graciousness, took the note and handed it to the interpreter who copied out the brief text in English which Stalin then initialed. He handed it back without expression.

Now Rayna rose and thanked him and bowed her head in gratitude and, clutching the vital order to her chest, followed Krupskaya into the long hall.

As the two women were escorted out, Rayna was faint with excitement. The guard moved them down some stairs and then to a side door, but when Krupskaya tried to dismiss him, he refused. "Comrade Stalin has directed me to escort you to your quarters." So the two women were only free to exchange glances. Krupskaya insisted that she accompany Rayna to the Spassky Gate.

There, as the guard stepped out to hail a taxi, they had a brief moment alone. Krupskaya murmured, "You plan to take it to her tonight?" Rayna nodded. "She must not wait too long. Koba is notorious for changing his mind. And see it becomes public." Then the guard returned and Rayna had only a half second to kiss Krupskaya's soft cheek.

She had no money, having lost her purse. But the driver was too frightened to protest about a penniless passenger picked up at the Spasskey Gate and let her off at Sun Yat-sen University without so much as a backward glance. She wrapped Krupskaya's gray shawl around her and looked down at her oversized boots. The gold dress was muddy and wet to the knee. She had no idea where Mme. Sun slept, having only visited her office quarters. The night watchman was as likely to report her as to help. Besides, she spoke no Russian. It occurred to her that many of the Chinese cadets spoke English and so she set about scraping in the frozen slush for gravel. She tried the ground floor first, scratching the frost to see if there was someone awake inside. It turned out to be only class rooms so she stepped back and threw her handful of stones at the window above. When that got no response she gathered more handfuls of slushy gravel and threw them one by one at the sequence of windows. By the fourth, she detected a figure turning on a dim light. She threw another handful and began waving for the cadet to lift the window sash. This took a while as the window was frozen shut. Finally the glass went up and a head came out.

"Do you speak English?"

A pause, a conversation with someone inside. "What can I do for you, Miss?"

"I must find Mme. Sun. I have an urgent message."

More consultation with the second person and then the head said, "Is very bad, against rules."

"I know, but it's urgent."

Another long wait and then the window went up all the way and the young man and his companion, both in cadet uniform, climbed down the brick and stood in front of her making deep bows.

Now Rayna felt the cold. "Thank you. Mme. Sun will thank you."

There was a conversation in Chinese and then the first young man said that Mme. Sun was in seclusion. Rayna knew that when the Lady was in seclusion it was absolute. "Her maid, can you get in touch with her?"

Another show of regret.

"How about the cook? Can the cook talk to the maid and get her to come out and see me?"

They agreed to try. The cook lived in the women's quarters, and getting to her involved waking one of the female students. By now there was light in the eastern sky. It must be past the time when cooks would be up anyway. They gave up on the female student idea and went directly to the kitchen which turned out to be well lit and bustling with activity. One of the cadets went in and returned shortly with Mme. Sun's personal cook. He explained that the American woman needed to get a message to Mme. Sun.

Mrs. Ma recognized Rayna and seemed willing to accommodate her. Rayna was loathe to part with her precious order, however, and did not want anyone to see what it was, so she wrapped the folded paper in the cook's apron and tied it with the apron strings and told Mrs. Ma, through the cadet, that she was to take it directly to Mme. Sun and return to assure Rayna that the message had been received and read.

They waited outside for another half hour, the cadets getting nervous because they were supposed to be lining up for morning roll call. All the energy and excitement had evaporated. Rayna was both numb with cold and tingling with nerves. She wondered if she was getting frostbite and longed to ask the cadets to put their arms around her, lend her their warmth. Finally she saw Mrs. Ma returning, her face bobbing up and down with pleasure. Much back and forth in Chinese and then the cadet turned to her and said, "The message had been received and Mme. Sun thanks you."

It was done. When she was in the middle of clutching their hands to thank them, the last bit of will holding mind and body together collapsed. First her knees buckled and then she blacked out.

CHAPTER 24

She was being carried over someone's shoulder through heavy snow and her arms were dangling and a man's hands were on her rump. Not a bad feeling, the rump part, except for the way his shoulder dug into her stomach made her want to vomit, and she was worried about puking down the back of his scratchy coat.

The next thing, a warm lobby, confusion about where to take her, the mirrored elevator panels making her eyes hurt, and then bed. They were striping off her beautiful gold dress and putting on something huge and pink. When she awoke it was afternoon, the sun streaming through a curtained window and Jimmy Sheean was at her side.

"Thank God!"

She started to protest that she was a bother, that she shouldn't have walked out on him, but he interrupted her with a stream of apologies of his own. He never should have let her go off like that, she'd been feverish in the restaurant, anyone could tell.

"Where's my dress?"

Jimmy didn't seem to know. Anna Louise had taken it, he said, and then put on the nightgown.

Rayna looked down at the heavy cotton housecoat that buttoned down the front. "This belongs to her?"

"Yes, it will keep you warm."

She waved her hand, a weak protest that was all she could manage. "Where am I? How did I get here?" It was all coming back, the late night outside the kitchen at Sun Yat-sen, the interview with Chairman Stalin.

He told her he'd come upon her by accident. That he'd been tying one on and was making his way back to the Savoy when two Chinese cadets appeared, one of them carrying her over his shoulder and the other holding her shoes.

"My shoes," she groaned, thinking of the sodden straw sandals she'd started the night in. Then she remembered the felt boots. "What kind of shoes?"

He was surprised at that question but humored her. "Some kind of black things."

Ah, she hadn't dreamed it. She really had done the impossible, stood up to Chairman Stalin, guaranteed Mme. Sun's means of escape. She smiled. "I had a rough night."

He took up her hand in a way she wasn't inclined to reject. She closed her eyes to think. He was telling her she was in the Metropole, in Anna Louise's room, that they had arranged to move her next door.

She protested she felt fine, that all she needed was a good sleep. "I told the evil landlady I was staying until Monday and then it's off to the Soviet nunnery." She tried to laugh but her throat constricted and she started to cough.

"You're not going anywhere," he said with a voice that brooked no disagreement and she realized that this illness, or whatever it was, suited him just fine. He was in a stalling game, and the sicker she was, the more unlikely she could make her induction at the Lenin School.

"I want to speak with Bee." Might as well use being sick to get what she wanted. "And after that, Mme. Sun."

Jimmy said he'd do what he could. Then Anna Louise arrived and started acting like a matron in a boarding school and Rayna couldn't stand it so she announced she was going to sleep and only woke when they were carrying her wrapped in Jimmy's coat on a rolling chair to the next room.

She sat on the little chair, holding on to the radiator to keep from falling over, while the two of them unmade the bed from the last tenant and put on new sheets from a pile on the dresser. A porter watched but did not participate. Jimmy bundled up the used sheets and stuffed them in the porter's hands and then helped Rayna sit on the bed. But the sheets weren't tucked in right so he pulled at the bottom one to retuck it. That tangled the whole mess and brought it half on the floor.

"Nuts." Anna Louise surveyed the scene and turned on the porter. "Find us a hot water bottle." The porter claimed to speak no English. Anna Louise muttered to Jimmy that she couldn't remember the word, so clapped her hands and tried German. The porter gave a shake of his head and responded in a torrent of Russian. Anna Louise reciprocated with one of her well known outbursts. "Heat up some rocks, bake potatoes, I don't care — do something to help us get her warm!" He backed away, leaving the door open to a brisk draft.

Anna Louise closed the door. "We've got to start over." They lifted Rayna, put her back on the rolling chair. Jimmy held her shoulder with one hand while Anna Louise got the bottom sheet tucked in, then he moved Rayna back on the mattress and tucked the top sheet around. Then came a blanket, Jimmy's coat, and Anna Louise's on top of that. Rayna felt wet stringy hair plastered to her cheeks.

"She looks like an igloo." Jimmy observed, "but at least she is in no danger of freezing."

But she was shivering inside and felt herself drifting.

Then what sounded like a sob came from Jimmy. "Sit down," Anna Louise instructed him. "The doctor should be here any minute." His cold fingers fished under the coats to pull out her wrist to check a pulse.

"I shouldn't have let her get chilled!" Jimmy's voice rose to a wail. Anna Louise cut him off.

"Don't blame yourself. After she left me was when this all happened. She must have spent the night on the streets."

Jimmy was holding up the matted felt boots. "She wasn't

wearing these earlier — do you know where they came from?"

"No, but thank God she had them. Why did you let her out in those straw things?" Then, "Last night, did she seem entirely well?" Anna Louise was using her careful voice. "I mean, you spent time with her, was there any hint of irrationality?"

Again that wail. "Irrationality? Irrationality?" His breathing was jagged. "If you call enrolling in the Lenin School — becoming a Bolshevik spy — if you call that irrational, I suppose." The outburst seemed to quiet him.

"Interesting," was Anna Louise's only comment. "I didn't know."

Rayna could hear him making his way over to the window. "A nun, a fucking Bolshevik nun." Then the two of them began speculating about where she had gone, what her mental and physical state had been for the last few days.

At that moment Fanya Borodin appeared with a cooking pan, some kind of heating coil and a string bag. Rayna smelled lemons but where on earth did she get those? Mrs. Bee waddled past and put the electric coil on the dresser, the pan on top, and then busied herself searching for an electric outlet. She found it and began unpacking her string bag. "My rink," she announced. "Always I travel with my electric rink." Rayna let herself be amused by the thick accent, now free to think of her as Mrs. Bee, not Madame Borodin. Now she was just a *hausfrau* stuck in Moscow, not the wife of a Soviet commander.

"Ring," Jimmy corrected. He never would have done that in China.

"And lemons," Mrs. Bee continued. "Always, always you must carry with you lemons. You have a knife?" She addressed this to Anna Louise while aiming the pan at Jimmy. "Here. Go to the faucet and get me some *vater.*"

"Water," Jimmy said, not moving.

"Qvick!" That was a command. "Two inches." She shoved

the pan into his hands, lifted his elbows to push him in the direction of the bathroom. "Now I chop onions." Rayna found herself starting to laugh, relieved that she could find this funny.

Mrs. Bee was making up a surgical table, laying down newspaper, taking a knife from her pocket.

"What are you doing?" Rayna asked, thought she knew well enough.

"Poultice," Mrs. Bee declared. Chop, chop, chop. In seconds the onion and lemons were reduced to mush. "Now I boil." She took the pan from Jimmy and put it on the heating coil. "Mustard." She fished a packet of yellow dust from a pocket and added it to the mix. "Now garlic." Two cloves appeared to endure another bout of chopping, "Next wintergreen—"

A sharp memory of wintergreen, the year they had treated her with camphor. The wintergreen had been used to disguise the smell and the medicine itself had nearly killed her.

"I place it here on the chest, and also here—" Mrs. Bee motioned to Rayna to open her nightgown.

"No poultice," Rayna told them, but they ignored her.

Jimmy had gone back to the window to stay out of the way. "My grandmother used oatmeal and honey," he said.

"Also good." Fanya was fishing for Rayna's wrist which was well hidden under the covers.

"No poultice." Rayna threw her head side-to-side and arched her back. "You can't make me."

Mrs. Bee's face contorted with disapproval. "Such a silly stubborn girl."

At that moment a Russian doctor arrived. He took off his muffler and placed his cracked leather bag on the dresser next to the abandoned poultice. There was a three-sided conversation in Russian between Anna Louise, Mrs. Bee and the doctor.

Fanya was pointing out the rejected poultice. In a dismissive gesture, she turned to Jimmy who had come over to take up Rayna's hand. "The doctor has other responsibilities besides American girls who don't take care of themselves."

"She was unconscious, had been for at least an hour when I found her," Jimmy told the doctor. "Must have been out in the cold for hours." He was trying to keep his voice calm, but it rose again to a shout. "She was blue, totally blue and hardly breathing! Something happened. This is not a case of not knowing enough to come in from the cold!"

Rayna gave a little sound of agreement. She could feel her mouth shaping into a smile. Fanya glared at them both, pulling the pan off the heating coil, unplugging it and marching off to the bathroom to dispose of the mess.

The doctor asked Anna Louise something in Russian, ignoring his patient and her defender. Rayna tried to be obedient, opened her mouth for the thermometer. Jimmy snatched it out before it could fully register and whispered it was 104, or close, he wasn't so hot on converting from metric.

Rayna sat up to observe what would happen next. The Russian doctor was a glum man in a frayed overcoat, which he still wore, even though the room seemed hot. His huge leather valise creaked at its hinges and spewed out dry flakes when he opened it. He set to extracting a great variety of tools, laying them out on the dresser, oversized implements that looked like the ones her father's vet used. Finally he produced a dozen brown bottles with handwritten labels. Anna Louise eyed all this and decided to go into the bathroom to help Fanya.

Jimmy was still gripping Rayna's hand in what seemed like terror. Her thoughts were elsewhere. She was transfixed by the brown bottles. "I'm allergic to camphor," she said to no one in particular. "They gave me shots of that when I was ten and I became deathly ill."

"Did you hear that?" Jimmy seized on this to fend off the doctor and his implements. "She's allergic to camphor." Even as he said it, Rayna knew it was hopeless, because the man didn't speak English.

The doctor came over to his charge. Without any attention to modesty, he pulled open her night gown and surveyed her. She grinned an apology, there was so little there and all of it covered with freckles. He took out a stained wooden tongue depressor, pried open her mouth and checked her throat. Then shined a light in her eyes, used a tin funnel to check her ears, and made show of thumping her chest and back. It was just like the half-dozen exams at the Lenin School. Finally, he folded back the covers and motioned for her to scoot down. With one hand he pulled down her underpants while, with the other hand, he palpated her belly.

Through all this Rayna remained wide-eyed and quiet. Then the doctor went back to his table and began examining his collection of bottles. Mrs. Bee had reappeared and the doctor spoke to her. She nodded and took up a place by the bed. Jimmy was clutching Rayna's hand so tight it was beginning to hurt. Then he was pushed aside as Mrs. Bee turned Rayna over to expose her backside.

"I'm allergic to camphor," Rayna repeated. "Even to smell it when I've got a cold. Don't let him give me camphor."

Jimmy went over to the doctor who was back by the dresser and they had a long discussion about what was in the various bottles with neither understanding the other.

Just then Anna Louise reappeared and the doctor pulled out a long length of tubing and a red rubber bag. Anna Louise nodded and went back to the bathroom, presumably to fill it. Rayna closed her eyes, knowing what came next. Jimmy said something about getting fresh air, and Rayna was glad to see him go, given the next part of the show.

She was concentrating on that, the indignity of an enema, and so missed the real event. As she was listening to Mrs. Bee bark questions at the doctor, the man snuck up and pushed a huge needle into Rayna's behind. As the fluid went in she could smell it, the smell like mothballs, but it was too late. She began to go rigid along her spine, then her legs went numb and she started to retch yellow bile.

The next thing she heard was Jimmy. Apparently he hadn't left. "Fool!" She could hear a crash of bottles and implements. "Quack!" The sound of two men struggling. "Get out of here. Get out! Out!"

A lot of self-justifying Russian.

"She told you she was allergic to camphor!" Someone kicked the doorjamb, then she could hear the doctor darting back in to grab his valise. Through half-open eyes she could see Jimmy tucking his arms under his armpits and flapping them. "Quack!" The doctor seemed startled by this performance. "Quack, quack!" Jimmy played the menacing goose as he advanced on the frightened man. The doctor grabbed his muffler and ran out the door, which Jimmy slammed behind him.

Then he went over to Rayna, bending to see her awake through the puffy slits of her eyes. "You're awake. Thank God. The man nearly killed you."

"I know." Maybe she whispered this or maybe she kept it to herself. But she didn't tell the really important thing she'd just realized. They had asked her about camphor, her allergy to it, at the Lenin School. Those doctors knew everything about her medical history. Every weakness.

Mrs. Bee reappeared from the hallway and made a point of defending the doctor, saying he was the best in Moscow, that he had been sent over especially from the Kremlin Hospital. Jimmy launched into a second tirade, denouncing the Soviet medical establishment, then added a full scale indictment of the revolution and threw in all of Russian culture for good measure. Rayna, weak and numb as she was, enjoyed the show. Jimmy told Fanya he hadn't had a decent meal or a decent conversation since he'd left Berlin, and as far as he was concerned the whole damned country could rot in a bog. Mrs. Bee made weak protests and Anna Louise kept hissing for Jimmy to shut up. It seemed they'd lost track of Rayna entirely.

Then Anna Louise remembered the patient and said they should have some kind of doctor. Jimmy said as long as it wasn't a Russian. Rayna was feeling far away and warm for the first time in hours. She could hear Fanya announcing that since he, Mr. Expert, had driven the last doctor away, he could find a replacement. Then she left with a flounce. Jimmy announced that Anna Louise should stay and he would go find one. When she awoke they told that she had been sleeping for two days.

They had found a doctor at the German Embassy who was coming again that afternoon. Her fever was still high and he was worried about dehydration. Jimmy had been sleeping on the floor and Anna Louise checked in every two hours.

"Where's Bee?" she asked. "I want to see Bee."

"That's the other thing," Jimmy told her. "All hell's breaking loose. Last night the Central Committee voted to expel Trotsky."

CHAPTER 25

There were flowers, two great baskets of them, lilies and asters and snap dragons. Mme. Sun had come while Rayna was sleeping but Jimmy told her that today the Lady was at a funeral for General Joffe.

That didn't mean much to Rayna's tired brain. What she was worried about was Mme. Sun. "Has she got her exit visa?"

"I don't know. She didn't want to talk."

Rayna pointed to the ceiling light.

Jimmy nodded. "Could be."

Rayna settled into her blankets, she now had two, a grudging concession from the hotel management, as well as a bedcover, peach colored, of the smoothest silk. Another gift from Mme. Sun. She ran her hand along the delicious weave and asked about her gold dress.

"Anna Louise sent it out to be laundered. God knows what condition it will be in when it comes back."

There was grief about her poor dress but part of her felt proud of the damage. A big sigh. There was only so much she could worry about. Jimmy was offering her a day-old copy of *The London Times* to read about Trotsky. She examined it for a minute and then said she'd read it later, not telling him the entire page was smeared beyond a blur. Instead, she tried to reconstruct what they'd been talking about. "You said there was a funeral."

"Yes. Joffe shot himself. Despondent about his health, they say. But it had to be a protest about Trotsky. His arrest came just hours before Joffe's suicide."

Joffe was Bee's mentor, the man who had sent him to China. "I want to see Bee," she said quietly. "It's very important."

Now it was Jimmy's turn to sigh. "I'll try. Mrs. Bee is guarding the gate. I don't suppose you want to see her."

"Good God, no!" They both laughed, but then her laugh turned to a cough and then she blacked out for a few seconds. She didn't tell Jimmy, just pretended she was catching her breath.

He tried to get her to eat a few crackers, but her stomach revolted at the thought. Since the bitter sip of Turkish coffee she had been throwing up like clockwork.

The German doctor seemed trustworthy. He had on a pressed suit, for one thing, and his breath smelled of mint instead of heartburn and he had recently shaved. He asked her who the American President was and what date was Christmas. Made her count backwards but she gave up after 92. He said she needed to drink fluid and gave her something for gastric upset, then mentioned to Jimmy that there was something else going on, but first they had to get her back to eating. He asked about mood swings, did her thoughts race? Had she had blackouts? A history of drinking alcohol to excess?

That last she could answer in good conscience. In a deadpan voice, as dry as she could make it, she said, "Tell me, doctor, am I losing my mind?"

He didn't take the bait, but didn't laugh either.

After the German doctor left, she tried to entertain Jimmy with tales of her childhood. She told him about Reddy, how the man from the beer tent had turned her upside down. About Planter and the thrashing machine, volcanic fights with her father. The fantastic dreams about her mother during the year she'd spent in bed.

266

"I saw her lit up on the wall like an angel." She was playing with the edge of her silk cover. "Had long discussions with her about what to do with my life. I knew from the whispers that they supposed I would die. So I asked my mother what it was like. She said not to worry, I should do my best and make sure my time on Earth counted for something."

She looked up. "I wrote my friend Helen about you. She has a husband named Dan, that's why I named my dog Dan, even though it was a girl. I wanted someone like him, who loved me and let me do whatever I wanted." She was silent and then started on another topic. "I told Helen you reminded me of Raph. If I die I want you to write Raph and tell him I think of him all the time. Also, at my funeral, I want to wear the gold dress."

Jimmy said, "You're not going to die." And then, "I thought you didn't like Raph."

She gave him a wide smile. "Raph's wonderful in his way. Talented. Driven. So sure of himself and yet not so sure. That's what reminds me of you."

"Thanks, I guess."

"But there was a flaw, something missing between us that took me a while to figure out. It wasn't his fault. He was who he'd always been. But with him I couldn't find my mother, could no longer summon her presence."

"You lost yourself."

"I guess. And then along came Bill, that's another story, and I won't go into it except to say he was very insistent and charming and also talented in his way." She was silent and then made a confession. "I don't love him anymore. Never did, not really. I admired him and thought I could have a marriage that would be like my friend Helen's. Don't tell him I said that. Tell him I miss him terribly."

"I don't want to hear this. You're not dying."

She didn't argue, didn't think that was important, just summoned up the last of her energy and said, "Maybe not, but right this minute I'm going to sleep."

When she woke it was getting dark, and Anna Louise was sitting with a nurse they'd found somewhere. "I don't want a nurse. I don't want anybody in this room I don't know."

Anna Louise tried to hide her irritation. "Don't be a pill. She's very competent. The German doctor ordered her."

"Does he know her?"

That produced a crack in Anna Louise's confidence. "I don't know. She was sent by the Kremlin Hospital. The German Doctor wants you to go there for some tests."

"I'm not going to the Kremlin Hospital."

"Well, you need to get the tests."

"What tests?"

"I don't know exactly."

"I'll go to Switzerland. Has anybody told the Lenin School why I didn't show up?"

"I believe somebody said something."

"Did I mention the Lenin School? I don't remember saying anything. You know they make you keep everything secret."

"I believe someone from there inquired."

Rayna settled into her covers and once more looked over the soft expanse of peach silk. "I want to see Mme. Sun. She left all these flowers."

"I'm sure she'll stop by again."

"I want to see Bee." This last in a faint voice, the edge of fear she'd been trying to keep away at last nudging in.

The next morning when she woke, the nurse was sitting at the far end of the room checking pill bottles. Jimmy was there too, asleep on the floor in his nest of blankets. "Jimmy, wake up. I want you to go down to the hard currency shop and buy me something to eat."

He was still trying to focus. "I'll order something sent up."

"No, I want those special crackers." She tried to remember the name of the brand. "The ones with the gold and blue wrapper. They come in a roll, like poker chips."

He was up now, straightening his shirt and looking around for his shoes. "Anything, Madame. And when he comes, I'll tell the German doctor you are past your stomach upset."

"Yes, do that. And tell him I am going to Switzerland. To take whatever tests he wants."

The doctor, when he arrived an hour later, was dubious she was well enough to travel, but Jimmy said he'd accompany her and arrange everything. She sent Jimmy off to wire Helen, and also, at the last moment, added Raph. "You remind me so much of him," she repeated, although she wasn't sure what she meant by that. Mme. Sun would be visiting that afternoon and Rayna wanted all these arrangements set. Then she would write Bill.

She was feeling invigorated when Jimmy and the doctor left, alone except for the heavy-faced nurse in the corner. She supposed she might try to make friends. "Excuse me."

No response. "Do you speak English?" Then she tried in her execrable Russian.

No response, just a defensive outpouring and a rearranging of all the pill bottles. "I want to see Commander Borodin," Rayna tried again. "*Comrade Borodin.*"

The woman smiled and nodded, then pointed down the hall in the direction of Bee's rooms. Rayna knew where his rooms were, but why did the nurse? She rose from her bed, disobeying the cardinal rule that she was only allowed up to go to the bathroom and then only with support. Blood drained from her head and she was unsteady but reached for her robe. Or, rather, Anna Louise's robe. Pink, very warm, though needing a wash. She clutched it firmly around her, eyeing the Russian nurse, daring her to intervene.

The woman began to advance. Rayna wondered if she had it in her to get as far as the door. Instead, halfway there, she collapsed. The nurse hauled her up. "I want to see Commander Borodin," she protested as she was frog-marched back to the bed.

She had a second plan, to enlist Mme. Sun to carry a message to Bee, and waited in her covers until late in the day. There was a soft knock. Jimmy had returned earlier and Rayna was pretending to sleep. The nurse had retreated to her corner. Mme. Sun opened the door with another huge array of flowers. "Rayna! I have been by twice but you were asleep. I'm so glad you are feeling better."

She settled on the edge of the bed and stroked Rayna's forehead. Rayna closed her eyes just for the sensation of the cool hand. Now she could feel her mother's presence. "I've been asking to see Bee. He hasn't come. Do you know why?"

She could sense Mme. Sun considering what to say. "I saw him at the funeral, a sad time. You know General Joffe was the link between us. He negotiated the arrangements with my husband that brought Commander Borodin to China."

"I know." Rayna wanted to spill out what was welling up in her but was afraid that Jimmy would hear. "There was a time," she began in a low voice, "when he was everything to me."

"I know."

"I'm so worried. If they are being this hard on you, what—" She didn't finish. Who knew whether the Russian nurse spoke English. "Jimmy," she called out. "Can you come over?"

She whispered in a low voice that she and Mme. Sun needed to talk and she was afraid the Russian nurse was a spy. Jimmy shrugged, there was nothing he liked better than thwarting a spy. He went over and stood in front of the Russian nurse and began speaking in loud English, gesticulating and making a pest of himself. The nurse kept trying to look around to see what her charge was doing.

"The flowers are wonderful," Rayna whispered to Mme. Sun, "but next time you must send food. Anything. I think they are trying to poison me."

Mme. Sun took this in without surprise. "Then you must be very vigilant. And leave here as soon as you are well. I will send Chinese medicines. We know about such things."

"The German doctor seems trustworthy. He's from the Embassy. Jimmy is making arrangement for me to go to Switzerland."

"Excellent. When you recover, I should welcome your company."

"I will be honored."

"But first you must recover."

"Yes." A pause. "The German doctor thinks there's something else wrong. He wants to send me to the Kremlin Hospital." She broke off and looked toward the nurse. "That's why I need to see Bee. I need to tell him."

Mme. Sun spoke slowly. "I believe he is under orders not to see you. He was not supposed to talk with me either."

"Can you go to him? Tell him it's urgent?"

"I will try." She thought a minute and then whispered, "You must explain to me how you arranged that letter from the Chairman."

Rayna started to giggle. "I can't. You shouldn't know." For the first time she squarely faced possibility of being poisoned. Was it at the Lenin School when they had so magnanimously offered her lunch? Or the single sip of Turkish coffee? The bumbling Russian doctor with his camphor? Who knows what the wretched nurse was doing while she was asleep. "What you can know is that for the first time in my life I felt brave."

Mme. Sun pressed her hand and promised to send over some herbs that would aid digestion. Jimmy came over and gave Mme. Sun an account of his arrangements for Switzerland.

"Remember Bee," Rayna reminded Mme. Sun as she prepared to leave. "I must see him." Then the Lady was gone and the German doctor came and did his thumping and peered in her eyes and asked whether it was hot or cold in the summer and what color did the leaves turn in the fall. She was tired, exhausted from all the events of the day, and when he said he wanted to give her a sedative she did not object. "Make sure it's one from your bag," she insisted. "I don't want anything from those pill bottles over there."

He said he had given those bottles to the Russian nurse, but she insisted and he gave in, took out a new bottle from his black bag and went to get some water from the bathroom. When he gave her the pill, she had a hard time swallowing. The last thing she remembered was seeing him stop and talk to the nurse before getting the water. Had he kept that bottle in his hand the whole time?

CHAPTER 26

Rayna awoke fretting about Bill. Anna Louise was there, and sometimes Jimmy, and she heard them speaking as if from down a long hallway, words echoing as they huddled with the German doctor. Her bed was soaked and she remembered the nurse changing the sheets. Remembered facing the white wall, rocking back and forth while feeling deathly cold. But maybe she had dreamed all this. She could no longer keep straight what she imagined and what was real. She asked for a mirror and studied her snarl of damp hair, the red welts on her cheeks. "Bee won't like this," she said, handing the mirror back to Anna Louise. And then, "Where is he? Did he come while I was out?" They assured her he had not.

She put her finger on a welt. "Bill never liked my skin." Then, asking no one in particular, "Do you think he's lonely?"

Anna Louise said of course he was, but not to worry.

"It's all my fault."

Anna Louise tried not responding but Rayna fixed sorrowful eyes on her and waited her out.

"Well," Anna Louise began, "if you think we should cable."

"No cable." Rayna was adamant. "That's too cold." A letter. But what to say? That she was going to Switzerland? That she was dying?

"Whatever you think."

"I should say I'm sorry." Rayna thought for a while and then added, "I've pulled him awfully far out of his channel."

Anna Louise tried a different tack. "Are you sorry you came to Moscow?"

"Oh, no!" Rayna fixed a serious expression on her face. "It has been absolutely worth it." She started to cough, then, giving up, turned her face to the wall and pretended to sleep. When Anna Louise bent over to check, she kept her expression slack.

Later that afternoon, when it was Jimmy's turn to sit, she opened her eyes and began telling him about Reddy and the greenhouse. It was when she was nine and they'd broken all the glass in the roof and had been marched into their father's study. How Reddy had been so scared he'd peed his pants. "But I wasn't scared. Just like I wasn't—" Here she stopped, remembering the urge to pee in front of Chairman Stalin. Then she took up again. "I looked my father straight in the eye and stared him down, said I wasn't sorry, that it had been an accident, that Reddy and I were playing Seven League Boots and the roof gave way. He gave Reddy a whipping, he liked to give whippings, but didn't touch me. Because I wasn't scared. But later I got sick and he decided to keep me in bed for a year and force feed me cream to build up my strength and that's when I started having tantrums."

Jimmy didn't know how to respond so he just took up her hand.

Then she announced, "My mother, I bet she had tantrums, too." Then, "Jimmy, do you love me?"

That caught him by surprise. His face turned pink and she watched the color rise and deepen, then let him off the hook. "I forgive you for yelling at me and making me eat my carrots." Then she veered in another direction. "Something's happening, Jimmy. I'm losing track of who I used to be." She grinned to make him feel better.

"Revolutionary Instrument Number — what's the number you gave me? Anyway, that number is reporting for duty."

"Soon as I'm well," she added, waiting while his face registered the fact that she wasn't going with him. She reached out for his hand. "Jimmy, all of us are called upon to do something, even though it's not always clear what it is." She made a sad clown face. "You tried to be a revolutionary but it didn't work." Then she laughed, as if this were the world's greatest joke. "You are a journalist, Jimmy. Face it, that's what you are. So, for heaven's sake, be a good one!"

After that she slipped into deep sleep, knowing now that she would stay with Bee, that he was the one who needed her, that Mme. Sun would be able to take care of herself. Then she woke with a jerk, sat up and stared at the street lights outside the window. "Jimmy?"

When he said, "I'm here," she started to cry, not making a sound, just letting the tears slide down her face. "I can't see," she whispered. And then, "Promise — don't tell."

The next morning when the doctor tested it, her vision seemed fine. He felt her neck and all down her spine, then turned to address Jimmy and Anna Louise. "The process I have envisioned has begun." But he said no more, just closed his bag and said he'd be back the next day.

Anna Louise decided both she and Jimmy would spend the night, but when the night nurse arrived Rayna insisted they both leave. She was firm, turned childish, said she wanted only the nurse, and when Jimmy whispered to Anna Louise, presumably the story about the tantrums, they decided to go.

When the door closed, Rayna turned her back on the new nurse, snuck a look to make sure she wasn't being watched, opened her mouth, stuck in her thumb and began to talk with her mother.

Hours later, when the moon was casting broad blue stripes across her bed, Rayna cleared her throat. "I want to see

Commander Borodin." The new nurse made a point of not responding. Rayna thought about a tantrum but didn't have the strength so succumbed to what was now a habitual deep sleep.

Later, when she awoke, the moon was still splashing its eerie blue light around the room. She was afraid. There was a nameless something; she felt it assemble into fingers, become a huge hand that pressed down and begin to push the life out of her. She fought her fear of the blue light, the weight of the hand. In desperation, she bargained, offered to let it push through her, wrap itself around her pounding heart. Willed herself to welcome it, held herself still while it was within her, a moment, an eternity, all in the hope that it would release her and move on.

After a time she was able to sit up. She looked around. The new nurse was napping by the window. Rayna's mind began to race. She must get out, she must find Borodin. And so, blood pumping, she folded back her covers and placed one foot, then the other, on the floor.

The creak of bedsprings woke the woman. Rayna let out a cry. The nurse rose. Rayna lunged for the door, but her foot caught in the sheet and she stumbled, crashing hard against the metal bed stand.

The nurse caught her and maneuvered her back, scolding her in some language that was not Russian. Ukrainian? Lithuanian? "I must see someone," Rayna pleaded, trying to make this sound like a practical problem. "I'm dying. It's very important." The woman's burbling language overrode her and against Rayna's weak protests she was tucked back into bed.

"I need to write a message. I must have paper." Rayna wrote with a finger in the air, then tried French, adding an extra syllable, *papier.*

"Ah, *papier!*" The woman knew enough French for that. So by scribbling on her palm Rayna was able to get a pad of paper and pencil. She still didn't know what language the woman spoke or why she had decided to trust her.

"Comrade Borodin," she said, folding the note in half and then quarters, writing his room number on top. "Take it to him, please," then repeated the instruction in French. But the woman's French didn't extend that far, so Rayna had to resort to pantomime again, pointing down the hall toward the elevator.

The woman looked doubtful.

"Very well, I'll go myself." Rayna swung her legs back to the floor. Got as far as the door before she collapsed. That did it. The nurse, with shrugs to an invisible employer, tucked Rayna back in bed, took the note and peered out to see if the hall guard was awake. She turned with a glance to make sure Rayna promised not to get out of bed while she was gone.

"Absolutely," Rayna agreed. "Scout's honor," giving the remembered salute as the nurse closed the door. She was still grinning when Borodin arrived, a few minutes later, tucking in his shirt. "I should have thought of this sooner," she told him.

When he realized she was not in death throes, he became cross. "You are a very bad girl."

"I hope so," she said, pleased with this thought. Then, "I'm glad you're here." She patted a spot on the bed for him to sit.

He hesitated a moment, then moved a chair out in the hall and motioned for the nurse to take it. With that bit of privacy, he came back to take up her hands. "They are cold," he observed. And then, "I'm not supposed to be here. They told me not to see you."

"I know."

"You will get me in trouble."

"I already have." And then, pulling his head down, relishing the feel of his dark hair in her fingers, she whispered the whole story of her night interview with Joseph Stalin.

He pulled back to look at her in disbelief. "Krupskaya did this?"

She nodded.

"For what reason?"

"For the same reason I did. To help Mme. Sun."

"To believe this is impossible."

"I know."

Then she whispered about the Turkish coffee, the warning look from Krupskaya, the unexpected meals at the Lenin School. "Maybe I'm being poisoned. Though the German doctor seems to think it's organic."

"What does that mean?"

"I don't know. Everyone talks in riddles. My brain is addled, that's for sure. I'm not much use to you anymore."

"Nonsense." And here he took up her hands again and stared at her with a peculiar intensity. "You are very dear to me. You know that."

"Yes." She did know that.

"And very dangerous." To me, he meant.

"Yes." Her head bowed in acknowledgment. "And my eyes aren't right. I have wild, scary dreams. Before you came I dreamt I was dying."

"It's the fever."

"No." Then, "The first doctor, the Russian one? He gave me camphor. I'm allergic to camphor. They knew that at the Lenin School."

A sharp intake of breath. "You know what you are saying?"

"I'm saying the whole thing is rotten. Rotten to the core." She saw how her words stung and added a consoling note. "I know you're stuck. With your sense of duty. Fanya and the boys."

"Not stuck. It is a matter of belief."

"I know that. And love you for it."

He stood and spoke in a normal voice. "Well, thank you for telling me this bedtime story. It is usual for the visitor to tell the patient stories, but you always were contrary." He ran his finger up her cheek, across the feathery area above her lip. Then to the far side of her neck. Her cheek turned to caress the motion.

"Yes," she said, "a bedtime story."

There was a silence. Borodin bent to kiss her. It was a clumsy moment, something awkward in the gesture, as if he were trying to mend something hopelessly broken. Grief surged. She felt cut away. His hand, as he touched her, felt numb on her skin.

Then he plucked a smile from God knows where and arranged it on his face as he reached out to touch the tip of her nose. "Cold nose, healthy dog." Then he pinched her cheek in a soft farewell. "Ach, a little color. That's good." Then kissed her cold forehead and said, "The nurse, she's Latvian, like me." As an afterthought, "There will be no more camphor. I promise."

"No more," she repeated, then slipped into a half-sleep. She could feel him fluffing her pillow and smoothing down the silk coverlet and looking at her for a long moment.

"Sleep," he commanded, "so you will get well." Then added, "I'll come tomorrow night. Not so late, but after the moon comes up." He remembered an old poem. "I'll come to you by moonlight..." then stopped. She knew why, knew the next line: "though death shall bar the way."

The next night when he came she asked, "What took you so long?" her tone seeming so imply that everything had returned to normal.

"You are feeling better?" He slid into the same spot on her bed, while his hand under the blanket traced the curve of her hip. She cupped her body close as he stroked the sharp bone. "Thin, so thin, like a little chicken."

"I'm sorry," she began.

"For what?" He seemed absorbed in the feel of her hip.

"For dying." Then, to set the agenda straight, "Sorry for you, not me "

He tried to say something but couldn't.

She shifted so she could look up at him. "I do. Feel badly, like I started something I can't finish."

He shook this off, muttering that it wasn't important, but she moved her head back and forth to make clear that he should take what she had to say seriously. "You love me, you said so. You can't take that back." She tried to make this matter-of-fact. "And now it's an impediment, something you have no earthly use for, that's what I am sorry about. The waste of it."

He stole a look at the door, at the nurse whose job it was to report on their doings.

She caught the glance, and again shook her head. "Not to worry. I'm the one who's babbling, not you."

His fingers once again found her hip. "Shouldn't I be the one to babble just a little bit? So as to keep you company?" His voice cracked, his eyes stared down at his hand on top of the silk coverlet. She took in the fabric's weave, how the folds lapped peach and purple in the moonlight, how his hand, heavy against her body, seemed almost not to exist.

"No." Her answer to his question was sharp. "You don't have to babble to keep me company. You've got work to do, not very nice work, this duty of staying alive, but necessary. So don't apologize for anything."

He seemed afraid to ask the next question. "Staying alive, that is my duty?"

"To wait for what unfolds in China. The long view, for China. This country, too." She frowned as she whispered, "If I knew more, I'd tell you, honest." Then she smiled. "I told Jimmy his life's work is journalism, that he is hopeless as a revolutionary. Here I am, Lady Bountiful, propped up, dispensing famous last words." Her giddy mood shifted, became forlorn. "I don't have any last words for you. Just that I'm sorry I made you love me, jumping in that lily pond. It wasn't very thoughtful of me. It's just going to make things harder."

Rayna felt hot blood surge through him and patted him to keep him quiet. "Anger wastes energy. Think of it. All my life I wanted to mean something. Now I do. Not in the way I expected, but there it is. You gave me a mission and I've done it." She looked at her fingers and then pressed them into his side, into the ribs near his heart. "I'm planting myself in you, so you can keep me forever."

He held himself erect and very still.

She continued. "Somewhere along the way, you'll have a moment when you can do something for China. You'll do it and be at peace. That's all I can promise." She pulled back her hand and curled herself into a warm crescent around him. "It's not much, but it's the best I can do."

As he kissed her forehead and began to make his quiet way out, she rose from her half-sleep one last time. "About the lily pond – don't tell!"

The End

HISTORICAL NOTES

I first came across the story of Rayna Prohme twenty-five years ago after reading Vincent Sheean's *Personal History*, which details his visit to Hankow in the spring of 1927 where he met a red-haired American girl who was an aide to the Russian advisor Mikhail Borodin. Rayna followed Borodin to Moscow, traveling with Mme. Sun Yat-sen, and Sheean followed Rayna.

Sheean and Rayna met again by accident in the lobby of the Hotel Metropole in mid-September. The rest of the story between them is more or less as recounted in this novel, although I gave Sheean a better understanding of the struggle between Stalin and Trotsky than he had at the time.

According to Sheean's account, she was due to report to the Lenin School on November 15 but collapsed on November 12, was taken by some Chinese cadets to the Hotel Metropole and was there tended by Sheean, Anna Louise Strong and others. Her condition had its ups and downs, but she died on November 21 and was cremated at the Donskoia Monastery. Mme. Sun led the funeral march. Borodin sent flowers but did not attend. However, he sought Sheean out a day or two later and delivered an emotional tribute to Rayna that was both personal and professional.

That was the story Sheean told, that he had fallen in love with a red-haired girl, an American who was dedicated to the Chinese revolution, followed her to Moscow, tried to persuade her to return to the West, but then she died.

I was hooked. Five years of research led to a draft of a novel that had Rayna embarking on an affair with Borodin (there is some sketchy evidence this might have been so) and leaving her second husband (Bill) under the pretext that she needed to accompany Mme. Sun to Moscow.

In writing an historical novel there are many choices to be made. A compelling fictional narrative has to be shaped from the messy historical record. Events must be simplified, motives, relationships, dialogue and decisive actions must be bent to serve as building blocks of story. Much must be imagined. Here is a list of the major fictions, as well as some important facts, that make this story hang together:

Fictions:

Rayna may have had a romantic encounter with Borodin at Kuling (that was certainly the rumor), and resuming that affair may have been the motivating force for her decision to go to Moscow. She certainly was taken with him. On the trip down the Yangtze, this is what she wrote to Raph regarding Borodin and where she would go next: "The greatest man I have ever known... He knows my geographic desires and wants to see them satisfied."

The reasons Bill stayed behind are unclear but there is ample evidence that Rayna was at least conflicted as to whether she wanted Bill with her in Moscow.

The meeting with Krupskaya was invented, as well as Rayna's meeting with Joseph Stalin, but Rayna did make a pest of herself trying to help Mme. Sun get an exit visa for Berlin (where General Teng escaped to after his unsuccessful meeting with Joseph Stalin).

Facts:

Rayna had typhoid fever as a child and suffered headaches all her life. A Russian doctor did give her camphor treatments (which were used medicinally at that time) but camphor is also a poison which can be fatal and there was passing reference to Rayna being allergic to it.

Yagoda, Stalin's nominal head of the secret police at that time, was known as "the pharmacist" because of his fondness for poisoning people.

An autopsy report from the Kremlin Hospital found that Rayna died of a brain abscess arising from a weakness remaining from a childhood illness.

In 1930 Anna Louise Strong and Borodin were named coeditors of an English language newspaper, *The Moscow News*. In 1946, after having spent the war years in the United States, Anna Louise traveled to China to interview Mao Tse-Tung. In the resulting article, she quoted Mao as mocking the Stalinist 'hegemony' argument that peasants couldn't lead a communist revolution. Against Mao's advice, she tried to get the article published in the Soviet Union and was rebuffed. In 1947, she asked for Borodin's help to reverse that decision. For her temerity and his help they both were arrested. Anna Louise was expelled as a Chinese spy, and Borodin was transported to a gulag where, in 1953, he died.

Mme. Sun (Soong Ching-ling) went to Berlin in 1928 (she delayed her departure so as not to imply approval for her sister's December, 1927, wedding to General Chiang). In 1930, she and General Teng returned to China to try to build a "third way" political party. In 1931, Teng was arrested and executed by Chiang. Mme. Sun continued her refusal to recognize General Chiang's government until the Second World War when the Chinese Communist Party made temporary alliance with General Chiang and she consented to become part of the coalition government. After the war, when the Chinese Communist Party pushed Chiang's armies onto the island of Formosa, she became the only official in the government of the People's Republic of China who was not a member of the CCP. She died in 1981, becoming a member of the CCP only on her deathbed.

Soviet and Chinese Communist Party conflicts over the matter of the authenticity of a peasant-led revolution forestalled any public discussion in Russia of events in China during Stalin's reign of terror in the 1930s. When Anna Louise returned to Moscow with her famous interview, Borodin had his chance to act. By helping Anna Louise try to get her Mao interview published, he was finally able to express, in a small but significant way, his love for China.

Borodin, a fascinating character, has made his way into my other novels, *A Snug Life Somewhere* and *A Desire Path*. The best historical record of his life is found in Dan Jacob's book, *Borodin: Stalin's Man in China*, although that title does a disservice to Borodin. He was in China at Lenin's behest, and when the Chinese revolution collapsed, he got blamed as part of Stalin's self-serving policies to thwart Trotsky.

As for the sources of Rayna Prohme's story, in addition to Sheean's *Personal History*, I've relied on two other books that deal extensively with Rayna's time in China: an annotated collection of her letters, *Reporting the Chinese Revolution*, by Baruch Hirson and Arthur J. Kodel, and a memoir about that time in China by Millie Bennett, *On Her Own*, written in the late 1930s but only recently published. I also consulted other historical records including Anna Louise Strong's book about her trek across the Gobi with Borodin, *China's Millions*, Percy Chen's *China Called Me*, Si-lan (Sylvia) Chen Leyda's *Footnote to History*, Sterling Seagrave's *The Soong Sisters*, and *Soong Ching-ling*, I. Epstein's magisterial biography of Mme. Sun. In addition I consulted the papers of Samson Raphaelson (Rayna's first husband) which are housed in the Columbia University manuscripts division, as well as many books about Lenin's early doings, the Stalin era, and the rise of the Chinese Communists.

About Jan Shapin

Jan Shapin has been writing plays and screenplays for nearly thirty years, in the last decade concentrating on fiction. Shapin has studied playwriting at Catholic University in Washington, DC, screenwriting at the Film and Television Workshop and University of Southern California, and fiction writing at a variety of locations including Barnard College's Writers on Writing seminar, the Sewanee Writers' Conference and Bread Loaf Writers' Conference.

Her plays have been produced in the Northeast and Mid-Atlantic states. She has received grants from the RI Council for the Humanities and has served as a juror for the Rhode Island State Council for the Arts screenplay fellowship awards.

She lives in North Kingston, RI with her photographer husband.